CORRUPT CITY

CORRUPT CITY

TRA VERDEJO

www.urbanbooks.net

Urban Books, LLC
78 East Industry Court
Deer Park, NY 11729

ISBN 13: 978-1-60162-436-9
ISBN 10: 1-60162-436-0

First Printing February 2011
Printed in the United States of America

10 9 8 7 6 5 4 3 2

Distributed by Kensington Publishing Corp.
Submit Wholesale Orders to:
Kensington Publishing Corp.
C/O Penguin Group (USA) Inc.
Attention: Order Processing
405 Murray Hill Parkway
East Rutherford, NJ 07073-2316
Phone: 1-800-526-0275
Fax: 1-800-227-9604

Praise for Tra Verdejo

"Tra Verdejo's sophomore novel, *Corrupt City,* is such a great read. I haven't enjoyed urban literature with so much suspense in a very long time. Tra has penned a phenomenal page-turner."
Rukyyah J. Karreem
Author of *Princess & Princess II*

"Breathless, explosive, exhilarating. *Corrupt City* is the perfect combination of spine-tingling and heart-pounding suspense. Tra Verdejo is definitely an author to look out for."
Silk White
Author of *Tears of a Hustler & Tears of a Hustler 2*

"A peek into the reality of the streets. Tra Verdejo will take you directly there. A man on a mission, he is determined and enthusiastic about 'keeping it real.' "
Jennifer Robinson
Expressions Book Club

Dedication

I would like to dedicate this book to all the innocent lives lost at the hands of police officers with quick triggers. Also to all the police officers killed in the line of duty while protecting us. Rest in Peace.

Acknowledgments

Peace to the Gods and Earths.

I first want to thank everyone who purchased this book. Thank you for the support. I mean that from the bottom of my heart. I will always put in 100 percent. Love is love.

Without a doubt I have to thank my mother, **Mirta Davila**. I hope you are resting in peace. I want to thank the second most important woman in my life, **Purified Earth**. You complete me, and thank you for two beautiful boys, **Omighty** and **Destin**. Everything I do is for them, my family.

I also want to thank my father, **Pedro Verdejo**, the man who taught me how to work hard. Next, I want to thank my sister **Ana**, who is holding it down on her own. Single parents, stand up. My little sister **Nichole**, I'm so proud of you, doing your thing and running your own business, too. My eldest sister, **Tee**, what's good? I want to shout out the future of our family tree, my nieces and nephews **Ray, Destine**, **Tyler**, **Nelly**, and **Kenya**.

I also want to thank **Freddy "Tone" Garcia**. Many thank God for their second chances; I would like to thank this man for my second chance. Love you, Brah. You already know that. **Melissa Edwards**, I remember telling Eric when we were younger I would buy you a house. Trust me, I haven't forgotten that promise. Thank you for stepping in there and providing shelter when I needed a home. I will love you forever. I also want to thank my entire family in Puerto Rico, especially my *abuela,* **Carmen Alomar**.

Now it's time to show love to my other family, **Remy Rich**, **Ray Rocca**, and **Daddio** (Wagner Projects, stand up). Peace to the **God-born Knowledge**. I love you, Brah. My cousin **Ruddy**. My CNS family—**Snypes**, **Ron**, **DB**, **Smoke**, **Last Breath**, **Buddha Bride**, **Ill Murda**, **Kauso**, **Lizzy Long**, **Boo Bizzy**, **Rob-U (RIP)**, and **Gutta (RIP)**. And 119th Street and Lexington Avenue, stand up, baby!

Now the literary love. I first want to thank all the authors who believed in my vision and were part of the 2009 Sexy Scriptures calendar. Those authors are **Kwame "Dutch" Teague**, **K'wan** (good looking for all the love), **Deshaun "Jiwe" Morris**, **Sexy**, **Julie Ojeda (BX Bookman**, what's good?), **Kerry "Mr. Wagfest" Wagner**, **Dex**, **Shani Greene-Dowdell**, and **my Bronx connect**, **Iesha Brown**.

I can't forget all the beautiful models. I want to thank Mrs. January. **Tish Love**, for helping in finding most of the girls and our locations. I only had a few slots for the calendar, but there are a bunch of authors in the game I break bread with, and I have to shout them out as well. Authors **Rukyyah J. Karreem**, **Silk White**, **Maxwell Penn (Peace God)**, **Dex**, **Antoine "Inch" Thomas**, **Tenia Jamilla Conrad**

Glover (let's make this movie). I also want to send love to authors like **Ingrid**, **Winter**, **Robert T. Sells**, **Don**, **Dashawn Taylor** & the many others who have done book signing at my spot in Baltimore.

To all my book vendors and distributors, good looking for the love, especially the ones that pay up front, **Black & Nobel** (Philly, stand up), **BX Bookman**, **Purgo** on 149th Street and Third Avenue, **Black Star** in Harlem, **Charles** in Baltimore (the Wise brothers), **Shane** by Lexington market, Cliff at **Expression** bookstore in Baltimore, **African World Book**, and the list goes on. I really appreciate the love.

On the other hand there are a lot of bookstores and vendors with bad credit and reputations. I'm not going to blast you, but please stop bull$hitting. I want to send a shout-out to all my co-vendors at the **Patapsco Flea Market** in Baltimore. Love is love.

I also want to thank two ladies, **Jeannie Hooper** and **Helen Andrews**. We spend a lot of time critiquing books. I gave these ladies the opportunity to read and review my book first. I also want to thank my weekly supporters who stop by the flea market. Thanks for the love.

Shout-out to **Flowers High** in Largo, MD, whose seniors did a book report on my first book, *Born in the Streets But Raised in Prison.*

I also want to thank all the people who have hated on me. Yah are the reason why I stay motivated and work so hard. I know it must burn inside watching my success blossom the way it has. Get used to the feeling because I'm just getting started. Many thought my first book was just a one-hit wonder. I'm sorry to burst your bubble. But please remember one thing—**Yah could kiss my Puerto Rican A$$**.

Chapter One

10/22/2003

"Damn, we have been out here for like forty-five minutes, Toothpick. What's taking them so long?"

"I don't know. Maybe they changed their minds."

"Changed their minds? We have a bag filled with money. How can they change their mind? It's too late for that. They got fifteen minutes, or we out."

Cash and Toothpick had placed an order for two kilos of cocaine and four guns, two of which were semiautomatic rifles. They were getting a bit nervous waiting for the drop. All kinds of scenarios ran through their heads, and they were hoping they weren't being set up.

"I hope they're not trying to pull any funny moves, 'cause I have a full clip," Toothpick added.

They both took a deep breath and leaned back on their seat, both exhaling like two little bitches. They were in the Hunts Point area of the Bronx, parked in an empty parking lot behind a large agriculture warehouse between Garrison and Longwood Avenue. It was close to midnight on a breezy Friday night, and there wasn't a soul in the area. That's how cold it was. But it still felt strange because, usually, you would see at least a few crackheads roaming around. To the criminal-minded, it was one of those perfect opportunities to pull off a hit—no witnesses, and in the middle of nowhere.

After another twenty minutes went by, they finally decided to leave. In all honesty, they both were nervous and thought it was a bad idea to meet there, anyway.

"Fuck this! They're not coming. Let's go," Cash said as he turned the car on.

"Wait. Look. Here they come."

Cash looked to his right and saw headlights approaching. The lights blurred both their vision, and they couldn't see the car. Both Cash and Toothpick placed their hands on their guns, just to be on the safe side. As the car got within twenty feet, they finally had vision on it but couldn't see inside because of the dark-tinted windows.

After the car pulled up parallel to theirs, the passenger lowered his tinted window and told Cash, "Follow us."

"First of all, who the fuck is you?" Cash shot back. "And where is Scratch?"

The window from the back started to roll down, and that's when Toothpick pulled his 9-millimeter. He cocked it back so quickly, the window only rolled halfway down and stopped.

"Chill, Toothpick. It's me, Scratch. I'm in the backseat. It's all good. Put the gun away. Just follow us. We know a safer place. This shit here looks too creepy."

Toothpick lowered his gun and told Cash to follow

the car. For a moment there, it almost got ugly. Toothpick was seconds away from pulling the trigger.

While they were following the car, both of them were quiet, their minds were heavy with suspicion. Not knowing where they were going added to the suspense. They could be driving to a setup where more goons with guns could be waiting for them. This criminal life was full of surprises, and your reflexes had to be quick in order to survive. Second thoughts would get you killed in this game. Your first instinct was the first and only rule to live by.

Toothpick and Cash both knew something was wrong, but they were both strapped with loaded guns, so they risked it anyway, knowing the odds were against them. They knew it was a big mistake, but once you've committed and you've passed a certain point, there is no turning back.

They got off at the Castle Hill Avenue exit. They parked across the street from Castle Hill projects and both looked at each other.

"Toothpick, how in the fuck is Castle Hill projects safer?"

They both laughed.

"I don't know, but we about to find out. These cats are fuckin' amateurs, but keep your eyes open. Don't even blink."

As Cash was parking, Scratch jumped out and walked up to their car.

"Toothpick, you come with me. We're going in this building behind me."

"Scratch, what's up with all these last-minute changes? You sure you have the bricks and the guns? Don't fuck with us."

"Toothpick, just trust me on this one. Calm down. We're going inside to my cousin's apartment. That way, you get a chance to check everything out while I count the money."

"A'ight, cool. C'mon, Cash, grab the money."

"Just you, Toothpick. Your boy has to wait in the car."

"C'mon, Scratch, that's my partner, we roll together. I'm not going upstairs alone."

"Listen, either you come alone, or the deal is dead. It's your decision. My driver is also waiting in the car. Don't worry, your partner will be okay."

Toothpick looked at Cash and waited for his approval. Once Cash nodded his head, he jumped out of the car with a bag of money. Toothpick kept looking back as he walked with Scratch, making sure no one was following.

As soon as they got in the building and pressed for the elevator, two gunmen emerged from apartment 1B. It happened so fast, Toothpick didn't have time to react or reach for his weapon. They pulled him inside the apartment, took his gun, and threw him on the floor.

Scratch leaned over him as he pressed the cold barrel against his cheekbone and asked him, "How long have you known your boy outside?"

"What the fuck is going on here, Scratch? Are you crazy? We are boys. What's going on? Why are you asking about Cash?"

Before he could answer, about five to six shots rang out. Toothpick knew those shots were intended for Cash. He wanted to break loose and reach for his other gun, but he had to play it cool and wait for the right moment. There were three people in that apartment with guns in their hands. He wasn't stupid.

"Were those shots? What the fuck is going on here?" Toothpick asked with a clueless expression, trying to work his way out.

"Answer my question. How long have you known Cash?"

"Not for long. My cousin set me up with him when I came home two years ago. Why?"

"Cash is police. He's undercover. Please tell me you are not a cop as well."

"A cop? Get the fuck outta here. Cash can't be police, and if he is police, your boy just shot him. Why the fuck is you still here? That means police was either following us or on their way here. We need to bounce the fuck outta here. Let me go. You know I'm not a fuckin' pig. Get off me, nigga. I'm not trying to get locked up today. Let's bounce and handle business another day."

Scratch looked into Toothpick's eyes for about four seconds and couldn't read any lies. He believed him and decided to let him go. "My bad. I had to make sure," he said, helping Toothpick up and giving him his gun back, but with the clip and the bullet in the chamber. "Nowadays, you never know who's undercover. Wait about fifteen seconds after I leave before you bounce. We'll make the deal another time. Keep your money. No, as a matter of fact, give me this fuckin' money. Next time, pick a better partner," Scratch said before running out.

Toothpick waited for about five seconds before he reached for his second gun and ran out. He kicked open the front door of the building so hard, he got the attention of Scratch and his boys. By the time they realized where the noise came from, Toothpick was already approaching, shooting rounds from his 9mm Glock. Instantly, he dropped two of them with single shots to the head. Now it was just Scratch and his driver left.

It was an all-out war at one o'clock in the morning in the middle of the streets in the Bronx. Half the neighborhood was up watching the action from their windows, some ducking bullets. These projects were known for their high crime rate, but neighbors never saw anything like this.

Toothpick was in the battle of his life. He had to run for cover behind a parked car when Scratch's driver pulled out a MAC-11 and emptied the entire clip at him. Bullets were flying all around Toothpick. All he could do was stay put and pray they didn't go through the car and hit him.

He caught a break when the MAC-11 went silent for a few seconds because it ran out of bullets. As soon as he heard a pause in between shots, Toothpick jumped up, quickly let off two shots, and ducked back down. He'd shot the driver in the neck and shoulder.

Scratch realized he'd lost his crew. Now it was just him left. But he was still hanging, going out like a soldier, letting off rounds from his .40-caliber. When he noticed Toothpick reloading, he jumped in the car and tried to make a quick getaway.

Before he was able to switch gears, Toothpick ran up on him and pressed the hot barrel on his temple and yelled, "Freeze, muthafucka! You are under arrest. You have the right to remain silent. Anything you say will be used against you in a court of law—man, fuck that! And fuck you!"

Toothpick, whose real name was Donald "Lucky" Gibson, shot Scratch twice in the head then quickly ran toward his partner, praying for a miracle.

"Nine-one-three, nine-one-three. Officer down! I need a bus, and I need it now, goddamn it! Now! Officer down, I repeat, officer down. I'm on Castle Hill and Randall Avenue!" he yelled.

When he got to Cash, real name Michael "Tango" Scott, he was still breathing, but there was blood everywhere. He noticed Tango had been shot a few times in his chest. When they took this undercover assignment, they knew they couldn't wear a vest. Tears overcame him because he knew his partner's destiny.

Tango kept mumbling for Lucky to call his wife. "Please call her. I want to hear her voice before I die."

"You are not going to die. Help is on the way. Hang in there," Lucky replied, reaching for his cell phone.

Lucky started dialing the number, the phone rang once, and his wife, Tammy, answered. When he went to pass the phone over to Tango, he was already gone. He didn't know what to do. Should he hang up or tell Tammy what happened? He couldn't hang up because Tammy knew his phone number.

"Hello," Lucky said, sounding like a scared little boy.

"Hello, Lucky? That's you? What's going on? I hear sirens in the background. Where is Michael? What's going on, Lucky?"

"Tammy, I'm sorry. I'm so sorry," a teary Lucky said.

Tammy became hysterical because she knew it only meant two things—he was either in critical condition or dead. "Lucky, goddamn it! Tell me the truth. What happened to my husband? Is he okay? Oh please, God, help me. Please, God."

"I'm sorry, Tammy, our cover was blown, and Tango, I mean Michael, didn't make it."

The phone went dead.

Tammy had yanked the cord from the socket. She was throwing a tantrum at the house. Her twin boys, only eight years old, woke up asking their mother what happened and why she was crying. She was speechless. She didn't know how to tell them their daddy was never coming home.

Meanwhile, back at the crime scene, Lucky, still in shock, was trying to put the pieces of the puzzle together. Two questions kept bugging him. How did they know about Tango's identity? And why was it taking so long for backup to arrive?

Lucky was starting to get a major headache and was feeling weak. He dropped to one knee, and that's when another cop at the scene noticed Lucky had also been shot. They rushed to his aid and treated his wound on the spot.

He was hit on the side of his stomach, a flesh wound, nothing serious. His adrenaline was running so high, he'd never felt the shot. After a fifteen-minute conversation with his captain, he finally agreed to get in the ambulance and head to the hospital as a precaution.

The Present (2006)

Lucky woke up sweating and out of breath. He was dreaming about the night one of his ex-partners, Tango, was killed three years ago. That was one memory he would carry with him for the rest of his life. Till this day, he suspected it was foul play that led to Tango's cover being blown.

Today was a big day for Lucky. He turned on the TV and listened to the news reporter, while getting dressed for court.

"Today, June 21, 2006, the biggest case against the State of New York is set to hear the prosecution's main and last witness, Donald Gibson, a former, fifteen-year veteran police officer, was one of the four officers present the night Perry Coleman, a twenty-five-year-old Black man, was gunned down by the NYPD. The other three officers are all being charged with murder.

"Perry's case has drawn national attention, and the entire state of New York is behind the Colemans. New Yorkers, already sick and tired of thugs roaming the streets, don't want to have to worry about these trigger-happy rogue police officers running wild in their community.

"Even the great Minister Al Muhammad has joined the family and their legal team. We all know the minister's reputation for bringing attention to police brutality cases.

"Today, the jury will hear the shocking testimony of Mr. Gibson, where he indicates Perry Coleman was murdered on the night in question for no apparent reason. The courtroom will be filled with supporters, police officers, and politicians. Everyone is anticipating what will take place today.

"Rumors are circulating that Donald has been hiding under his own protection, without the help of the government, because he knows how crooked the system has become. In another forty-five minutes, we will finally hear what happened the night

Perry Coleman was murdered. I'm Destine Diaz, live from the courthouse, Channel 5 News."

Those three officers were confident the charges would be dropped until Donald "Lucky" Gibson re-appeared and agreed to testify.

Meanwhile, it was pandemonium outside the courthouse. There were news stations parked everywhere, and reporters were interviewing anyone who wanted to get in front of a camera. The crowd was asking the same questions over and over. "Will this be the case that will rock the state of New York and shine the spotlight on police brutality? How many more innocent bodies need to drop? Better yet, how many more minority bodies need to drop?"

Inside the courtroom, there were barely any seats available. The NYPD tried to take up most of the seats to prevent supporters and protesters from entering the courtroom. Court officers had to ask police officers to move to the right side of the courtroom or exit.

Police officers were not happy, and some even argued their point. The police department knew their future relied on the verdict of this case. Though the evidence against these three cops was not in their favor, they strongly supported their own. The cops involved were all suspended with pay, which was nothing but a paid vacation.

The people demanded more severe punishment, not a slap on the wrist. However, Mayor Ralph Gulliano and Police Commissioner Brandon Fratt made it their business to point out that Perry Coleman had a criminal record on file and the people shouldn't rush to judge and crucify these officers who were doing their job. Both the mayor and police commissioner received harsh criticisms for their stance. Blacks and Hispanics were not shocked, because the lack of support in their communities had always been evident.

The mayor tried to smear Perry's image. Perry Coleman had been working at the same job since he was nineteen years old and had no record of felonies or misdemeanors. They were referring to a juvenile robbery charge. Perry and a few of his high school friends got caught running out of a store with jewelry when he was fourteen years old. Part of his plea bargain was that his record would be sealed, which meant closed, and would never resurface again, after he completed eighteen months of probation. But the following night after Perry was killed, newspapers were already printing stories about his juvenile record, hoping the court of opinion would at least convict him of being a thug.

The public didn't care about what he did when he was fourteen. He turned out to be a good human being and role model to others. Perry was a manager at a furniture store and was a year away from earning his bachelor's degree in business communication. He was survived by his wife, Kim Blackburn Coleman, and their three-year-old son, Perry Coleman III. Perry's family promised that his name would never be forgotten and that his story would be told across the world.

Perry's mother, Laura, said it the best. "You can't change destiny, but you sure can change your life. My son is a prime example that one mistake shouldn't ruin your future. Perry was a great son, father, and husband. He worked extremely hard to stay positive and keep his family happy. Now, because of racist, trigger-happy cops, my son is no longer alive. We will carry the torch from here and educate the world, not just on police brutality, but on racism as well, because it's still alive in our communities, in our everyday lives."

Chapter Two

Lucky's Testimony

Around 8:15 a.m., the judge, who had a reputation for handing out harsh sentences, walked out of his chambers. He was six feet, five inches tall and weighed about two-sixty. His white beard matched his old, white, long hair. He barely smiled in a courtroom. A lot of protesters were against him hearing the case because he was rumored to be a racist, and Perry's family was concerned they wouldn't get a fair trial.

"All rise," the bailiff said. "The Honorable Judge Henry J. Lewis presiding." A few seconds later, he added, "You may all be seated."

"Good morning to all. Counselors, are we ready? Mr. Johnson, you may call your witness."

District Attorney Jonathan Johnson had over fifteen years of experience and had worked on more than a few high-profile cases in the past. He was considered a celebrity. He once graced the cover of *Essence* magazine, and was ranked number two on the top ten of single Black men in law. The smooth-talking prosecutor was the lead counsel on two cases that brought down The Young Kingpins, a million-dollar street gang in Spanish Harlem. He'd also taken down a few mob figures and dirty politicians. His resume had Perry's family feeling confident. If anyone could get a conviction, it would be this man.

Mr. Johnson had a history of going for the maximum penalty without a second thought, and barely offered deals to offenders. In his first public statement about this case, he made it known he hated dirty cops.

African Americans all felt they had the right prosecutor. Whites, on the other hand, were bitter and had mixed feelings. Ever since the trial started, it had been a racial war. The courtroom was packed with angry supporters from both sides. Yet people of all colors were rooting for a guilty verdict. With the anger and tension across the courtroom, the smallest thing was going to set it off.

District Attorney Johnson got out of his seat and said, "Your Honor, I would like to call the state's last witness to the stand, Mr. Donald 'Lucky' Gibson."

The courtroom exploded, some cheering and clapping, others yelling and using obscene language.

"You fuckin' nigger rat!" an officer in uniform yelled.

"How could you betray the brotherhood? We should hang you," a White man dressed in a three-piece suit yelled.

A few supporters on Perry's side were yelling at the officers. They couldn't believe the trash coming out of their mouths.

The judge started banging his gavel so hard, court officers came marching in.

"Silence in my courtroom!" a furious Judge Lewis

said. "Officers, get the crowd under control immediately. Whoever doesn't obey my order, escort them out of my presence. I will not tolerate this behavior in my courtroom. I'm extremely shocked at the police department's outburst. I'm sure Commissioner Fratt will be embarrassed when he hears of this. Any more interruptions and I will clear this courtroom. Mr. Johnson, will you please proceed?"

Extra security was on hand because of the high media attention. In fact, the media had been coming down hard on the NYPD. And some experts were saying the outcome of this verdict was meaningless because the court of opinion had already convicted the police officers.

It took about five minutes to get the courtroom back in order after a few were escorted out, one in handcuffs, but none of the officers were thrown out. Perry's family was heavily protected by the Nation of Islam security, the FOI, the Fruit of Islam, known to provide excellent protection.

Perry's mother, not rattled by the mini outburst, sat there motionless as she held her husband's hand. She didn't even look toward the altercation. Her only concern was getting justice for her baby who was gunned down by those dirty cops.

Once there was silence, the trial proceeded.

"I would like to please the court and call my final witness, Mr. Gibson, to the stand," Johnson said nervously, hoping another outburst didn't occur.

Lucky came in the courtroom from the back, from where inmates entered. As he walked to the stand, you could tell he was a buff brother. Lucky's suit didn't hide his biceps, which were huge. He was known as a weightroom rat, and it was obvious. He didn't have that prototypical cop look. At six foot, one, and weighing about two hundred and twenty pounds, he looked more like a professional athlete going to a business meeting, or a superstar rapper. His jewelry and swagger gave the impression he was a street cat, not a detective. Which was probably why he made one hell of a detective. His thuggish appearance was so believable.

As he was walking with swag toward the stand, he turned to the crowd. He couldn't believe the amount of people in attendance. Then he turned toward the defense table, where his former partners were all sitting. He slowed his walk and gave each one of them eye contact. He read through their eyes. He knew they were all nervous. Lucky smirked at them because he knew his partners had searched hard, hoping they could kill him and prevent this day from ever happening. But he laid low right under their noses. He'd never left New York. He was hibernating, cooking up a plan of his own.

"Mr. Gibson, we don't have all day," the judge snapped. "Please sit down, so we can proceed."

After Lucky sat down, a few police officers stood up and walked out as he was being sworn in. One of them said, "Die in hell, rat!"

The DA waited for the officers to exit before he began his questioning. "Can you please state your name, for the record?" Mr. Johnson said.

"My name is Detective Donald Gibson, but everyone calls me Lucky," he said as he slouched on the chair. Lucky had a laid-back demeanor about him, like an old-school pimp, but without the funny-looking hat. His body language was hard to read.

“Why do they call you Lucky?”

“In this line of work, I’ve brushed death a thousand times,” he replied as he looked at his former partners. “I’m lucky to be alive right now.”

“Tell us about your resume, Detective.”

“I have worked for and dedicated my life to the NYPD for the past fifteen years. I started in 1991 as a streetwalker. I was a rookie straight out of the academy at twenty years old. I’m now thirty-five. I’ve always wanted to be a cop. It was a childhood dream of mine. I was hoping by being an African American police officer, I could change the bad image in my community.

After my second year on the force, I was promoted. I was transferred from the Twenty-fifth Precinct to the Twenty-third Precinct, still in Spanish Harlem. I was assigned a new partner and given a new police cruiser. After four years of protecting the streets of East Harlem, I finally made homicide detective in 1999. After I solved a few murder cases in Queens and I received guilty convictions in all, I was assigned to a special elite unit called Operation Clean House.”

“Mr. Gibson, can you please explain to the court the qualifications needed in order to be even considered for such an elite team?” Johnson asked.

“Sure.” Lucky turned toward the jury. “To be honest, the qualifications are not written in stone. I was told, because of my excellent performance, great attitude, distinguished record, and high conviction rate, it made me an easy candidate. Like I stated earlier, I dedicated my life to the badge. For me it was a way of life, not a job to pay bills.”

“So, is it safe to say before you joined Operation Clean House, you were an honest police officer?”

"Yes."

"I object, Your Honor. He's leading the witness," Defense Attorney Matthew shouted it.

"Overruled."

"Thank you, Your Honor. Donald, for the past three weeks, the jury got an in-depth explanation of why we are here. Today, they will get a chance to hear the truth about what happened to Perry Coleman."

"I object, Your Honor. Is this necessary? Are you going to allow the counsel to make a mockery of your courtroom?"

"Mr. Johnson, please ask your question. Save any additional comment for your closing statement."

"Donald, do you consider yourself a dirty cop?"

"I object!" Matthew interrupted again. "He's leading the witness."

"Overruled. Mr. Matthew, I'm eager to hear the truth."

"What kind of police officer are you?" Johnson asked again.

"By the book, until I joined Operation Clean House. I mean, I'm a man, and I take responsibilities for my actions. I knew what I was doing was wrong. Operation Clean House was like a crackhouse. It's impossible to live in a crackhouse and not smoke. I became part of the environment."

"Donald, let's start from the beginning. Take us back and tell us about your first day in Operation Clean House."

Lucky reached for the cold water in front of him and slowly sipped it, hoping it would prevent the sweat from pouring down his face. He was about to commit suicide by testifying against his former employers. He finished the glass, cleared his throat, sat up, and began talking.

"I remember my first day on the job. I received mixed feelings from my new partners because I was the only Black guy on the team. They didn't hide how they felt about my presence either. I extended my hand out to all four men in that room, and only one of them shook my hand, Detective Michael "Tango" Scott. Tango became my closest friend on the squad, but died in the line of duty. His cover was blown in one of our many dangerous assignments. My other partners are all sitting right there." Lucky pointed at the defense table. "Captain William 'Tuna' Youngstown, Steve 'Loose Cannon' Stanley, and Jeffrey 'Speedy' Winston."

Captain William "Tuna" Youngstown had been in the police force for close to forty years. He was six foot three and weighed two hundred and ninety pounds. He had long blond hair, which he kept in a ponytail, and evil dark brown eyes. He looked more like a bouncer at a nightclub than a police captain.

Detective Jeffrey "Speedy" Winston, a ten-year veteran, was five feet nine and barely weighed a hundred and sixty pounds. He was built more like a sprinter than an officer. His low-cut hair and clean-cut attitude gave away his military upbringing.

Detective Steve "Loose Cannon" Stanley, a seventeen-year veteran with tattoos all over his body, didn't look like a cop. Just less than six feet tall, he looked more like a biker or the leader of a dangerous gang.

"My first assignment was taking down a notorious heroin gang called M&M, which stood for Murderers and Millionaires. The captain wanted to throw me in the fire quickly and test my ability. Since we were going after a Black gang, I was made the lead detective, even though I was basically a rookie on the team. I guess they wanted me to fail and throw me off the team.

"Michael and Jeffrey were going in as undercover drug addicts, and my job was to infiltrate their operations. M&M was making about twenty to fifty-thousand dollars a day in the Bronx. They called their product 'cliffhanger.' Fiends were dying off this powerful drug. There was no cut—straight, raw dope. A violent drug war started behind the success of cliffhanger. Bodies were dropping daily because other drug dealers were losing profit. The city was losing control on the war. The mayor called our captain and told us to take down M&M at whatever cost."

"The mayor of this city said, 'at whatever cost'?" Johnson interrupted.

"I object, Your Honor. That's hearsay, third-party speculation."

"Sustained. The jury will ignore that last question. Counsels approach."

After counsels approached the bench, the judge said, "Don't you dare implicate our great mayor through a third-person statement, Mr. Johnson. Your action could lead to contempt of court, and you could be disbarred in the State of New York. Are we clear?"

"We're clear."

Johnson didn't like that the judge came down hard on him, but he understood. This case wasn't about the mayor. He walked back to the center of the courtroom and proceeded.

"Let's get back to M&M. Please continue, Mr. Gibson."

"M&M was a gang that was well organized. Their leader, Money Mike, was a smart criminal. We label these individuals as organized thugs. He ran his operation out of one building on 139th Street and Third Avenue. He had so many lookouts, his team barely got arrested. Tango and Speedy, I mean Michael and Jeffrey, never got a chance to buy from the dealers directly. M&M would have the neighborhood kids deliver the drugs back and forth from the building and serve the addicts.

"These kids were making anywhere from one to three hundred dollars a night. That's more than what an average cop makes today, or even their own parents. These kids were not going to school. M&M basically ran a twenty-four-hour operation. Anyway, after ten months of surveillance, we had nothing on M&M, not one wiretap, only a few photos. We arrested a few members with bogus charges, but they didn't talk. That was strange because usually there is always one who wants to talk, but not this crew. Not even the little kids we arrested would talk. We were up against one of the most loyal organizations in history.

"This made our job a lot harder because we rely on information to solve at least ninety percent of our cases. From the intelligence we gathered on M&M, we only knew who was calling the shots, but there were six to seven other members who were still a mystery. We didn't know their ranks or true identities. Truth be told, we could have been wrong about who was calling the shots. We needed to come up with a better strategy. Meanwhile, the crime rate was rising like the sun. This is when I first learned that our department worked under a different set of rules."

"What do you mean by 'a different set of rules'?"

"We did as we pleased. We didn't report to no one. Don't get me wrong, we were good at our jobs. We just took the law into our own hands, even if that meant planting drugs, tampering with evidence, assault, or murder. Whatever it took to get the job done, we did it."

"Murder? Do you mean others besides Perry were innocently murdered as well?"

"Yes."

You could hear the oohs and ahhs all across the courtroom.

"The only reason why this case is getting national attention is because Perry didn't have a criminal record and was a working parent. Had he had one felony, forget about it."

Matthew quickly stood up. "I object. The witness is using the stand as his personal platform to speak for his personal feelings. I move that the witness be removed, and I ask that his testimony be made inadmissible. It is obvious his intent is personal."

"Overruled."

"Your Honor, but this witness has a personal vendetta against my clients."

"I said overruled," Judge Lewis shot back in a slow, loud voice. "Your objection was heard and denied."

"Okay, let's get back to M&M. Donald, please continue," Johnson said.

"Since we couldn't get close to M&M, we decided to set up one of their key members. M&M ran Patterson Projects, but they had beef with their neighbors, Mott Haven Projects. We did a sweep one night in Mott Haven Projects and locked up about ten members of the RSB, which stood for Red Slab Boys, a crack gang.

That same night, we pulled over Money Mike's black Mercedes Benz, and one of M&M's key members happened to be driving his car.

"We later learned he was the captain of the crew. His name was Derek Bailey, better known as Thirty-eight. He loved and used his .38 handgun so much, that became his nickname.

"That night when we pulled him over, we didn't care about the gun or drugs. Around that time, a gun charge against a high-profile criminal was like a misdemeanor charge. Money Mike would have spent good money on attorneys to get his captain out and charges dropped. All we wanted was for Thirty-eight to spend one night in jail, so we made up a story about an arrest warrant, took him to Central Booking, and we locked him up. I was undercover in the cell waiting for him, so were the ten RSB members we picked up. The plan was to drop Thirty-eight off in the cell, and when all hell broke loose, I'd jump in and help him out.

"The plan was perfect because not a minute went by after the CO closed that cell before one of the Red Slab Boys approached Thirty-eight and started swinging. Ten against one is no match for any one, so within seconds, Thirty-eight was on the floor getting stomped. Since they all had their back toward me, I jumped toward them and pushed the whole pile toward the metal bars, and Thirty-eight was able to get back on his feet. We were both swinging to save our lives. After the correction officers saved our butts, the RSB boys were moved to a different cell, and Thirty-eight thanked me. He wanted to know why I helped. I told him because that's how I get down, and by his reaction, I knew I had him in my pocket.

"The following morning right before Thirty-eight's

court hearing, we had a few COs from Rikers Island come in and scoop me up, making it seem like I got transferred to there. Before I left, Thirty-eight told me to look him up when I got out. I told him once I posted bail I would. I waited a week before I went to Patterson Projects, looking for him. When I got there, it was like they were expecting me. They were showing me a lot of love for helping Thirty-eight. That same day, I was introduced to Money Mike and the rest of the crew, and Thirty-eight spoke highly of me.

"Within days, I knew their whole operation. Five months later, I had a wiretap on the whole organization. With my intel, we were able to identify all the top members and their ranks. We knew where the stash house was located, their connections, plus drop-off and pickup locations. I had so much information on them, we didn't need a snitch for this case. It was a slam dunk."

"Impressive. So what happened next? Did all the members from M&M get convicted?"

"No."

"What do you mean? I can't believe you. Why not?" Johnson fired back with a puzzled face.

"Deals below the table were cut. Information was leaked about how we illegally arrested Thirty-eight. A lot of charges were dropped, and my evidence was not admissible in the court of law."

"You mean to tell me the wiretaps were not accepted?"

"I had Money Mike on tape ordering hits and talking about his operation. I recorded meetings between all the members and Money Mike. They were all incriminating themselves, talking about murder, kidnapping, and money laundering. You name it, they talked about it on my wiretap. We all heard the tapes together."

"Donald, can you please clarify for the court who you mean by 'all of us'?"

"I'm referring to my partners sitting over there. We all heard the tapes together. We played those wiretaps over and over, like a Marvin Gaye record."

"So everyone from M&M walked, how?" Johnson asked.

"Not everyone. But Money Mike only did eighteen months, and four others were sentenced to only two to six bids. I don't know how, especially with all the evidence we had, but you would have to ask my former employers sitting over there why." Lucky pointed at his former partners.

"So you are testifying today that there was foul play?"

"I object, Your Honor. This testimony has nothing to do with the current case. This is an irrelevant testimony."

"I agree. Counsel, get to the point," the judge stated.

"I'm just trying to bring to light the criminal behavior of these police officers, including Donald Gibson himself. Donald, you may continue," Mr. Johnson said.

"I recorded those wiretaps myself. I felt betrayed. Everyone in my department turned their heads. I risked my life, and it seemed like no one cared. A few days later, our captain called a meeting to discuss our new target. I tried to ask about the M&M case, and he snapped at me. They wanted me to turn my cheek like they did. At first I couldn't, but after a while, it became old news, and I just went with the flow."

"So just like that, you were given a new target? Who was the new target?"

"This delivery service company located in Manhattan, called Mr. G Express. We got a tip they were delivering cocaine all over New York."

"Who provided the tip?"

"We used to pay all our informants lots of money if they provided good information."

"How much did it cost for this tip?"

"Around twenty thousand dollars."

"Twenty thousand? Wow! Where did the money come from?"

"Like I said, we were governed by a different set of rules. We never once turned in drug money we seized, not once."

"I object, Your Honor," Matthew yelled. "This is all speculation."

"Overruled."

"Go ahead, Donald, finish what you were saying," a cocky Johnson said.

"We never turned in confiscated drug money. We created our own budget. For example, once we paid this informant on a tip about a Dominican crew smuggling drugs through fifty-four-foot trailers coming up from Miami. We infiltrated the buy. We confiscated 450 kilos of cocaine, over fifty brand-new guns, and 1.5 million dollars in cash. We only reported the 400 kilos and the guns. We never turned in the money."

"What happened to the money and the fifty kilos of cocaine?"

"We split the money. Tango was no longer with us at the time. We each took $200,000 for our personal use. We put the other $500,000 in the budget along with the drugs. In our line of work and how deep undercover we worked, we needed to produce cash, drugs, and guns quickly, so I will say at times, it was necessary to have that amount of money and drugs. We abused the system, using and keeping a lot of money for our own personal use."

"No one ever questioned your team or made you guys follow guidelines?"

"No. It was like we were given the green light to do whatever we wanted."

"Whatever happened to M&M?" a curious Johnson asked.

"Karma. Money Mike was murdered, and his crew fell apart."

"What about the Mr. G delivery business? Who led that investigation?"

"Loose Cannon—I mean Steve. I don't know how or why, but I kept my mouth shut. We didn't call him Loose Cannon for nothing. We spent about four months trying to find a lead, but we couldn't. We really thought we were taken for a ride by the informant. We followed every delivery boy on foot, bike, and car. We had nothing, until we illegally got access to Mr. G's computer and his network."

"What do you mean by illegal access?"

"I object, Your Honor. Witness is testifying to a third-party conversation."

"Overruled. This is all credible testimony."

"I don't know how Steve got the access. I just know he showed up with a disk full of information. Mr. G's computer became our personal informant. His company seemed legal, at least to the naked eye. We couldn't digest all the computer language, and he had a bunch of codes and passwords, so we hired an ex-con computer geek, and he was able to hack the files. We'd found the break we needed.

"One of the first things we noticed was, Mr. G had another warehouse we didn't know about. This warehouse was located in Long Island City, Queens. That same night, Jeffrey, Steve, and I watched the new warehouse all night. About four in the morning, the main gate opened up, and a white van with tinted windows drove out.

"We followed the van all the way to East Harlem. The van stopped at 110th Street and Lexington Avenue. We parked on 111th Street. Five minutes later, we noticed a Hispanic man walk up to the van, and an exchange was made. We thought we were following the van because they were making a drop. Come to find out, the driver was a heroin addict just out buying a quick fix. We pulled the van over right before he jumped back on the FDR Drive on 116th Street and Pleasant Avenue. We arrested the driver, and if my memory serves me correctly, his name was Robert, yeah, Robert. We were hoping the van was dirty, but it wasn't. All we had on Robert was the few bags of heroin. He was not cooperating either. We needed him to talk, so we started offering him all kinds of deals."

"What kind of deals?" Johnson asked.

"Money. We started at a thousand and offered as much as five thousand, but he didn't want the money. All he wanted was his heroin, so Steve went into the captain's office. Ten minutes later, they are letting Robert shoot dope right in the interrogation room."

"Donald, you mean to tell me you guys let a heroin addict shoot up just to get information out of him?"

"We did whatever it took to solve a case. I didn't agree with it, but it worked. Robert gave up all the information we needed. Even though we had Mr. G's files, we still couldn't read them correctly. Mr. G had a very large clientele list, and Robert helped us figure out who were the cocaine customers and who weren't. His VIP customers either owned or ran Fortune 500 companies. He was averaging about one million dollars a week, since he didn't deal with small-time customers. To buy drugs from him, you also had to use his mailing services. That's how he was able to stay under the radar and make his business look legit. We also learned he made out-of-state deliveries as far as California and Las Vegas. He was larger than what we'd originally thought. Robert agreed to wear a wire, but things got ugly quickly. Two days later after our meeting with him, he was found dead in an alley, and Mr. G disappeared."

"What do you mean, he disappeared?" Johnson asked.

"He was gone. After Robert got murdered, Mr. G and his files disappeared."

"Wait a second, Donald. How can your main suspect, his operation, and all the evidence you had on him disappear?"

"That's a good question."

"What do you think happened?" Johnson asked.

"I object, Your Honor. He's not an expert witness. He is asking him for his opinion."

"Overruled. Though he's not an expert, he was part of the investigation and has firsthand knowledge on the matter. I think his opinion does count in this matter."

"When we started to carefully read the list and check out some of these VIP customers, too many important names were surfacing. We are talking CEOs, VPs, and politicians. My honest gut feeling, these people were able to pay their way out."

"I object, Your Honor. Witness is speculating, based on hearsay."

"Sustained."

"You didn't make any money off these deals?" Johnson asked.

"Not off the Mr. G case. I never received one dime. I was told to erase the whole operation from my mind."

"By who? Who said erase it from your mind?"

"My captain." Lucky pointed at William.

"How much money you think they made?"

"I object, Your Honor!" Matthew shouted.

"Withdrawn, Your Honor," Johnson shot back before the judge gave his ruling. He walked back to his desk and consulted with his assistants. He was getting ready to ask about the night in question.

Lucky took advantage of the break and poured himself another glass of cold water. He knew the heat was coming.

Johnson waited for Lucky to finish his glass of water before he proceeded with his case.

"Mr. Gibson, tell us about the night Perry Coleman died. What really happened? Do you remember that night?"

"How can I forget? It still haunts me at night. Anyway, we were all having drinks at this strip club called Tops Off. We normally hang there when nights are slow."

"Were you guys drinking while on duty?"

"Yes, we arrived around seven p.m. It was Captain William "Tuna" Youngstown, Steve "Loose Cannon" Stanley, Jeffrey "Speedy" Winston, and me. We didn't leave till we heard the call. We were drunk and high off cocaine. All of us were."

"While still on duty, you guys were high and drunk?" Johnson asked as he turned to the jury.

"Yes, that was a regular routine for us. We got a call about a robbery on 103rd Street and First Avenue. By the time we arrived at the scene we didn't see any perps. We had a description on the suspect, a young Hispanic male in his early twenties, wearing a red shirt with blue jeans.

"We drove around the area for about fifteen minutes, but we came up empty. Steve was pretty upset about it. He was having a blast at the strip club and didn't want to leave. He kept repeating to himself, 'Someone is getting locked up, and I don't care who.' While we were sitting at the light, he yelled, 'What's that?'

"We all looked toward our left and we saw this Black male wearing a white shirt with black jeans walking out the store. He was reaching for his cell phone, not a gun, and he clearly didn't fit the description. I was driving, Captain was shotgun, and Steve was sitting behind me with Jeffrey to his right. Steve and Jeff were the first ones to jump out the car, with the captain right behind them. All three had their guns drawn, yelling for Perry to get down on the ground."

"Wait a second, Mr. Gibson. Are you saying that Perry never shot at the officers first?"

"Correct. Perry never shot at us, because he never had a gun."

The courtroom erupted again. This time, it took about fifteen minutes to control the crowd. Everyone who supported the Colemans was on their feet, demanding and screaming for justice. The police officers in attendance were still sticking up for their brothers and began arguing with a few protesters.

Through the ruckus, you could see Perry's mother

still in her seat, her head down. She was in tears and crying out for help under her breath.

"Why, sweet Jesus, my Lord and Savior, why did you have to take my son away?"

By the time the mayhem was over, the courtroom was half-empty. A few more protesters were arrested.

During the disturbance, Lucky had looked over at his old partners and read the lips of his former captain.

"*You are dead.*"

Lucky just smiled and gave him the middle finger.

Once order was restored in the courtroom, the judge banged his gavel and said, "This will be my last warning. One more, and I will empty the courtroom and postpone this case. Mr. Johnson, you may continue."

"Thank you, Your Honor. Lucky, please continue. What happened next?"

"I parked the car right in the middle of the street. When I jumped out, I noticed Steve approaching Perry and he was discharging his weapon. The captain and Jeffrey followed like a domino effect. They were also firing their weapons. As I'm running toward them, I was able to stop both the captain and Jeffrey from shooting. Steve stopped only because he ran out of bullets. I was in complete disbelief because I knew we messed up pretty bad. As I'm yelling at the Cap and Jeff, Steve, who I thought had had enough, was trying to reload his weapon. The Cap tackled him to the ground and was able to calm him down for a few seconds.

"Meanwhile, Jeff ran back toward our unmarked car to retrieve a .357 revolver we kept in the trunk for dirty work. The serial number was scratched off. He took about four to five steps back from the car and shot at the back driver-side window twice. He then ran back over to Perry and placed the .357 in his hand. As soon as I approached Jeff about his actions, other units showed up to the scene. It was too late."

Lucky stopped to wipe a tear coming down his cheek. He looked around and Perry's family was also in tears. A few jurors had watery eyes as well.

"Mr. Gibson, did you discharge your weapon?"

"No."

Matthew shouted, "I object, Your Honor. Our forensic witness made it clear that there were other shells found on the scene. This witness is committing perjury."

"Your Honor, their witness also confirmed those shells did not come from Donald's service nine-millimeter weapon."

"Overruled."

"And are you positive Perry never had a gun that night?" Johnson asked.

"I'm positive. We planted the gun. We shot him first and continued to shoot him while he was on the ground."

The crowd started whispering. Lucky's testimony was firing them up again. Even the judge thought another eruption was about to take place, but everyone kept their cool this time.

"What made you come forward?"

"Even before the shooting, I was having a hard time sleeping. It almost felt like I was in too deep to turn back. I wanted out, but I couldn't find a way, but this case here is my way out. When Perry was killed, I realized then how important it was for me to stand up and come clean. These past few years, I have nothing to be proud off. I wanted to give back to New York. I have taken so much as a dirty cop. Hopefully now, I'm able to rest in peace in the afterlife."

"No more questions, Your Honor. The State rests its case," Mr. Johnson said.

Judge Lewis looked at his watch. "It's now eleven thirty in the morning. Let's break for lunch. I will see everyone back in here at one p.m. Mr. Matthew, you will get a chance to cross-examine the witness at one p.m."

Chapter Three

Lucky's Roots

Lucky was led back to the holding cell for his own protection. He had just made himself a whole new set of enemies with his testimony. It wasn't just police officers who felt betrayed, but correction officers as well.

Even the prisoners hated him. They didn't care that he was helping Perry's case. He was still a dirty cop and a snitch, and was now what they would call easy prey.

Lucky just sat inside his single cell, his head leaned back against the graffiti-covered wall. He tried to figure out where things went wrong for him. He thought about his ex-girlfriend and daughter, also hiding somewhere safely.

Lucky kept his family business to himself. No one in the police department knew about them, he made sure to keep their identity a secret. Hurting a cop's family was high on a criminal's wish list. Lucky was starting to have second thoughts about his decision to come forward.

He stood up and began pacing back and forth in that tiny cell. "What did I get myself into? They are going to kill me for sure," he kept repeating to himself.

He sat down and tried to relax his mind. He leaned his head back against the wall again and reminisced about his past, his childhood. Reflecting on his painful past had always helped him get through any issues he was dealing with in the present.

Donald was born and raised in the South Bronx. An only child, his mother, Dawn Gibson, was a Southern lady, born and raised in New Orleans up until she was seven years old. That's when her family moved up to New York.

Dawn met Lucky's father when she was sixteen years old. Four months later, she noticed her stomach was getting bigger, and she was dealing with morning sickness. She was devastated. She didn't tell her sex partner until she was six months pregnant. Right after she told him, he got up, got dressed, and walked out. Dawn never saw Lucky's father again. From that day on, she never looked back.

Young Donald was a witness to his mother's suffering, and he made himself a promise to help her out as best as he could. All she'd ever wanted for him was a good education. He made it through elementary and junior high school unfazed. He was an honor roll student and was loved by his peers because he wasn't a follower. Everyone considered him a leader.

By the time he reached high school, the smooth-sailing ride was over. Not having a father figure started catching up to him.

Donald was into girls heavily. Popular and good-looking, girls were throwing themselves at him. There were some questions he thought his mother couldn't answer. He needed a male's advice. He wanted to know how to handle them, and he didn't want to listen to his friends.

His mother had always said, "Leave those fast girls alone. They're nothing but trouble." But, in reality, Donald wanted the attention. The word *sex* was now in his vocabulary, and he wasn't waiting until his prom to lose his virginity.

He had sex for the first time after a home game with a cheerleader he really liked. She was his girl for three weeks, until the next one threw him some new pussy. He kept switching girls as they came. If his mother had any idea he was having sex with so many different girls, she would have had a heart attack.

He maintained a 3.9 average through high school. He lost his love for karate and grew a passion for football and basketball. He played safety for his school football team and shooting guard for the basketball team, breaking several school records. His senior year he ran for school president and won. All the faculty members wanted him to get into politics, while the coaches were arguing about which sport he should play in college. Everybody wanted to make a decision for him, but he stunned everyone with his decision to attend a community college and join the police academy.

No one understood why he would join the academy with such a bright sport career ahead of him. No one but his mother. She knew Donald grew a passion for his community and wanted to help turn his neighborhood around.

He'd joined the academy in hopes of having other African-Americans follow his lead. The police department had an image of only nerds and rednecks in its ranks. He figured once the public noticed a basketball and football star had joined the force, it would bring better qualified applicants. And he was right.

Everything was on track when things took a turn for the worse. The summer right before he was to start college, Dawn was involved in a very bad car accident. While she was driving home from her second job around 2:30 in the morning, she was involved in a head-on collision with a pickup truck. The other driver fell asleep behind the wheel. By the time Donald reached the hospital, his mother was pronounced dead. He didn't even get a chance to say good-bye to her. Her last words were a voice mail she left him.

"Okay, baby, don't you forget dinner is in the microwave. Mommy will be home late. I love you."

Donald changed after his mother died. He never made it to college that year. He was lucky his mother had a $150,000 life insurance policy, with which he was able to pay off bills and survive for the following eighteen months in isolation with no problem. For an entire year and a half, he basically blocked the world out and only went outside his house like an inmate, an hour a day.

Donald had blocked the world out, but he didn't shut down his mind or body. He kept exercising them both and grew physically stronger and mentally tougher, working out at least five hours a day. He was growing muscles he didn't even know existed.

He read all the "survival" books, and would actually live out the drills in them, sometimes starving himself for a few days. He was trying to become a superhero cop. He restarted his karate training and learned how to live in the dark, and for four months didn't turn any light on at the house and kept all the blinds down.

Lucky woke out of his daze when the district attorney, wanting to prepare him for the bombs the defense team would throw at him, came by to see him.

"Listen, Lucky, get ready to talk about your whole past. If you have any secrets, they are about to get exposed on that stand. Matthew will do everything in his power to damage your credibility, trust me. The important thing to remember here is your poise. Stay cool, calm, and collected under his attack. If you lose your cool in front of the jury, you could damage our case. Are you following me?"

"Yeah, I hear you. I'm ready. It's not like I'm lying. I can handle Matthew, don't worry."

"Well, we got five minutes. Good luck. I will talk to you after court."

"That's funny, Mr. Johnson. As soon as court is over, I'm going back in the hole I crawled out of. You won't see me anymore."

"You just can't disappear again. We could protect you, Donald. Give us a chance. We may need you again."

"We got five minutes before court begins, right? We don't have the time to talk about this bullshit right now. My decision is made. Thank you, but no, thank you."

"Have it your way," Johnson shot back and left the cell.

Lucky's hands started sweating. He sat back down

on the metal bed and placed his hands over his head. He didn't have a clue on what to expect once he took the stand.

When the bailiff called his name, his heart dropped. He knew it was time to face the music one last time.

Chapter Four

Cross-Examination

This time when Lucky entered the courtroom, he didn't take his time. He walked straight to the stand and was sworn in.

"Counsel, you can cross-examine the witness when you are ready."

"Thank you, Your Honor," Matthew replied.

Tyler Matthew walked toward Donald and stared him right in his eyes, hoping to intimidate the former detective, but Lucky wasn't fazed by the staredown. He held his ground until the fancy defense lawyer looked away.

Tyler Matthew first got his license twenty-five years ago as a public defender. He became famous when he was able to get all charges dropped against Al "The Stallion" Soprano in one of the biggest Mafia cases to hit NY in the '80s. He even won a civil lawsuit against the city. Ever since that case, he had been defending high-profile clients who could afford his rate, which was anywhere from $5,000 plus, an hour.

"Donald, can you please state for the court and jury your last employer."

"You mean who I worked for?"

"Correct. You do remember your last employer, right?"

"For the past fifteen years I've worked for the New York Police Department."

"Are you aware of the brotherhood code in the police department?"

"What brotherhood?" Lucky asked, confused.

"Testifying against one of your own is against the brotherhood."

"I object, Your Honor!" Johnson interrupted.

"Withdrawn, Your Honor. Lucky, today you made some accusations in this courtroom. You have implicated my clients' involvement in all sorts of criminal activities. It is my job to make sure those accusations are nothing but the truth. How old are you?"

"I'm thirty-eight years old."

"Are you a family man?"

"No, I'm not. My job didn't permit me to have a family. I worked too many hours."

"But, all three of your partners, they have a family. I don't see why you couldn't. Any reason as to why?"

"I object, Your Honor. His questions are irrelevant to the case."

"Your Honor, I'm just trying to see if Mr. Gibson is a credible witness. I'm trying to establish his character, that's all," Matthew shot back

"Overruled. Counsel, I hope you are going somewhere with this. You are running on thin ice."

"Thank you, Your Honor. I understand. Please continue, Mr. Gibson."

"I understand my partners are all married, but trust me, you don't want to use them as examples or role models. They are horrible husbands and fathers. They have all committed adultery. The clients you are defending loved having sex in our department. It didn't matter where—in the police car, holding cell, right on their desk. You name it, they did it." Lucky chuckled.

"But you still haven't answered my question. Why are you avoiding answering me? Why don't you have a family?"

"I don't want a family, and I don't need a family. When my partner was killed in the line of duty, I had to call his wife and tell her about the murder. I wouldn't want my wife to receive a call like that. That's why I avoided a family. I still dated females. I just stayed away from serious relationships."

"You don't have any kids?"

"No."

Matthew paused and walked back to his desk.

Lucky took a deep breath, hoping they didn't know about his daughter. He poured himself a glass of water. He knew he was in an awkward situation, but he kept his composure because the jury was still watching him.

"Donald, you know you are under oath. Once you make a statement, it becomes a record of the courts."

"I understand."

"Let's go back to the M&M case for a second. You stated you couldn't comprehend why Money Mike was let off the hook and his members received short sentences. Could it have been because of you?"

"What? Are you serious?" Lucky shouted back. "I did what I was told to do. I did my job."

Mr. Johnson caught Lucky's attention from his chair and hand signaled him to calm down.

"Did they tell you to go around killing rivals?" Matthew asked.

"As an undercover detective, you have to play whatever roles you need to in order to keep their trust and to stay alive. That's nothing new. We killed if we had to, just to stay in character."

"You still didn't answer my question. Did you kill rival members with the fella you call Thirty-eight?"

"I object, Your Honor. He's leading my witness."

"Overruled. C'mon, Mr. Johnson, you know you can lead in cross-examination."

Lucky, looking for help, was hoping Johnson's objection didn't get overruled. Matthew had him trapped against the wall.

"We are all waiting for your answer, Mr. Gibson."

"Yes."

Lucky knew his credibility was shot. Even the body language of a few jurors changed a bit.

"Is it true that some of your wiretaps also included your voice in the background?"

"Of course, they did. They were strapped on my chest. You could hear my heartbeat."

"Mr. Gibson, let me refresh your memory."

"I object, Your Honor. Where are these wiretaps? There could be anything on those tapes."

"I agree. Sustained. Counsel, don't talk about mysterious wiretaps in my courtroom. Unless you are submitting new evidence, please proceed."

"Is it true your captain approached you about your conduct during the investigation?"

"No, he never approached me about my conduct. He patted me on the back and told me to keep my mouth shut."

"He wanted you to keep your mouth shut about what?"

"They didn't want me to talk about my involvement with M&M. They thought my behavior was a bit much."

"Over the edge, you think?" Matthew asked with a friendly smile, hoping Lucky would bite.

"I guess a little too much."

"I just asked you if you were approached by your captain about your behavior and you said no."

"No, I didn't. I thought you were referring to IA, Internal Affairs."

Lucky's credibility took another hit. Perry's family was all sitting on the edge on their seats. They knew Lucky was messing up, and that was hurting their case.

"I warned you earlier that you are under oath. Secretary, read back for the records."

"Counsel," she said. "'Is it true your captain approached you about your conduct during the investigation?'

"Witness. 'No, he never approached me about my conduct. He patted me on the back and told me to keep my mouth shut.'"

"Mr. Gibson, how can we trust anything that's coming out your mouth is the truth? In the past few minutes, we all have witnessed you change your testimony. Were charges dropped against M&M because your wiretaps also incriminated the police department?"

"No, I don't agree. I was asked to do what's necessary to bring down M&M. I acted as a gangster, only to build the trust I needed to shut down their operation. My behavior wasn't a mystery. It was necessary to perform at a maximum level."

Matthew walked right up to the jury, and without

looking at Lucky, facing the jury and smiling the whole time, he said, "Mr. Gibson, today you could go to jail for perjury. Did you know that? You have lied to us all," Matthew spread his arms like wings.

Johnson jumped in, hoping to save Lucky from himself. "I object, Your Honor. He is bashing my witness."

"Overruled."

"Earlier in your testimony, you stated you don't have any children, Donald. Again, were you lying?"

"I object, Your Honor!"

"Withdrawn." Matthew walked toward Lucky. "Is it true you have a pretty little daughter?"

Lucky just sat there. Once he heard the word *daughter*, he automatically assumed the worst, that maybe they got to her. No one knew about his baby girl, so for Matthew to bring it up meant he knew something.

After this trial he was going have to move his daughter to a new house. He was stuck in a tough situation. He didn't want to admit he lied again and hurt this case even more. He assumed the defense had some type of paperwork to prove he was the father, but he took his chances anyway.

The judge snapped, "Mr. Gibson, please answer the counsel!"

"No, I don't have a daughter. I have a god-daughter, who I haven't seen in years."

"Is that your final answer?"

"I object, Your Honor. Counsel is delaying this case in hopes he could trap my witness in his own words. It is obvious to the court the defense is hoping for a miracle mistake."

"Sustained. Counsel, let's speed things up. We are not here on a paternity case. We would need a DNA test, and we don't have time."

“I understand, Your Honor. I was trying to prove to the jury that Donald Gibson has no credibility.”

Matthew walked back to his table and consulted with his team about the next step. They were hoping to keep pushing and hurting his credibility.

Right before the judge banged his gavel, Matthew jumped up from the chair and continued his questioning.

“Mr. Gibson, you stated you accepted bribes from criminals and important businessmen, correct?”

“Yes, I did. Personally, from criminals only. The businessmen always dealt with my captain.”

“If you weren’t present in those meetings, how can you accuse my clients of making under-the-table deals?”

“I always waited in the other room while these meetings took place. Once the deals were made, I was always given a black garbage bag filled with money.”

“But you never heard the bribes. You are only assuming.”

“I don’t know the details of the negotiation, you are right, but if my cut is one hundred thousand, that’s more than assuming.”

“Donald, for how long have you been snorting cocaine?”

“Maybe five years. I was working on a case, and in order to join their organization, I had to snort cocaine. Only problem is, after that, I became addicted.”

“So you are an addict?”

Johnson jumped in again. “I object, Your Honor!”

“Withdrawn. Do you have a problem with cocaine, Mr. Gibson?”

“No, I’ve been clean since I left the force. Cocaine became a part of our job. We would snort every day, before we hit the streets. As a matter of fact, we snorted all day long, but those days are behind me."

"On the night in question, how much drinking and cocaine did you do before the shooting took place?"

"I don't recall how much cocaine, but it was a lot. Maybe three grams."

"You snorted three grams of cocaine?"

"Not just me. Between all four of us, we used about three grams, and we all had about three to four shots of vodka."

"Is it safe to say that maybe you were too high to remember what you saw?"

"No, it's not. I clearly remember what I saw."

"But you were high and drunk, yet you want us, the jury, and the court of law to believe an ex-dirty cop and former drug addict. Sitting over there, we have three honest cops, fathers, and husbands. Why are you trying to sabotage their careers and families?"

"What about Perry's family? Who's thinking about them?" Lucky stood up as he replied. Matthew finally got to him. "Listen, I know what happened that night. We killed an innocent man for no reason, and now we are hiding behind our badge, this city, and the law."

"Mr. Gibson, if you don't sit back down, I will hold you in contempt!" the judge yelled at him. "Are we clear?"

"Yes, we are clear," Lucky said as he sat back down.

By this time, everyone in the courtroom, including the judge, was losing a little patience. Matthew was trying his best to avoid asking the main questions he should be asking.

The judge said, "Mr. Matthew, please get on with your case, so we could move to closing arguments by tomorrow morning."

"Mr. Gibson, didn't you shoot your gun that night as well?"

"No, I never drew my gun from the holster."

"All of my clients testified you were the first one to shoot back. Remember, you are still under oath."

"I never drew my gun, and I never shot it. There were no shell casings found on the scene that matched my gun. Those three officers over there killed Perry out of pure hatred. 'Another dead, Black criminal. Who cares?'—Those were the words my captain used that night."

Again, the courtroom exploded. This time, some even rushed the three officers charged. They'd had enough and couldn't hold back their anger. The extra court officers available were able to control the crowd rapidly, but not before Steve "Loose Cannon" got hit with a chair across his back that threw him to the ground, but he was okay.

The judge banged his gavel and adjourned court until the following week. He then made his way out of the ruckus and ran straight into his chambers.

Lucky didn't want any part of the rumble. He made his way back into the holding cell, more concerned about disappearing again.

Meanwhile, the police officers on the scene were slapping handcuffs on anyone that moved or supported the Coleman family. It was like something out of the movies.

It took about forty-five minutes to finally get the courthouse under control. Those who weren't arrested were sitting in their seats not knowing what to do next, shocked at the way things turned out.

Lucky had some quick words with the DA.

"Listen, Lucky," Johnson said in a soft, worrying

tone. "They're going to try to move this case to another county, maybe upstate or Westchester. If we continue, I expect a hung jury. The judge will give me a date to hear the closing argument, but I guarantee that day will never come. They don't want a deadlocked jury. This case will get moved, especially after the ruckus that just took place in the court."

"There's nothing you could do to stop it? C'mon, brother, this is the time to step up. You sound like you giving up," Lucky shot back in disbelief.

"Giving up? Listen, I worked my ass off for this case. I believe your story. I know they killed that poor kid for no apparent reason. Since this case started, I have noticed the loopholes in our great government. I'm getting pressure from the fuckin' mayor to plea-bargain down to a misdemeanor."

"What? That's only a twelve-month sentence. They'll be out in six months."

"I know, Lucky. I'm glad you came forward. You sure you don't want to hang around a little longer? We could really use your help."

"Man the fuck up. They are testing you to see how far you will go. If you show fear to take chances or risk everything you have, they will own you. I can't hang around. I now have a hit on my head for stepping on that stand. I won't disappear quietly—I could promise you that."

Before the district attorney could reply, Lucky was already heading for the door. Once he heard about the case being moved, he automatically knew the charges were going to get reduced or maybe even dropped. He made his way outside the courthouse and disappeared into the downtown Manhattan crowd.

There was nothing Johnson could have said to keep Lucky around, but Johnson had a funny feeling he wouldn't be too far away either.

Outside the courtroom, Perry's mother was getting ready to speak to reporters, while her husband, and Perry's wife and son stood by her side.

Chapter Five

The Phone Call

Laura took a deep breath when she saw there were over thirty media personnel waiting for her on the front steps of the Supreme Court, where many celebrities had held their press conferences. Laura dreamed about this moment. This would be her first shot at redemption, closure. She knew the world was watching. She wanted to make sure she kept her composure and chose her words wisely. The last thing she wanted to do was come off as a hateful woman who had a vendetta with the entire police department.

"Today, we learned the truth about what really happened to my son," she said. "We heard it from one of the officers who was present when the shooting took place. He testified against his former partners, and finally painted a picture for us. Now we know what happened that night.

"Since the first day my son was murdered, I was told by everyone, the mayor, police commissioner, and even you guys, the media, that my son had a weapon. I didn't raise him to shoot people. I'm not saying I'm a better mother than any woman, or that Perry is a better son than anyone's, but the portrait you guys painted of my son was untrue. Today, it was a blessing to hear Donald Gibson come clean and tell the truth to the world. I know my son didn't shoot at the police officers. He didn't even own a gun. He made one mistake when he was a juvenile with some school friends, but since then, he has blossomed as a respected, positive man.

"At today's hearing I was shocked to hear the racist language coming from other police officers who were showing their support. It's sad that we still face racism, like we are still in the fifties and sixties. I hope today's ruckus doesn't dilute the jury's decision when it's time to hand down the verdict. These animals must pay for what they did to Perry, his family, his wife, and son. A guilty verdict won't bring him back, but at least he will be able to rest in peace.

"I'm curious now to see what you guys will print in the papers tomorrow. I hope one of you apologize for jumping to conclusions and defaming my son's name. That's all I have to say right now. Any other questions, our family lawyer will answer them for you. Have a good day."

As Mrs. Coleman, her husband, Kim, and little Perry walked down the steps of the courthouse, reporters followed them, hoping for one more statement. They all quietly jumped in a black Lincoln Town Car and drove away.

While in the car, Laura leaned back, closed her eyes, and exhaled. She was hoping when she woke up, her baby Perry would still be alive, and this would all be one big nightmare. On their ride back home, they kept hearing a phone ring.

"I know I'm not going crazy. Can someone please answer their phone?" Perry Sr. said.

"I hear it, too, honey. Excuse me, driver. Is that your phone?"

"No, Mrs. Coleman, that's not my cell phone ringing. I have mine on silent."

They all looked puzzled and confused and started searching for this cell phone. Perry Sr. was riding shotgun and didn't see anything in the front.

Kim reached under her seat and pulled out a black RAZR, still ringing. "I found the phone. It's ringing. Should I answer it?" Kim asked.

"Wait, not yet!" Laura shot back in a scared tone.

"Someone left it here because they want to communicate with us," Kim argued. She flipped the phone open and answered the call. She had a gut feeling the caller had information to provide.

"Hello?"

"Put Mrs. Coleman on the phone, please."

"Who is this?" Kim replied, looking over her shoulders. She knew whoever was on the line was watching them, because they knew she wasn't Laura.

"Listen, I need to speak to Mrs. Coleman. Please pass her the phone."

Kim attempted to pass the phone to Laura, but she didn't want to take it. The past few weeks all kinds of nutheads had been calling her. She was tired of the harassment.

Her husband had to encourage her to take the call. "Go ahead, honey. Speak to them. See what they want. The minute they say anything crazy, just hang up."

"Okay." She pulled the phone close to her mouth. "Hello?"

"Mrs. Coleman, no matter what you do, please don't say my name until we hang up."

"Who is this?"

"Mrs. Coleman, it's me, Donald Gibson, the cop who just testified."

"I don't understand why you are calling me."

"Just listen. First, I want to apologize for what happened to your son. You have my deepest sympathy and condolences. I'm calling you because I wanted to warn you about a few things. If I know my partners, they already bugged your car and house. They know I would be contacting you guys, so in other words, they are listening. However, they can't hear me. That's why you can't repeat what you hear. Are you following me, Mrs. Coleman?"

"Yes." Laura sat up on her seat.

Perry Sr. was getting a little concerned about the conversation. By her body language, he knew she was uncomfortable, but not frightened. He held back from grabbing the phone.

"Okay, listen, I have some bad news. The defense is going to try to file a motion to move the trial to another county. That's going to hurt your case, if they approve the motion. Let's meet. I have something to give you. Meet me tomorrow morning in Central Park. You know how to get there?"

"Yes."

"Let's meet at nine in the morning on 110th Street and Fifth Avenue. When you get off the phone, I want you to say out loud my name, and a fake address where we're meeting. Good day, Mrs. Laura. I will see you in the morning. Oh, before I forget, remember, you are being watched. I would say, at least a ninety percent chance, you are. I would come up with other ways to communicate without making it obvious. Good-bye, Mrs. Coleman."

"Wait, I don't—"

"Shhhh. I will answer anything you want to know when we meet. Are you coming?"

Laura had to take a deep breath. She grabbed her husband's hand, squeezed it, inhaled, and said, "Yes," like she signed her life away. She exhaled and leaned back in her seat.

Perry Sr. was very concerned. "Honey, you okay? Can you hear me, sweetheart? Who was that on the phone?"

Laura just sat there for a good two to three minutes in dead silence. She knew her husband and Kim were both talking, but she couldn't hear a thing. Finally, she snapped out of it and told them what Lucky said.

"You won't believe who was on the other end of that phone."

They both asked, "Who?"

"That was Donald Gibson. He said he wants to meet and hand me some evidence that would help our case."

"You mean to tell me that was Donald and he wants to meet? It doesn't sound right, baby. What the fuck is going on here?"

"I don't know, but I guess we will soon find out."

Perry Sr. pointed his finger at his wife. He looked like he had the devil in his eyes.

Even Kim sat back and held Li'l P tight on her lap. She'd never seen him act this way. The stress of this whole ordeal had to be wearing him down.

"Listen, woman, we are not meeting with that cop. You heard the things he said in that courtroom. He's a murderer. Who knows what kind of trick he's trying to pull?"

Kim jumped in. “I think he’s right, Mrs. Coleman. You might want to think about it.”

“Think about what? My baby is gone.” Her voice started cracking. “This man called me and said he has something to give us. Plus, I have some questions of my own. We are meeting tomorrow morning at nine, at Penn Station on Thirty-fourth Street.”

“You never listen to me, woman. You are not going alone. I’m coming with you.”

“I’m not going,” Kim quickly added. “You guys could just fill me in later.”

They all sat quietly for the rest of the ride.

Laura thought about different communication strategies.

Lucky’s hunches were right. Captain, Loose, and Speedy were determined to capture him. They’d hired their own surveillance crew, two brothers who called themselves “The Watcherz.” Their names were Hack and Little Hack, and their rap sheet could stretch a mile. They were the best underground hackers in the game. Their specialty was tracking people down and hacking into systems. They’d made millions helping the mob locate witnesses. It was rumored they hit a bank for about twenty million, right from their living room, and just by hitting the enter key on their keyboard. That was before they both got busted and served over twelve years apiece in federal prison.

The Watcherz were back in business after they had been paroled, but they kept a low profile. They didn’t take those high-paying jobs, because they wanted to stay under the radar.

Until Captain Tuna approached them about the job of tracking down Lucky. Their mission was to find him and the whereabouts of his daughter. The captain wanted Lucky and everything related to him dead.

They bugged the Lincoln Town Car the first day of trial and struck gold. As soon as they heard Laura say Lucky was on the other line, the captain was contacted on his cell phone.

"Who the fuck is this? It better be good. I'm in no fuckin' mood."

"We got Lucky," said Hack.

Tuna's attitude did a three-sixty. "You did what? Great job. I'll be right over."

As soon as Tuna pressed the end button on his cell phone, he speed-dialed Loose.

"Cap, what's up?"

"The Watcherz, they found our boy."

"You're shitting me!" Loose yelled back.

"Find Speedy and meet me at the spot in forty-five minutes."

The spot was an old, beat-up apartment building on 102nd Street and Lexington Avenue with five floors, each floor with a four-bedroom apartment. Tuna's uncle owned the building. He rented the fourth and fifth floors to Tuna for his operation, he lived on the third floor, and the second and first floors were rented out to only family members. The fifth floor had nothing but state-of-the-art surveillance equipment, most of it illegal.

The fourth floor was basically a bachelor's pad/safe house. One room on the fourth floor kept all the money, guns, and drugs. Only the captain knew the combination to the safe. Speedy and Loose Cannon arrived at the spot early so they waited in the car until Tuna pulled up. Then they all went in together. They sat down, cracked open a few beers, and listened to the tape, evil smiles on their faces.

"We finally got this muthafucka, Cap. I'm going to cut his fuckin' tongue out!" Loose yelled.

"I knew he would slip up. Good job, boys. Now find his daughter," Cap said to The Watcherz. "We got a lot of work to do. The meeting is tomorrow morning, and it's going to be a madhouse in Penn Station. He picked a good location, but his ass is still fried."

"Wait a minute, Cap. Play the tape one more time," Speedy requested.

"We already know the drop. What else we need?"

"You see, Cap, that's the problem right there. Everything is too easy. Lucky is a lot smarter than that. We all know that."

After listening to the tape again, Speedy stood up and paced the room back and forth. He knew something was funny about the location. He asked The Watcherz if it was possible to pick up the conversation on the cell phone. They nodded their heads and asked for fifteen to twenty minutes.

The captain and Loose were starting to see Speedy's point.

Within three minutes, The Watcherz had the cell phone conversation playing through the speakers:

> *"Okay, listen, I have some bad news. The defense is going to try to file a motion to move the trial to another county. That's going to hurt your case, if they approve the motion. Let's meet. I have something to give you. Meet me tomorrow morning in Central Park. You know how to get there?"*

"Yes."

"Let's meet at nine in the morning on 110th Street and Fifth Avenue. When you get off the phone, I want you to say out loud my name, and a fake address where we're meeting. Good day, Mrs. Laura. I will see you in the morning. Oh, before I forget, remember, you are being watched. I would say, at least a ninety percent chance, you are. I would come up with other ways to communicate without making it obvious. Good-bye, Mrs. Coleman."

"Wait. I don't—"

"Shhhh. I will answer anything you want to know when we meet. Are you coming?"

"Yes."

"Damn, Speedy! You a bad son of a bitch," Loose said. "That was a great pickup. We would have been at Penn Station like assholes, while the real meeting is taking place in Central Park."

The room got quiet after they heard the real meeting location. Everyone was in a daze, thinking about tomorrow morning. Lucky had almost fooled them, but Speedy was on point. They quickly started getting ready.

They all had been waiting for this day since the night Perry Coleman was killed and Lucky disappeared. They'd searched for him all throughout the city. They had a million-dollar bounty on his head. No one knew his whereabouts. That's why they were so nervous when he'd showed up in court.

The captain started pulling out different maps of Central Park. Loose and Speedy cleaned and loaded all their guns like they were being deployed to Iraq.

This was the day they would get payback on a disloyal member.

The Watcherz were back on the computer, looking for the second targets while the Cap, Speedy, and Loose went down to the fourth floor to celebrate. These officers didn't care that they were each facing murder charges, they still partied hard. They'd stopped going to strip clubs, so they called strippers to the apartment. These NYC police officers were living and acting like gangsters, legal thugs.

While they were snorting coke, taking shots of vodka, and getting lap dances, someone else was busy preparing for the meeting.

It was one o'clock in the morning, and Lucky didn't plan on sleeping. He also set up his own spot like his former partners. His equipment wasn't as fancy and expensive, but good enough.

He'd bought a house in the Bronx, in the Pelham Bay area, a three-floor house he shared with Diamond, a twenty-three-year-old woman. Everything was under this girl's name. Her real name was Tracey Sanders, and she was a runaway from Alabama. She'd come to the Big Apple six years ago at seventeen.

As soon as she stepped off the bus, a pimp snatched her up and had her turning tricks that same day. She was working for only six months the night Lucky bumped into her. He was coming out the strip club in Hunts Points when she walked by and offered him a blowjob.

"Hey, big guy, would you like for me to suck your dick?"

Lucky looked around to make sure she was talking to him. His dick was already hard from all the lap dances.

"Hell yeah. How much is it going to cost me, baby?"

"For you, forty dollars, but if you get a room, I will suck and fuck you for seventy-five. You could even go inside my tight ass."

At that point, it wasn't hard to convince him. They started walking to Lucky's car and headed to a nearby run-down motel called Crown Inn, right off the Bruckner Expressway. Diamond was hot, even at a young age. She was five-six, with long, black, silky hair, caramel complexion, and juicy lips. Her body was right and tight for a young thing. Her baby face and pretty, chinky eyes made her desirable to any man. Her ass was big enough, and her tits were perfect.

Lucky had a feeling she was young, but he also thought she was old enough to get fucked. He knew he was paying for the sex, but he still felt special being with such a gorgeous girl.

When they got in the room, he told her, "Go ahead, baby girl. Jump in the shower. I want you fresh, baby girl, but please get undressed in front of me."

"I hope you know we are wearing a condom, so do it really matter how fresh I am?" Diamond quickly said.

"Of course, we are. I just don't want to smell the streets on you. Go ahead, take your clothes off."

"Okay, but turn the lights off. I'm shy. You could leave the bathroom light on, but turn this one off," she said, walking toward the light switch.

She was hesitant about taking her clothes off with the lights on. Being the detective he was, he sensed something was wrong. Why would a pretty girl with a body like that be so self-conscious about how she looked? He played it cool and told her it was okay.

Right after she dropped her panties, he quickly jumped up and flicked the light on. Her beautiful, young, tender body was covered with bruises. Her pimp apparently loved beating on her. Once Lucky saw the marks, it blew his high. His dick went soft, and he thought about his own daughter.

Long story short, he took her in that night, and she'd been living with him ever since. Three days after he took Diamond in, he went back to Hunts Point in the Bronx, where he found and killed her pimp.

Lucky treated Diamond like a woman from that day on. He took care of her and offered her a place to stay. All she had to do was maintain his house and not tell anyone about him or where they lived. She basically became his student, studying his every move. She became so good at it, she even committed crimes with him.

Diamond was his eyes and ears in the streets. He transformed her into a new woman. First, they became best friends, then partners, which led to them falling in love with each other. It wasn't until her Twenty-first birthday that they finally had sexual relations; that's how much respect and love Lucky had for her.

She was the one who'd planted the phone in the Colemans' car, distracting the driver with her sexy self. She would also be the one who would be watching the cops in the morning in Central Park. She was a rider, and since Lucky saved her life, she owed it to him and did what he asked without hesitation.

While Lucky was plotting in the basement, Diamond was in the kitchen fixing a late-night meal. It was going on two in the morning, and she was in there fixing fried chicken, French fries, and bisques.

That's why he loved that young tender. When she came downstairs with the food, she gave him the boost he needed.

For a moment, he was sitting there spaced out. When Diamond came downstairs, he snapped out of it and started eating like a beast.

"Damn, nigga! Slow down. Save some for the homeless." She laughed.

"Thanks, baby, I needed this right here."

"I know." Diamond leaned forward and kissed his greasy lips.

As Lucky ate, Diamond browsed through his paperwork on the table, catching up on the latest.

Fifteen minutes later, Lucky was back on his feet, ready to finalize the plan. "Diamond, everything on your end is ready to go?"

"Yes, baby."

"Good girl. Well, take your pretty ass to sleep. You got about three to four hours. We're leaving at six thirty in the morning."

"Okay, baby. Don't worry too much. We got this. The plan is perfect. Just come to bed for dessert."

"Not right now. Pussy is the last thing I need. No distractions. You know better than that. When we get back, we could do something special. Whatever you want."

"Sounds good. I'll see you in a few hours."

As soon as she went back upstairs, Lucky got back

to work, going over all the details. He wondered how hard his former partners were working. Little did Lucky know, his former partners were all drunk and passed out. However, The Watcherz were still up, trying to get closer to the little girl.

Chapter Six

The Meeting

When the clock hit nine in the morning, no one was at the Penn Station location but uptown, on 110th Street near Central Park. It was the moment of truth. The action was about to kick off.

The captain and Loose were both hiding in the bushes inside the park and had a clear view of the street, where Speedy was parked in an all-black surveillance van.

Speedy noticed the Coleman car pulling up. He reached for the radio and called his boys. "Hey, fellas, Elvis is in the building. They are parking as we speak."

"Which car? The red Chrysler parking behind the green truck?" the captain asked.

"Affirmative."

"Perfect. They parked right in front of us. We will be able to see Lucky when he approaches the car," the captain radioed back.

Diamond, watching from the rooftop on 111th Street, also saw the Colemans' car. She sent the signal to Lucky that the target had just arrived.

The Colemans were as nervous as hell, not knowing what to expect. Perry Sr. kept looking at his wife with a face that didn't need words.

Laura was now regretting the idea. She was seconds away from telling her husband to drive away, until she saw someone approaching.

That's when Speedy got back on the radio. "Here we go, boys. The mouse is coming right at you guys. He's wearing a black jacket and blue Yankee hat. I can't tell if it's Lucky, but he's built just like him. That's him, fellas, it has to be."

"We see him, Speedy," the Cap fired back.

"Let's just rush him now!" Loose yelled.

"Are you crazy? Right in front of the Colemans? We finally have a visual. We are going to sit here and follow him then kill him. Understand?" the captain whispered in an angry tone. He wanted to make sure Loose, who had a tendency to not follow directions, understood his orders.

"We clear. I just hate that double-crossing bitch."

As they watched Lucky walk up to the car, his back was toward them.

"Hey, Speedy, he has his back toward us, we can't see the transaction. He's going to give her something. Keep your eyes open. We'll follow Lucky, you follow the Colemans and retrieve whatever he gives them."

"How in the world can I retrieve the property, Cap?"

"I don't know. Think of something. Call your cousin over at the Thirty-first Precinct. He's blue and white. Have him pull them over or something."

"Cap, I just saw the drop. He passed her what looked like a CD jewel case. There must be a disk inside. He's walking away now, and I just heard the Colemans' car engine start up. I will follow the car, and you take care of Lucky. Cut out his dirty tongue."

"With pleasure, trust me," Loose shot back, not letting Captain Tuna respond.

Tuna and Loose started following Lucky down Fifth Avenue.

Diamond was looking for them and finally spotted them when they jumped out the bushes. That's when she ran down the six flights of stairs, but by the time she hit the street level, with the heavy traffic going down Fifth Avenue and a lot of people walking the streets, Tuna and Loose were out of her sight.

The captain decided to follow as far as they could before they made their move. They were getting restless as they were already approaching 103rd Street.

"Look, Cap, he's turning into Central Park."

"I see him." The Cap reached for the radio. "Speedy, Lucky turned into the park. We are making our move now. Make sure you get that CD."

"Understood," he radioed back.

By Lucky turning into the park, it made it easier for Tuna and Loose to catch up to him. They began running. Loose was running with his gun out in his hand. When they made their turn, they started shooting.

The sound of gunfire had everyone running and screaming, making it look like a scene out of *Grand Theft Auto*.

Even Diamond's heart paused and skipped a beat when she heard the gunshots. She started running faster toward the shooting.

After about eight to ten shots, the captain wanted to leave, but Loose thought otherwise. "Hold on, Cap, I have to make sure he doesn't survive this one. We don't call him Lucky for nothing." He ran up to the body, which was motionless in a pool of blood. He kicked the body on the back. "What the fuck! Who in the fuck is that?" he yelled.

When Tuna saw Loose's reaction, he ran toward him. It wasn't Lucky, and they both were tripping the fuck out.

"Let's go. C'mon, Loose, let's get the hell out of here," Tuna said, pulling him.

They disappeared through the bushes before the cops showed up.

Diamond made her way to the scene and radioed Lucky. "You were right, baby, these muthafuckas want you dead in a bad way. They just killed my boy in broad daylight in Central Park. Anyway, handle your end, and I will see you tonight. Remember, you made me a promise. I will be waiting for you."

"Cool." He laughed. "Anyway, I'm sneaking into the Colemans' crib right now. I will hit you later. And I didn't forget about my dessert."

The Colemans owned a beautiful, four-bedroom house in Astoria, Queens. Kim and Little Perry were the only ones home. Kim had just put Perry to sleep and was in the living room watching television.

Lucky was standing about fifteen feet behind her, and she had no idea he was there. He was stuck because he couldn't figure out a way of approaching without scaring the shit out of her.

He decided to sneak up on her and place his hand on her mouth, to prevent her from screaming. "Kim, it's me, Lucky, Detective Gibson from court."

Kim struggled at first until she heard his voice and name.

"I came here to talk," he said as he removed his hand from her mouth.

“What in the hell are you doing here? They left to go meet you.”

“Listen, this was a setup all along, I wanted to talk to you. I don’t have a lot of time to explain. Can we talk in the laundry room?”

“Laundry room? Why there?” Kim looked at him up and down suspiciously.

“This house is bugged. With the washer and dryer on, they won’t be able to hear our conversation.”

“Okay, follow me.”

As he followed her to the laundry room, The Watcherz were on the phone calling the captain. At first he couldn’t answer because he was on the radio with Speedy, who’d told him the Colemans were at a restaurant eating.

When the captain finally answered the phone, he almost caught a heart attack when he got off.

“Who was that on the phone?” Loose asked.

“The Watcherz. They confirmed Lucky is at the Colemans’ house right now speaking with Kim.”

“Let’s go then. We need to hurry up.”

“Loose, they live in Queens. It’s going to take like an hour to get there.”

“Yeah, but maybe he thinks he has two hours. It’s worth the shot. Call Speedy. Tell him to meet us there.”

By the time they were on their way to Queens, Lucky was already fifteen minutes deep into his conversation with Kim. She had tears in her eyes hearing the story all over again.

“I’m sorry, Kim. Perry didn’t do nothing that night but reach for his cell phone. Anyway, in the basement you will find a white envelope I left with helpful evidence against these police officers. Wait a day or two before touching it or telling anyone about it."

"Why are you giving it to me and not the courts?"

"Listen carefully. You are going to have to explain it to the Colemans. They are going to move this trial to another county, basically an all-white county. That way, they get an all-white jury."

"What? They can't do that, right?" a shocked Kim asked.

"You can say it's written in stone."

Kim started breaking down. She couldn't believe her husband was murdered and the people responsible would get away with it.

Lucky knew he didn't have time to sit there and console her. "I'm sorry, I wish I could do more. Tell the Colemans to move forward with a civil case. You guys will be better off getting money from the City than a guilty verdict. The evidence I left, if you use it in the case, you will lose it. Trust me, it will disappear. Remember, your attorney is the district attorney for the City of New York. He's getting all kinds of pressure from politicians."

"I really don't understand everything you're saying to me. Wait for Laura and her husband to get home."

"Kim, you are not paying attention. You have to be strong. The City will do everything in their power to make this criminal case go away. They don't care if they have to pay money. They will offer to settle."

"So, that's the way it is? All my baby gets is money, no justice?"

"Unfortunately, that's the way it is here in this corrupt city. It doesn't matter that you have all these Black politicians and these big-name African-American organizations backing you guys up. It's all propaganda. Just listen to what I'm saying—Do it my way, and at least you will be financially set. Just think about what I said. I'm leaving now. I will be in contact again, but you will never see me in a courtroom. Oh, and tell the Colemans they deserve the gift."

"What gift?"

"You will see when they get home. Just tell them it was from me."

"You are leaving just like that? What if we need you to testify again?"

"I left you enough evidence. You don't need me anymore. And, to answer your question, no, I won't testify. Good-bye, Kim, and take care of little man, and again, I'm sorry."

"Wait. Before you leave, did he say anything?"

"Who did?" Lucky replied, looking puzzled.

"Perry, what were his last words?" Kim asked, hoping Lucky would say what she wanted to hear.

"I'm sorry, Kim. By the time I reached him. he was gone."

"That's okay, Donald. We also appreciate you coming forward and placing your life on the line to tell the truth. We thank you so much. We knew in our hearts he didn't shoot at you guys first."

Lucky gave her a hug, threw his black hoodie over his head, and he disappeared again.

The only image The Watcherz obtained was Lucky's backside leaving out the back door.

While the Cap and Loose were still stuck in Manhattan traffic, Lucky was making his way back to the Bronx.

Lucky arrived back at the house and quickly realized something was wrong with Diamond. "What's wrong, girl? Everything went perfect today. We executed the plan. Why the long face?"

"Perfect? What about Larry?"

"Who in the fuck is Larry?"

"I can't believe you right now." She got up and walked away from Lucky.

"C'mon, tell me what's wrong. Come here," he said, grabbing her hand. "Where you going?"

"He was twenty-three years old. Larry was the mark I used as your stunt double, remember? He was killed today."

Lucky felt like a bag of shit, only because he wasn't more sensitive toward Diamond's feelings. To him, Larry's death was just another body, but to her, he was something more. She committed the mistake of falling for the mark. He picked up on her emotions quickly, and instead of flipping and coming down hard on her, played his part.

"Listen, on some real shit, my bad. I was hyped, caught up in the moment because, you know, things went well. You are right. We lost someone who put his life on the line for us."

"Wait," Diamond said, interrupting Lucky. "He put his life on the line for us without knowing he did."

"You're right. These muthafuckas really want me dead. Hey, listen, girl, you know a mark is a mark. We knew, whoever we picked, we were gambling their life away. I see you felt for the mark."

"No, no, Daddy, I didn't," she said, frightened.

"It's okay. You felt for the mark in some shape or form, and you didn't want to see him dead. We all go through that. All I'm saying is, don't get caught up. Emotions in this game are a no-no. You could lose yourself in guilt and never find your sanity again.

Let's just relax for the rest of the day. Call up the Chinese spot and order us some food. I got a few bootlegs we could watch tonight, before we get it on."

"So you're not mad at me?"

"Not at all, baby."

Lucky gave her a hug and kissed her on the forehead. "I'll be downstairs until the food gets here." And down to the basement he went. He wanted to check the surveillance cameras around his neighborhood.

Lucky had installed ten cameras in a three-block radius. To sneak into his house, you needed a few 007 agents. It was safe to say he was one paranoid individual. On the day he became a cop, paranoia became second nature.

Lucky was also able to pick up and hear any conversation within eight hundred feet of his house. He wanted to make sure no one followed him home. After returning from every trip, he would always spend at least thirty minutes reviewing footage and looking for anything suspicious. He had ten different camera views, all on a fifty-inch monitor. He would lean back on his chair and watch the streets like a nighthawk, hoping to see his partners or any idiot who wanted to die.

Lucky's former partners were all back at Tuna's spot, scratching their heads at the events that took place before them. They were mad and they kept throwing the blame around at each other. They'd thought for certain they had Lucky, especially when they picked up the cell phone conversation, but they didn't know he was actually setting them up.

"This fuckin' filthy nigger is getting on my last fuckin' nerves," Loose said.

"I agree. We need to find him, and I mean yesterday," the captain added.

The Watcherz stopped their search for the little girl and refocused their attention on Lucky. Meanwhile, Speedy wanted to know exactly what Lucky had given the Colemans.

"Cap, we need to break into the Colemans'," Speedy said. "I know he left something at their house."

"Calm down. There's no need to worry. Whatever evidence they present in court, we will make disappear. I'm not worried at all."

"But we don't know what he gave them," Speedy shot back.

The captain stood quiet for a few seconds and realized Speedy was making sense, but he was too stubborn to admit Speedy was right. He quickly switched the conversation.

"What we need is a bigger team and a trap to bring the rat out of his hole."

"But who can we trust in the force?" Loose asked.

Speedy looked confused as well.

"We are going to have to reach outside of the force on this one. We need maybe two to three more bodies. Us three, we can't cover the whole city. With all the heat this case is catching, no one in the force would dare do anything stupid. We need to think, and come up with names."

"So now we are employing street criminals to join our movement? Are we giving them guns, too? I don't like this idea, Captain," Speedy said.

"That's why I'm the captain and you are not. Don't start questioning my tactics now. We have no choice but to reach out. We are not going to ask any asshole in the streets with a criminal record to help us. We are reaching out to professionals, maybe out-of-state help."

Loose and Speedy were starting to see the direction of the plan. They all sat on a black plush sofa and went into thinking mode.

While they were thinking, The Watcherz were having a difficult time on their end of the job. They were so frustrated, it got to the point where they started slapping each other. The two brothers were weird like that.

Speedy had to run between them to calm the situation. After about five minutes of struggling to get them to calm down, he ended up slapping both of them. Speedy wasn't known for having a temper, but Lucky had him stressed out.

The captain got up. "What the fuck is wrong with you, Speedy? Go home and come back tomorrow when your mind is right. You are not the only one going through it. We can't let this nigger win. This trial is bigger than us. We can't let this boy win."

"My bad, Cap. I will see you in the morning. Loose, see ya."

Loose walked Speedy downstairs, laughing his ass off the whole way. He thought it was funny that Speedy had slapped the brothers.

As they went downstairs, Tuna asked The Watcherz what happened.

"When Lucky went in the house, he went straight to the laundry room, and we couldn't pick up the conversation, so we don't have any visual or sounds," Hack said.

That was bad news for the captain. He was hoping they'd at least picked up some type of sound. Tuna was now stressed himself, and he needed a relief. He got on the phone and called up his usual spot.

“Thank you for calling The Candy Shop.”

“Hey, Dimples. What’s up? This is Tuna.”

“Hey, baby. How are you doing?”

“I had better days.”

“Well, you called the right place. The Candy Shop carries all flavors. You want the usual, baby?”

“Surprise me tonight. Remember, I don’t like caramel or chocolate flavor.”

“Don’t worry. I know how you like them. Give me about an hour.”

Tuna hung up the phone and noticed Loose wasn’t back yet, which seemed weird. He quickly reached for his Glock and clicked off the safety. He walked toward the front door of the apartment, which was cracked, but saw no sign of his friend. Tuna’s heart was pounding as he slowly walked up to the door. He managed to open the door with his foot while both hands were holding the gun.

When he reached the front door, he looked around and still didn’t see Loose. He started walking down the steps, not knowing what to expect. He was shitting his pants. What if Lucky got to both Loose Cannon and Speedy, and now he was in the building trying to get him?

Tuna was able to make it all the way down to the first floor without any signs of Loose Cannon. As he approached the front door of the building, he could see the shadow of someone leaning their back against the front door. Tuna couldn’t make who it was, but as he got close, he was able to hear Loose Cannon’s voice.

"What? You want more? C'mon, you think you tough. Bring it."

Once Tuna heard that, he ran and opened the door as fast as he could and pointed the gun at whoever was fucking with Loose. Tuna scared his friend, catching him off guard, and Loose jumped on Tuna. In the struggle Tuna's black 9 mm Glock went off, and they both fell on the ground. Tuna didn't know if he shot his best friend or not.

Tuna quickly jumped up and started checking him for gunshot wounds. He couldn't find any and didn't see any blood. He then looked up to see who he was arguing with. It turned out, he was play-fighting with a ten-year-old boy.

After thoroughly searching Loose, they both looked at each other thinking it was impossible for that bullet to have missed him. Loose got up and told the kid to run home before the cops came.

"Damn, Loose! God didn't want you tonight. You are blessed, my brother."

"Cap, why in the hell did you jump out like that?"

"I don't know. You took too long to come up, so I came down. I crept up on the door, and that's when I heard you say, 'You want more?' so I didn't want to take any chance."

"Lucky got us all fucked up in the head. What if the kid got shot? Let's go upstairs and relax. You need to call The Candy Shop."

"I'm already two steps ahead of you. They should be here in like forty minutes. Go upstairs. I'm waiting for the uniforms to show up."

"No, Cap, come on. Don't wait. We don't need the attention."

"You right. Fuck that! Let's go get ready for the girls. I told Dimples to surprise us with a new flavor."

"You told her no chocolate or caramel, right?"

"They already know."

They went upstairs, took showers, and got dressed like they were going out to one of the hottest clubs in the city. The captain walked to the back, toward the safe house room. Ten minutes later, he came out with about eight grams of cocaine, a few pills of ecstasy, and seven thousand dollars, mostly singles and five-dollar bills, for the girls.

Back at The Candy Shop, girls knew they were big tippers and they would fight over who was going over to their spot. One time, four girls walked out with about five thousand dollars each.

These above-the-law cops were living like kingpins, spending thousands on a daily basis, and killing with no mercy. And instead of playing it low-key until the trial was over, they were still committing crimes and partying like rock stars.

While the corrupt cops were partying, Lucky and Diamond were sleeping. They had watched a few movies and fucked each other's brains out.

The Colemans were still up and confused about what took place. They were supposed to meet Lucky, but instead met a stranger, who passed them a CD. When they opened the CD case, there was no disk, just a note ordering them to eat at a certain restaurant. They were hoping Lucky was going to show up. After a few hours, they decided to leave the restaurant and head home.

When they arrived home, Perry Sr. needed to get something out the trunk of his car. That's when he noticed a big black duffel bag. He called his wife over. "Laura, did you put this black bag in the trunk?"

She walked over and looked at it, "No."

When they opened the bag, they couldn't believe their eyes. It was filled with money. They didn't know how much, but they quickly closed it and agreed to keep it a secret between them. They went inside the house and acted like they never saw the money.

Kim wasted no time approaching and handing them a four-page letter. She wrote everything Lucky said word for word. Everything, except what he left in the basement. The Colemans took turns reading the letter right in the living room. Now they knew who left them the money in the car, but they weren't surprised.

Kim was looking around the living room, searching for the camera. She couldn't stand being watched. She knew they were watching them read the letter.

The Watcherz desperately tried to zoom in on the letter, but they couldn't get a good angle. They even tried reading the Colemans' lips, but were unsuccessful as well. They knew Kim wrote about her meeting with Lucky.

After the Colemans finished reading the letter, Kim burned it with a smile, knowing whoever was watching would be upset by her actions. Once again, she was right. The Watcherz were pissed.

The Colemans were getting ready for another long night. No one could sleep, not after going through the type of day they'd gone through. Laura and her husband were in the same bed together, but their thoughts were miles apart. They both had two things on their mind, their money and their faith. Perry Sr. was relying on his belief in God to get him through this, while on the other hand, Laura wanted those pigs killed.

"Honey," she said in a cracking, low voice.

"Yes, sweetheart."

"How in the hell did we get into this? First, we lost our baby. Now we're losing our privacy. I have so much hatred for those police officers."

"I really wish I had an answer for you, sweetheart. I been asking God why this has happened to our family myself, but I'm still looking for the answer. I don't understand how my son, who was unarmed, was gunned down like an animal," a choked-up Perry Sr. said.

"Honey, I've been asking God the same questions myself. I'm starting to question my beliefs. We are a good family. This is not supposed to be happening to us," she said as she sat up on the bed.

"I'm questioning my faith as well. I'm trying to stay strong, but it's hard. I wasn't there to protect him, but I will fight his death till the end," he said, also sitting up.

"I can't live like this anymore, Perry, knowing they are watching us. I can't sleep, use the bathroom, or change my clothes. I've had enough." Laura jumped out of bed.

"It's almost one o'clock in the morning, Laura. Why are you picking up the phone? Who are you calling?"

"I'm calling up the minister and our civil lawyer. They told me to call whenever I needed them, and that's what I'm doing."

Laura threw on her robe and walked down to the

kitchen for a cup of coffee while she dialed the minister's number. After the fifth ring, he finally answered the phone.

"Who is this?" Minister Al Muhammad said in a angry, sleepy voice.

"I'm sorry to bother you. This is Laura, Laura Coleman."

"Laura, my goodness! What time is it? What's wrong? I'm listening."

"We need help. I think we are being watched. No, we are one hundred percent sure we are being watched. Our house is bugged."

"What? Excuse me, come again?" Minister Muhammad quickly got on his feet. "Listen, Laura, I will send a few FOIs by your house."

"That would be great, but I'm more concerned about our house being bugged."

"Don't worry. I'm sending someone who specializes in surveillance technology. He will find anything. It will take him less than an hour to sweep your house for bugs. I will be on my way after I make all these phone calls. We need to act now because, if your house is bugged and we wait, they will find a way to clean their mess."

"Okay, I understand."

"Don't let anyone in your home. I don't care who it is. I will get there as fast as I can. FOI will be there guarding the premises until I arrive. Remember, don't let anyone in until I get there, not even my security."

When Laura hung up the phone, she was nervous. She didn't know what she'd started. She just sat in silence with her head down.

Perry Sr. walked in the kitchen and hugged his wife. "Are you okay, sweetheart?"

"Yes, I'm fine. The minister is on his way, and he's bringing us a bunch of security."

Perry Sr. started laughing. "That's why I married you. You are a determined woman. I love you, baby."

As the Colemans continued talking in their kitchen, waiting for the minister, The Watcherz had called Tuna on his cell a few times, but he was not picking up. They'd also tried calling Loose Cannon, but his phone was turned off and going straight to voice mail.

Hack walked down to the fourth floor and knocked on the door repeatedly. He even banged on the door, but still no answer. All he heard was the loud music playing in the background. He went back upstairs and told his brother. They didn't know what to do.

They decided to call Speedy, but he was no help. He was still upset and didn't want to hear about Lucky or the Colemans. He just hung up the phone on those two retarded geeks.

They continued watching the house, not knowing what to do.

When the minister arrived, he brought a few friends with him. They swept the house and cars and found five cameras in all with built-in speakers.

The Watcherz lost both audio and video. They were fucked. All the monitors went pitch-black.

The Colemans were shaken to see so many cameras. By this time, Kim and Li'l Perry were also up and shocked to see all the commotion.

The minister walked over to consult the family. "Laura, I'm glad you called me. I have with me one of my top lieutenants. He's an ex-Navy SEAL. He quickly identified those surveillance gadgets were not property of the NYPD. They look more federal, or bought in the black market."

"We already know who's responsible," she shot back.

"You do. Who then?" a puzzled Muhammad asked.

"Those dirty cops who killed my son. They were keeping an eye and ear on us, fearing that the other cop who turned on them was helping our case."

"And you are one hundred percent sure about this?"

"You don't even want to know what we've been through in the last twenty-four hours. Donald 'Lucky' Gibson himself told us. He was the one who tipped us about the cameras."

"What else did he say?"

"He told us there was going to be a hung jury."

The minister was in a state of shock. Not surprise, but shock. He couldn't believe the government was about to let those cops get away with murder. He preached every day about a better day to come, but this mess he was facing was setting those days back by a few years.

"Okay, look, I'm going to make a few phone calls. I have some powerful friends in the force who could verify if this stakeout is legit. I'm also calling up members of my board. We are going to organize a rally in memory of Perry. We are going to march down by One Police Plaza. We need to show White America we will no longer take it. We will get a lot of media attention, which we need to fight the case from moving to another county. That can not happen."

"That sounds good, a parade for my child. He would love that," Laura said.

"Now, we need to talk about your safety. Are you guys willing to relocate until the trial is over?"

"Nope, that's not an option!" Perry Sr. fired.

"This is our home. We are not letting these dirty cops run us away from our home," Laura added.

"I completely understand. In that case, I'm leaving four members from my personal security team. The lieutenant is also a personal friend of mine. Brother Noble, he will stay as well. But, before we move forward, let's get one thing clear. I need to know everything. No matter how small or big, I need to know everything. Anyone else have anything they would like to add?"

Everyone got quiet for a few seconds.

The Colemans didn't bother telling the minister about the money in the car that Lucky gave them.

Kim was in a daze, thinking about the package Lucky left. She didn't know if she should say something and didn't see any harm in telling him about it. "Wait, I have something," she said.

Shocked she was withholding information from them as well, the Colemans quickly looked at her.

"What is it?" Minister Muhammad asked.

"Lucky said he would get in touch with us again."

"When? How soon?" he asked.

"He didn't say."

"He didn't say, huh. Well, we'll have to wait and see," Minister Muhammad replied, knowing Kim was hiding information.

"Oh, before I forget, you guys need to get ready. I have a reporter coming in about an hour to run this story. I guarantee you the mayor and police commissioner will bang their heads against the wall a few times. I will shake the city with this report. Hopefully it will work in our favor."

"That's the thing, Minister, but what if it backfires and hurts our chances in court?" Laura asked.

"I doubt it will. We clearly have foul play, and you guys should not be under surveillance like criminals. This is unacceptable, and we will take action. I don't care if we have to march from City Hall all the way down to Washington, DC. We need to show our true character as a nation."

Chapter Seven

The Media

When Channel 5 News first came on at five o'clock in the morning, they reported the story on the early show. The news station titled the breaking news, "An Illegal Government Home Invasion." The news reporter stated they would go live with an exclusive interview with the Colemans at eight o'clock in the morning right from their home, along with Minister Al Muhammad, and their civil lawyer, Joseph Anderson.

The breaking news was the rush-hour gossip in all of the city's public transportation. Everyone wanted to know what happened and who was responsible for the invasion of privacy. New Yorkers were very concerned. No one knew what was going on, but rumors were already circulating through the grapevine. Some were saying the Colemans' house was broken into by a warrant squad looking for evidence that would damage Perry's reputation. Others were saying the Colemans were being watched by the federal government as a precaution.

People couldn't wait until the exclusive interview at eight o'clock. New Yorkers crammed into every businessplace with a TV. Some didn't care they were running late for work. They were not leaving their house until the interview was over. This case was real important to the people of NY. At this point, it didn't matter the color or gender of those involved. New Yorkers had had enough. A few were even calling for the resignation of the mayor and police commissioner.

Back at Captain Tuna's place, The Watcherz were still waiting to hear from Tuna or Loose. Around seven forty-five in the morning, Speedy zoomed in through the front door.

"Oh my God! Did you guys see the news? Where's the captain and Loose?"

"They are still on the fourth floor. They had a party, and the girls are still in there. We tried calling and knocking on the front door, but we didn't get an answer. We called you last night as well, but you slammed the phone on my ear."

Speedy raced downstairs and started banging on the door as hard as he could. He couldn't believe their whole operation was just shut down and the captain and Loose were in there celebrating like it was New Year's.

After about thirty seconds of banging, Loose Cannon finally opened the door. "Speedy, what the fuck is wrong with you? Why are you banging on the door so early? Where the fuck is your key?"

"Where's the captain? We have a fuckin' situation upstairs that needs immediate attention. Tell the bitches the party is over, and meet me upstairs in five minutes."

Speedy looked at Loose then looked at the naked girls passed out on the floor. He just walked away in disgust.

Loose knew it was a serious situation.

The captain woke up when he heard Speedy's loud voice. He turned over and asked what happened.

"I don't know, Cap, but we better get upstairs in five minutes before he comes back down here. He also said get rid of the girls."

"Get rid of the girls? They could wait down here. I'm not sending these pretty bitches back today. I'm paying for another night."

"I don't blame you. I had the time of my life last night, but I think you should get rid of them. I got a funny feeling we won't have time. You should have seen his eyes. I haven't seen him that spooked since our rookie years."

The captain was shocked to hear Loose agree with Speedy. He knew it was serious, so he told the girls to leave. They slowly made their way upstairs.

Speedy was waiting for them at the top of the staircase. "Hurry. We only got two minutes before showtime."

They both looked at each other, not knowing what to expect. When they entered the apartment, Tuna quickly noticed all the monitors were blank. The power was on, but the screens were pitch-black.

"Why are the monitors blank? What the fuck is going on? Why are you guys sitting in front of the TV?" Tuna asked Speedy and The Watcherz.

"The Watcherz tried calling you last night. They even banged on the door. Pull up a seat, the both of you. Watch the news and see why those monitors are blank. Laura Coleman has an exclusive interview coming up."

"What!" the captain yelled.

"They are calling it 'the home invasion,' or some shit like that."

"This can't be fuckin' happening right now!" Tuna yelled as he got up and threw a metal stool right through one of the big-screen monitors worth ten thousand dollars.

Loose tried to spit a few words out, but Tuna quickly rejected him.

"Shut the fuck up! Not right now! This right here, gentlemen, this interview, is about to send our asses to jail. I don't need to see the interview. If the monitors are blank, and the news is calling it a home invasion, then the Black bitch must have found our cameras."

"Let's hear what she has to say first. Once she finishes her interview, we will know what they're working with. Then we could figure out a plan. We're in this together," Speedy said, walking up and embracing his boss.

"I'm calm. Turn the TV up, and someone please find me a beer. Better yet, some fuckin' vodka. I got a feeling this interview will be a historic disaster for us, but a celebration for all niggers. I will bet you one million dollars that fuckin' scumbag, Minister Al Muhammad, is planning a rally."

"SHHHH! It's on, Cap. Here we go," Speedy said, his eyes glued to the TV screen.

Everyone was quiet and sitting still, except Tuna, who was the only one standing. He was about to watch an interview that would almost guarantee a guilty verdict in his court case. His heart was pounding, and his knees were shaking. The anticipation would have given any man a heart attack. They weren't the only ones watching. The whole New York City was. Plus, it was being broadcast via Internet as well.

Lucky was also up watching from his bed, sipping coffee, a smirk on his face. As the interview was about to start, he shook Diamond awake.

"Get up, baby. C'mon before you miss it. Get up."

"I'm up. My eyes are open. Turn the volume up," she replied in a low, grumpy voice

> *"Good morning, my name is Destine Diaz from WBZT Channel 5 News. Today, I have an exclusive interview with the mother of Perry Coleman. Perry was gunned down by three New York detectives. We have some new disturbing allegations made by the Colemans' family lawyer, alleging that the their house and vehicles were illegally bugged by surveillance cameras and listening devices. Hear for yourself as we roll the tape."*

The media did an excellent job in attracting the public attention through fear. This was the way to sell ratings and newspapers, coming up with catchy titles that would attract attention. By using words like *illegal* and *invasion*, the media sparked the attention they needed. The media still couldn't be trusted, but it couldn't be ignored either. The media's best attribute was their backstabbing motives and sneaky ways. All they cared about was ratings, but many felt they were still manipulated by politics.

Five seconds after the reporter said roll the tape, TV screens across the tri-state area went blank for three to four seconds, and then the weather guy came on with the forecast. While Blacks and Hispanics already knew the deal, a lot of White people didn't and were puzzled.

Meanwhile, the captain, Loose, and Speedy were all celebrating and whipping the shit out their asses. They knew they were still in deep trouble, but happy the media didn't air the interview.

Once the mayor got word of the interview, he called up Eric Macintosh, the station's CEO, and his golfing buddy.

"Hello," Eric said, on the way to his office.

"It's me, Ralph."

"Good morning, Mr. Mayor. To what do I owe the pleasure of you calling early this morning?"

"I need a favor, and I need it in ten minutes."

"Let me guess. This has to do with the interview airing at eight in the morning?"

"You know about it and you're letting it air?"

"Calm down, old friend. I received about four phone calls already. You know I don't screen every report. But don't worry, I already made some phones calls, and it won't air."

"Thank you. I owe you one."

"You bet you do."

"Damn, Captain! We are untouchable. Once these charges get dropped, I'll bet you, we all will get promotions. I love being a cop, I love it," Loose said.

"Let's not get too excited. I'm pretty sure a lot more heat is coming our way," Speedy said.

"Don't worry. They will do what they always do—yell and yell. Loose is right. Once these charges are dropped, things will get better."

All three of them went down to the fourth floor. They

wanted to relax and wait for the call. They knew the commissioner would either call or request a sit-down.

While they went downstairs, The Watcherz resumed their hunt for Lucky.

Lucky was in his bedroom doing exercises. He wasn't surprised that the network pulled the interview. Two corrupt moguls, the media and the government, pulled another fast one on the community. Lucky had bigger issues to worry about. His identity was back at risk once he showed his face in that courtroom.

He turned the TV off and continued working out, listening to music, and acting as nothing happened. He couldn't be rattled.

The real drama was taking place back at the Coleman residence, where Minister Muhammad quickly started making calls and trying to set up a press conference with independent outlets.

"I can't believe what we all just witnessed. White America just made a mockery of us. Brother Perry and Sister Laura, I apologize for this pain not going away. It just keeps pounding harder and harder. In the name of Allah, we will get justice, by all means," the minister preached.

"Well, I don't care who or which God, Allah, Jesus, Jah, whomever. We need closure, and it seems like we won't find it," Laura said.

"I understand, Sister. That's why we won't stop. We can't quit. At the press conference, we will tell the truth to the city. Trust me, the people want to know. Several media outlets will show up. Are you ready to start fighting back?" Minister Muhammad extended his hand to her.

She grabbed his hand and told him, "Yes, I'm ready."

When 10:00 a.m. came around, there were at least eight media outlets outside the Coleman residence. Laura, Perry, Kim, and the minister were all standing on the porch.

Laura took the center stage and told the world about the hidden cameras and microphones found in their home and cars. "We don't know how long the government has been watching us, but we discovered these devices last night. Donald 'Lucky' Gibson made us aware of the hidden show taking place in my home."

Reporters quickly began hounding Laura with questions, but Minister Muhammad stood up and said, "Please, ladies and gentlemen, one at a time, or your questions will go unanswered. We are here to talk. We will get to everyone's questions, but please, one at a time."

"Laura, hi. My name is Angela Stile. I'm with BETV Channel 20 News. Did you just say Donald Gibson, the police officer who testified in court, made you aware of the surveillance taking place in your home?"

"Yes, that is correct."

"Laura, hi. Channel 4 NBZ Prime Time. Let me ask you this—Are you sure the government is behind this?"

"Donald stated, the police officers who are on trial for killing my son are the same ones watching us."

"So it's not the Government, but these three police officers, correct?" the reporter shot back.

"Let me jump in here," the minister said. "When Laura called me out my bed and told me about the hidden cameras, I called in my very own friend, an ex-Navy SEAL who, for over ten years, specialized in surveillance tactics. He indicated the gadgets were top-of-the-line equipment. If these three cops are responsible, then they must be receiving federal help because the equipment we found is very expensive in the black market."

"So you don't know who's behind it?" another reporter asked.

"No, we don't. That's why we called this press conference. We wanted to share this with all New Yorkers and let them know how your privacy could be invaded. We are not pointing fingers, but these three officers and the police department are on the top of our list of suspects. We will launch our own investigation."

After a few more rounds of questioning the Colemans realized the media was out there trying to downplay the involvement of the government and police department. Minister Muhammad picked up on the media's intention and ended the press conference without warning. He had his FOI security escort everyone off the Colemans' front lawn.

Inside the house, Laura was having a nervous breakdown. The poor lady had had enough. Her baby boy got killed by police officers drunk and high off cocaine, and the whole system was against her. Now the media, which she thought was her only hope of spreading the truth, was turning against her as well. She was on the floor, kicking and yelling like a four-year-old child.

"Why? Why, Jesus? You don't need him up there. I need him. Please, bring my baby back. Why did You have to take him? Take me instead. I lived my life already."

Kim attempted to console Laura, but Perry Sr. stopped her.

"Let her be. Just let her be. This is the first time she has cried like this since our son was murdered. Just let her get it out of her system."

Kim held her ground but couldn't stand there and watch. She grabbed little Perry and went upstairs. Minister Muhammad and his people walked to the kitchen area.

Once Perry Sr. noticed everyone was gone, he approached his wife. "Just let it out, baby. I'm right here when you're ready for comfort."

Laura looked up at her husband, wiped her eyes, and hugged him like it was her last hug.

"I just want my baby back, that's all. I want him back."

"Come here, sweetheart," Perry said as he hugged his wife.

They both sat on their sofa crying together, rocking back and forth. They asked the minister to leave because they were tired and wanted to be left alone.

The minister left a few bodyguards behind before leaving. Then Laura and Perry Sr. went upstairs to their bedroom to catch up on their rest. The rest of the day went pretty quiet, which was exactly how they wanted it to be.

The captain, Loose Cannon, and Speedy kept it quiet for the night as well. For the first time ever, they finally realized they needed to keep a low profile.

The next morning, Diamond went out to the front door to pick up the paper, routine for her every morning around seven. She would brew coffee and get the newspaper.

Lucky would head down to the basement and go over his video footage from the night before.

This morning was a little different. Diamond was shocked when she saw the front page. She quickly ran down to the basement, calling out Lucky's name. "Baby, you are not going to believe this. Here, check the front page of the newspaper."

Lucky grabbed the paper and stared at Diamond for a few seconds. He was hoping he could read her eyes before looking at the paper. He couldn't read her eyes, but knew by her facial expression it was bad. When he finally looked at it, he laughed.

"Those dirty muthafuckas," he said, laughing.

"That's all you have to say, Lucky? I don't understand."

"There's nothing I could do about this. Now it's time to think about leaving. This will bring a lot of pressure our way. As a matter of fact, let me finish watching these tapes from last night. You start packing your shit."

"But, Lucky."

"But nothing."

Diamond walked away upset. She didn't understand why Lucky wasn't upset about his face being on the front page of the most popular paper in the city. The headline read: *NYPD issues warrant for Lucky's arrest in connection with bugging the Colemans' residence*.

Diamond went upstairs to pack, but she turned on the TV first. Lucky's face was on every channel. She turned the TV off in disgust and started packing. Things were moving too fast for Diamond. She sat on the edge of the bed to catch her breath. She was scared to death. She knew her life would be in jeopardy if she left with Lucky.

Actually, for the first time ever, she thought about staying behind and leaving him. But her love for him was too strong, and she wasn't about to let anything get in the way of her man. Whenever she was in doubt about her love for him, she always thought about the first night she'd met him and how he saved her life. Not only did he save her life, he gave her hope and a new beginning. He'd always treated her like a lady, and she knew he was in love with her. She also respected the fact that he waited until she was twenty-one years old to have sex. She didn't care about the age difference between them. They were in love with each other, so it was a no-brainer. She decided to roll with him. She didn't even know why she second-guessed herself.

An hour later, Lucky went upstairs. "Hey, baby, we are leaving in thirty minutes."

Lucky went back down and started to work out the final details for his new plan. With his face now being exposed, his privacy was next. Even though Lucky kept a private profile, he was sure one of his neighbors got a good look at him in the past. That's why he knew he needed to leave as soon as possible. He knew this day was coming, so he was prepared.

This was the risk he took by testifying for the government. He didn't know why he had trusted the government in the first place. He already knew they didn't protect witnesses.

Lucky had a disguise locked away in a suitcase. He didn't change his look too much, just adding a mustache, beard, and pair of run-down reading glasses, giving him the appearance of a nerd or a washed-up teacher that read every book in the world.

He called Diamond to get her opinion on his makeover. "Baby girl, come down to the basement for a quick minute."

"What is it?" she hollered back. "I'm still packing."

"Get your ass down here! Stop asking questions."

Lucky could hear Diamond stomping on each step on her way down. He knew she was still upset about having to leave, but he didn't care. He didn't let his emotions make his decisions.

When Diamond made it down to the basement, she took one look at Lucky and burst out laughing. "What the hell is that on your face? You look like bin Laden."

"Bin Laden? Don't play with me, girl." Lucky started laughing, too.

"Is this your new disguise, honey?"

"Yes. What do you think? Can I get away with it?"

"Since I know it's you, it's hard for me to give you an honest answer. But the disguise looks real. The facial hair is believable."

After a few more jokes, Diamond went back upstairs to finish packing.

Lucky started pulling out folder after folder from his safe. He placed them in a suitcase, along with all his computer software. He wanted to make sure he didn't leave any evidence that would link to him. He destroyed all three of his computer hard drives and grabbed his keys.

Diamond was done packing, and they headed out the door. "Where are we going? And why are we only taking clothes?"

"I have another apartment in Jersey City. Actually, a condo."

"A condo? You have a condo, and I don't know anything about it?"

"Baby, it's all part of the plan. Now hurry up. Let's get out of here. We will talk once we're in the car."

As soon as Lucky locked the door to his house and turned around, an SUV with tinted windows made an abrupt stop right in front of his house. Diamond ran for cover, while Lucky dropped his bags and reached for his .40 Glock sitting on his hip.

Both front doors opened on the SUV, and a Spanish man and woman jumped out screaming at each other. Lucky didn't see any weapons on them, so he didn't shoot, but he was pointing the gun right at them.

The Spanish couple was so busy arguing, they never noticed Lucky pointing a gun. Lucky also realized these two were not assassins, just a drunk couple fighting, so he called for Diamond, and they both jumped in his black Expedition and sped away, not waiting for the couple to stop arguing and get back in their truck.

"That was a close one, baby," Diamond said, exhaling.

Chapter Eight

Corrupt City

By the time Lucky reached his New Jersey condo, Diamond was asleep in the car. He drove around the block a few times, checking out the scenery. Lucky didn't have cameras around the area, so he didn't know what to expect. After about a good half-hour of driving around, he finally decided to wake up Diamond. He parked, and they went inside.

The condo was a beautiful two-bedroom loft with a view of New York City. The exterior wasn't impressive, but no one would have guessed the building was filled with luxury lofts. When he unlocked the front door, Diamond lost it.

"This is a beautiful place, Lucky. Wow! Are we going to live here? I want to stay here, baby, please. But I can't believe you never slept in here before. How come you never told me about this place?"

"You know how I am. I always have a trick up my sleeve. I bought this condo because I knew this day was coming. I always have a plan B. Shit, at this rate, I need a plan C and D."

Diamond walked around the condo, touching and feeling every piece of furniture. She kept grilling Lucky about purchasing this condo without her knowledge. She wanted to know when and how.

"So that's your story, and you sticking it to it?"

"What are you talking about, girl?"

"Don't play with me—this muthafuckin' condo. I want to know if you are telling me the truth."

"Lister, this young, hot movie producer and high-class customer, decided to move to Hollywood. He told me about the place and gave me a price. The shit came furnished and all that."

"So out the blue a movie producer sells you his condo?"

"Didn't I say he was a customer, a drug addict. Is not like he gave it to me for free. I paid a grip."

While Diamond was still fawning over the beautiful condo, Lucky quickly started mapping out the surveillance equipment he needed. He loved the view from his living room and balcony because it was easier to set up cameras. He turned on the news, and they wouldn't stop mentioning his name or showing his face. With a fifty-thousand-dollar reward on his head, a lot of people would be looking for him. He knew his house in the Bronx would be in the news soon, especially with the large reward. Lucky didn't want to waste anymore time. He grabbed one of his bags and pulled out all his folders.

Diamond walked over and started looking through them. "What's in these folders? You have guarded them more than your money."

"This here is the plan of all plans. This is how I'm

going to turn this city upside down. Three years before the Perry shooting and about five days after Tango was murdered, I decided to bug my own crew. For three fuckin' years, I wore wires and sometimes a video camera, and I recorded all our dirty deeds. You wouldn't believe what I have on tape, and the pictures I have in my possession."

"So no one hired you? You did this on your own? That's crazy, Lucky. Why risk your life?"

"When Tango was murdered, our cover was blown, and our backup showed up after the ambulance. I had a gut feeling someone in the crew gave us away. I didn't trust them, so I recorded their every move. I knew one day I would need everything in this folder to show the world how corrupt New York City police really are." Lucky opened up some of the folders.

Diamond couldn't believe her eyes. Lucky had pictures of politicians having sex and using drugs in hotel rooms with high-class escorts, and of high-ranking priests naked with little boys from their choir. He even had a picture of the mayor leaving a Hampton villa with an escort girl. Lucky also had evidence where they'd framed criminals for crimes they hadn't done.

"I don't understand. Why would you frame criminals for crimes they did?"

"No, baby, we framed them for crimes we did, not them. But since they were already convicted felons, no one cared."

"But why frame criminals?"

"Because it was easy. Sometimes we were hired to kill. We didn't want another open unsolved murder, so we solved the case by framing a convicted felon."

"Wow! That's fucked up, Lucky. How about these pictures? How did you get them?"

"Those are all cases I worked either alone or with my team. The escort agency was a real high-class organization. These weren't cheap whores. An average date will run you at least two thousand dollars. That was just a date. We are talking at least five thousand for oral, and fifteen for a sleepover."

"Get the fuck out of here. They were charging five grand just for head?" Diamond had a quick flashback about her days on the streets. The most she ever got from a trick was a hundred and fifty dollars, and that included everything.

"For real, girl. Some of these senators were spending around twenty thousand on just one date. These pigs were getting penthouse suites at five-star hotels and only staying two to three hours in those muthafuckas. They were blowing serious money."

"What about these filthy preachers touching little boys?"

"They all received slaps on the wrist. We reported those sick bastards. We weren't about to defend or help child molesters. But our great judicial system didn't think they deserved jail time. Some of these bastards were allowed back in their churches to resume their positions."

"I can't believe they let these sick people go. What? Pictures of them naked with little boys wasn't sufficient evidence?"

"I guess not. You can't trust this government. I'm not trying to justify my actions, but once I saw how dirty everyone else was, I joined the party. That's why I kept these pictures to protect myself, just in case I needed to blackmail myself out of trouble. I have politicians, state attorneys, the police commissioner, and the list goes on."

"Whatever happened to the whorehouse? How come they weren't charged with anything?"

"They paid us a lot of money. I don't know how much in total, but I was given sixty thousand dollars to keep my mouth shut. Before we destroyed all the evidence, I kept a few pieces as well. But that's not all I have. I also have a list of bogus corporations and non-profit organizations that our city officials used to launder money. Shit, I even know a few election campaigns that were funded by the Italian mob and a couple of cartels out of Mexico and Panama. And let's not forget the tapes I left with the Colemans."

"So why not go public with it right now and clear your name?"

"Baby girl, are you not paying attention? We are on the run because I came forward about a murder. Imagine if I accuse the mayor of this city of adultery, and the police commissioner of money laundering and murder. Do you really think that's a good idea? I'm leaving these papers and files with you. All things in life have a right place and time. They will get theirs, if my plan goes accordingly."

"Why are you leaving it with me? Here we go with this shit again."

"What shit?"

"You are leaving. I already know the rules. If something was to happen to you, you want me to make sure these files go public, right?"

"Something like that, but why the big attitude if you know the routine?" Lucky asked in an angry tone.

"When are you leaving?" she asked, tearing up.

"I don't know, but not soon. It all depends on the amount of heat I'm under. I'm staying indoors as long as I can. I don't want you to wait until I'm gone to mail out these folders. I want you to head to the post office in the morning."

"Oh, well, that's good to hear," she replied with a big smile.

Lucky and Diamond talked for a few more minutes then he gave her a list with names and addresses and specific instruction on how to mail each folder. It was a simple plan, and he felt confident she didn't need the pep talk.

Diamond still curious and wanting to find out more, kept flipping through the files, and each one seemed worse than the other. She discovered some graphic pictures of fatally shot victims.

"Who are these dead people?"

"Witnesses we got rid of for the DA."

"Damn! How corrupt is this city?"

"Listen, I personally took care of witnesses in five major drug and murder cases. I did a lot of dirty work that I'm not proud of. That's why I want to mail this information to the lawyers of each of those cases, and I want the truth to come out. They want to fuck with me? Well, they made a big mistake. I know I'm throwing myself in a deeper hole, but I won't go down alone or without a fight."

"This is a little too crazy for me. I see why you want me to stay away."

"Sweetheart, you wouldn't believe the things I learned in the NYPD. I was taught how to racially profile the minority. We had quotas we had to meet, and they were all targeted toward African-Americans and Latinos. We used to get bigger bonuses. It was unreal. I remember a partner of mine was fired because he arrested a White man who was smoking weed in the streets. Our captain, at that time, was upset at my partner because he didn't give him a fine or a warning, never mind that our holding cells were full of arrestees picked up for jaywalking, and beating the fare on the New York subway. It was a double standard rule. I remember we used to laugh at all the complaints we received for illegal searches. We used to shred those reports. No one cared. They trained us how to profile, so all complaints were irrelevant."

"Damn, Lucky! So it's really true? Cops profile Blacks and Hispanics?"

"It wasn't written in stone, but it was code among cops. It was hard for me because I'm Black, and here I am, harassing my own people. They brainwashed me to the point where I thought it was right to disrespect my own kind. I thought my paycheck was more important than my pride. I did so many of my people wrong. There were nights when we went on gun missions. Our job was to bring in as many guns and suspects as we could. We didn't care if we witnessed a drug deal in front of us. Our mission was to bring in guns. We would drive around and jump out on whoever was standing on the block. We'd search them illegally, and we were destined to find either drugs or a gun. If we didn't find either, we would harass them until they told us where to find suspects with guns. I remember one time I framed a seventeen-year-old kid."

"What do you mean by *frame*?"

"Well, one night we were out on our gun mission for like three to four hours and we didn't find any guns. Every time we jumped out on suspects, they were only carrying drugs. We would take the drugs from them, and if it was a large amount, we used to resell the drugs to other drug dealers. We were parked in the Bronx, by Yankee Stadium. It was going on two in the morning, and we were all upset and tired. I jumped out on this kid who was coming from a party. He was scared to death when he saw me approach him with my gun drawn.

"This little punk, instead of following my orders, started back-talking to me and calling me every name in the book. I threw his little ass on the floor and put my knee on the back of his neck. His tough talk quickly turned into screams for mercy. Two transit police officers heard his big mouth, and they quickly came up running from the subway. They noticed I was a detective by the color wristband I was wearing. They asked me if I needed help, and I told them yeah. I got off the suspect and told the officers I witnessed him removing some drugs from his pockets and stuffing them in his drawers right before he was going to enter the subway. I gave the officers some drugs, and they quickly arrested the teen. I felt bad, but the little muthafucka should have stood quiet."

"That's fucked up, Lucky. I can't believe you were out there like that."

"It came with the job. I agree with you, I was a scumbag, but at the time, I didn't see anything wrong. Truth be told, we really removed a lot guns and reduced crime by profiling our suspects. People could complain all they wanted, but the fact still remained that nine times out of ten when we did profile our suspect, we were right. They were either carrying a weapon or had drugs in their possession. Hey, listen, we didn't go around harassing working-class people. We harassed those who we saw on the street corners every day and night. If you are walking down the streets with your pants hanging down your ass, hat turned backwards, and visible tattoos around your body, expect to get harassed by police."

"I could understand what you mean, but you know there are a lot of followers in the hood. Just because they fit the profile doesn't mean they are criminals. But looking at your folder, I see a lot of criminals who should get life for what they've done. Why not go after them? Why only go after the Blacks and Hispanics?"

"I'm going to give you another reason. Because they are poor. We know ninety percent of our charges would stick because they can't afford lawyers or hush money. We went after the bigger fish that you see in those folders, but not to arrest them. We went after them so we could blackmail them and suck their bank accounts dry. We made millions off these pricks. My police duties changed after I joined Captain Tuna's team, and I became an aggressive businessman."

"What really made you realize you needed to change? I don't believe it was just the death of Perry Coleman."

"You know me so well, baby girl. It was a mixture of things, but the main reason was my mother. I wasn't raised this way, and it started to catch up to me. Since my mother passed away, I've always promised I would make her happy in heaven. But once I got a taste of that fast money, it blinded my common sense. The night Perry was killed, that was the final sign, my wake-up call. I knew in my heart I had to step up and come clean, not just about the murder, but also about the dirt I did as a police officer. That's the reason all the folders are set up. I would be able to help a lot of suspects that we arrested and tampered with their cases. I'm risking my life, because real talk, I have enough money put away to disappear. I don't have to do this. I didn't need to come back and testify, but I won't be able to live with myself if I didn't. Remember, the information inside these folders will also incriminate me as well."

"I understand, baby, and that's why I fell in love with you. You are determined and a go-getter. I will never judge you, but it was just a little shocking to hear about your behavior as a police officer. I'm starting to understand why you don't want me to come along. Just make sure you bring your ass back in one piece."

"I promise."

Diamond logged on the Internet to search for restaurants that delivered, and Lucky went back to work, organizing all the folders and stacking them away in a box. They decided to call it a night, and it was only 7:00 p.m. By the time the food arrived, they both had already taken showers and were ready to eat and go to sleep. Diamond fell asleep right after she ate, while Lucky stayed up and watched ESPN until he fell asleep.

Back in the Bronx, there was a twenty-man SWAT team posted all around his house, hate in their eyes. They felt like Lucky had betrayed their brotherhood. They were hesitant to enter, only because of the surveillance cameras they found around the area. They knew the equipment belonged to Lucky. They figured he was inside watching and waiting with all sorts of guns and explosive devices. Once the snipers were in position, the captain of the squad called for tear gas.

Four members ran up to the house and threw eight tear gas bombs through the front window of the house. They waited two minutes before entering. A total of ten were ordered to storm in and kick in the front door. The cops entered the house with only one thing on their mind—Kill Lucky and anyone else in the house.

Twenty minutes later, they realized Lucky wasn't home, that he had destroyed all his computers. When the officer in charge was informed of the bad news, he had to call it in and report the mission a failure.

By the officer calling it in, The Watcherz picked up on the call and alerted his boss. When Captain Tuna got the call, he rounded up his squad, and they headed up to the Bronx location as fast as they could.

Speedy was still confused about why they were rushing if Lucky wasn't there. "Cap, I don't understand why we are rushing," he said.

"I know they reported no sign of Lucky, but we could still find evidence that might help us. Nobody knows him like we do. Maybe a picture or a postcard could help us."

"Okay, now I understand."

"And knowing that muthafucka, he may be still hiding in that house in a secret wall, on some Batman shit," Loose Cannon added.

"You right." the captain said. "Lucky may still be there."

While they rushed to the house, Lucky was off his bed and watching the cops walk through his house. He left one little camera in his basement, a silent alarm attached to it. He was sitting on the edge of his bed laughing because the cops were trying to figure out a way to save his burned computers.

Lucky's laugh and facial expression changed when he saw his former partners walk into the picture. They had just arrived and quickly received permission to take over the crime scene. Leaving that one camera gave Lucky a big break. Once Lucky saw The Watcherz in his basement packing up his burned computers, he realized his former partners had hired them to track him down.

After The Watcherz packed up the computers, Lucky realized his captain was holding a picture frame. Lucky didn't have the capabilities of zooming in, so he couldn't see the picture the captain was holding. It was bugging him so much, he wanted to drive up to the Bronx.

The captain knew what he was doing. Loose Cannon and Speedy kept asking him why he was holding that same picture frame. The captain walked back upstairs and called Speedy and Loose up with him.

"Listen, I got a funny feeling that Lucky is watching us. If I know him like I do, he has a camera somewhere in that basement, so I figure I'd throw him off by holding this picture frame."

"Smart move, boss," Speedy said.

They all headed back down to the basement to finish up their walk-through. They wanted to make sure they looked through everything before leaving the scene.

Loose Cannon kept whispering stuff into the captain's ear, but he wasn't saying anything. He was just adding to the suspense.

Lucky kept asking himself out loud, "What the hell are they talking about now?"

The captain played along with Loose Cannon's idea, so he also whispered back in his ear. They all pointed at the picture frame as they left the house, leaving Lucky wondering what was really in that picture.

When his former partners were outside, they were hoping their little plan worked, and that Lucky would come out of hiding.

By this time, the media was already outside the

house and had reported in the news that Lucky made a last-minute blazing escape as a twenty-member SWAT team ambushed his residence.

Lucky went and woke Diamond out of her sleep and started asking questions about the pictures they had around the house.

"Slow down, Lucky. I can't understand you. Can you at least let me get up and rub my eyes?"

"No, I can't. Focus because this is serious. Listen to what I'm asking you. How many pictures we had hanging up at the old house?"

"Why?"

"Just answer the fuckin' question. How many fuckin' pictures?"

"I don't know, not many. I think four. Yeah, only four. The rest were just hanging up for decorations."

"Are you sure only four?"

"Yes, I'm sure, and I have all four packed in one of my suitcases. Why? What's going on?"

Lucky then switched the channel on the TV and let Diamond watch the news for herself. When she noticed police cars and camera crew in front of their old house, she realized why Lucky was nervous.

She got up from the bed and went into the kitchen, where Lucky was heating up some leftovers. "Lucky, what happened? Are you okay?"

"Yeah, I'm good. The alarm I set up back at the house woke me up. These clowns came at full force, and it looked like they were hunting to kill. I was only able to leave one camera, so I had limited vision, but I noticed my old partners were at the house as well. My captain kept holding this picture frame, but I couldn't clearly see the picture. That's why I was asking how many pictures in total we had at the house."

"What color was the frame he was holding?"

"I don't know. Everything was black and white."

"I know for sure I got all four picture frames we had up."

"I believe you. Maybe they were bluffing because they thought I was watching. Plus, I also noticed they had the two best underground hackers in the game with them. These two brothers call themselves The Watcherz. They are the best in the business. I remember the FBI once employed them to help locate some of the most wanted criminals in the country. They could find anybody."

"For real, I see they really want to find you, baby. What are we going to do?"

"For right now, I just have to wait. I know they are hoping I come out of hiding, but they will need a better tactic than just a picture frame. My only fear is that they find my daughter and her mother. I have done a real good job of hiding their identity."

"You really have, because I barely know anything about them. Hopefully they are bluffing with the picture frame."

"I need to be sure they're bluffing. I'm going to have to hit the city tomorrow and get a closer look at their operation."

"How are you going to do that? You just said they are using the picture frame as bait to get you out of hiding. Don't you think that's a bad idea? Just wait a day or two. You don't even know where they are located, so how can you look for them?"

"You're right, but I know where The Watcherz grew up. I figure I could go around their old neighborhood and see what kind of information I could get on them."

"I don't know, Lucky. It sounds risky, but you make

the final call. In my opinion, we should stick with the plan of mailing out these folders and sitting back and let everything else unfold."

Lucky knew Diamond was right, so they went back to the bedroom and watched some more TV.

Meanwhile, Captain Tuna was busy back at his place. He was hoping The Watcherz could get some type of information out of those burnt computers. The Watcherz tried for six to seven hours but couldn't retrieve anything.

The captain began screaming at the two brothers. "How in the world are you guys the best in the world, but yet, no sign of Lucky, and now you can't get anything out these computers? Am I wasting my fuckin' money? Let me know. Either you guys find Lucky, or I'm going to put a bullet through each of your heads. Do I make myself clear?"

They didn't answer, but by the look in their eyes, they knew the captain wasn't playing. The Watcherz got back to work and promised the captain they would find Lucky.

While they went back to work, the captain went down to the fourth floor to make some phone calls. He figured they needed a bigger team to catch Lucky and kill him. He called his cousin Floyd from Florida, who was dirty himself when he was employed as a cop in Florida. Now he ran his own bail bond and bounty hunting business.

"Floyd, it's me, your cousin Tuna."

Floyd was surprised to hear from his cousin, but not stunned. "Tuna? Captain Tuna from NY?"

"Yes, from NY."

"Cousin Tuna, I haven't heard from you in a long

time. I guess you are calling me for another mission. It's been like ten years since the last time you called me and asked for help. I knew this day would come. What's up?"

"Well, we can't talk over the phone. Let's meet."

"I'm not going to say no. Just let me know when do you need me up there, and how many men you need."

"I knew I could count on you, Floyd. I need at least four extra bodies. I need some real good people. Our target is a specialist. I will leave it at that. I will fill you in once you are here. I need you up here ASAP."

"Give me about three days, I'm up there."

Captain Tuna was excited about the extra help coming up. He quickly called Loose and Speedy and told them about the new hired help. Speedy didn't sound too happy, but Loose Cannon was excited. He knew his captain had war on his mind.

Chapter Nine

The Manhunt

Within two days, Floyd was in the city with three of his best men. They didn't know the details of the mission or who Captain Tuna was, but they were in New York with Floyd, ready to put in work. The captain sent Speedy to pick up the new squad. When the captain and Floyd saw each other, it was a family reunion moment. They embraced each other like brothers.

"Damn! Ten years. Come here, you bum," Tuna said.

"It feels more like twenty years," Floyd replied, hugging his cousin.

"I really missed you, Floyd."

"Okay, enough with the bitch talk. Let's get down to business." Tuna asked Floyd to follow him upstairs to his office. He took him to the fifth floor, where The Watcherz were busy at work. Floyd was impressed with all the high-tech equipment.

"I like what I see, little cousin. I see you have done really good for yourself, but I have to ask . . ."

"Ask what?"

"I'm sorry to switch topics, but I have to ask. Was the kid armed?"

Tuna took a deep breath. "No, he wasn't. I wish I could really take that day back, you know. But I can't."

"Hey, listen, you don't have to explain nothing to me. I know it was a mistake. Fuck the public and their opinion. They don't understand the risk of being a police officer, especially in New York. They don't think about the lives you saved by removing guns and drugs off the streets. What's the latest on the trial?"

"It's looking good, but we have a major issue. That's why I called you up here."

"I'm all ears," Floyd said as he pulled up a chair.

"Well, our ex-partner testified against us, and he didn't hold back on the stand. He told it all like a little girl, and raised a lot of eyebrows in the department. Even after we win this case, the heat will still be on us."

"Okay, so let's find and kill him!" Floyd yelled.

"Listen, I want him dead, but he's good at what he does, and we can't find him. By the time we found his house, he was long gone."

"His house? Wait a minute, you guys know where he lived? That's perfect. Let's go. Show us the house."

"We already checked the house. There's nothing there. If it wasn't for the burned equipment we found in the basement, you would have never known he lived there."

"No disrespect, little cousin, but my squad makes a real good living finding the unfound. Let's go back downstairs so I can introduce you to my team."

The Cap agreed, and they both went back downstairs.

It didn't take long for everyone to get accustomed to each other. When they walked back in the apartment, all the fellas were drinking beers and talking football.

"Okay, listen up. Loose, turn the music down. Hey, fellas, listen. For those who don't know, my name is Captain Tuna, and this is my team. Speedy, he would chase down and catch anyone. He's one hell of an officer. He's our forensic guru. He's the one who keeps us on our toes and makes sure we follow our plans. If it wasn't for him, I wouldn't be standing here today talking. I would be in a federal prison, serving life for all the shit I've done."

The room exploded with laughter.

"Then we got Loose Cannon. The name speaks for itself. It doesn't take much to set him off. Long story short, he's been my right-hand man for almost fifteen years. The 'Cleanup Guy' is his other nickname."

Tuna turned toward Loose and Speedy. "Listen here. I got some out-of-town boys to help us with our situation. My cousin Floyd will do the honor of introducing his boys, but it looks like you guys know each other already."

"What's up? Like Tuna said, my name is Floyd, and this is my team. That's Country, Ace, and Chucky. We are the best bounty hunters in the state of Florida. We hunt muthafuckas down. No one could hide from us. Their work speaks for itself. I'm not too big in telling stories. We just put in work. My boys and I are up here to help find this little bitch and rip his mouth off. Tuna was telling me you know where he lived. I need to get my crew in there and check out the premises again."

"No problem. Speedy will take two of your guys up there," Tuna said.

The captain sent Speedy, Ace, and Country back to

research Lucky's house. He was hoping Floyd was right and was able to find new clues to hunt down the traitor. The captain wanted his cousin to give out more info about his team. He wanted to trust him enough to not question their skills, but he had to ask just to make sure.

"Hey, Floyd, while we're waiting around, tell me a little about your team."

"Sure, no problem. We got Ace, who's my best man on the team. His nickname is 'Hound Dog.' He's able to track down anyone. It doesn't matter where or how. He once was able to track down one of Florida's most wanted criminals. He was wanted for smuggling over forty kilos of dope every week from Panama. Ace tracked him down in Brazil, in a small town called Rosita de Paz. Once he found him, he killed him. You see, cousin, I'm also a businessman, and I follow my own set of rules. I work for whoever pays more. It doesn't matter if they are the good or bad guys.

"Then we got Country. He's the only member who tries his best to follow the rules. He was born and raised in Louisiana. He moved to Florida when he was twenty-five years old. He joined the police force, and that's when I first met him. Country had assisted me in tracking down a homicide fugitive. I loved the way he carried himself and also liked the fact he was very muscular, a plus in the bounty-hunting business. I was able to persuade Country away from the police business and to join my team. Country is the guy that will break every bone in your body from just one punch.

"Now Chucky, he's another Loose Cannon. He lives on a short fuse and doesn't care about the law. If it was up to him, he will shoot and kill each fugitive we captured. He didn't care how big or small the case was, he wanted blood every time. They called him Chucky because of his red hair. He is one racist muthafucka too. He hates every race. He's the only one who was never a police officer. Is that enough information? I'm ready for a drink."

"Ha! I'm ready for one, too, and yes, that's enough information. Let me get some entertainment for us."

The Cap was up to his old tricks again. He got on the phone and called up The Candy Shop and placed an order for four girls. Within forty-five minutes, they were partying with naked call girls and high off a mixture of drugs. It was hard to tell which lifestyle they preferred, because these cops loved the gangster life.

Speedy, Ace, and Country were back at Lucky's house searching every inch. As soon as they walked in the house, Ace was examining every piece of furniture, even smelling some of it.

Speedy was looking at him like he was crazy. He called Country over to smell one of Lucky's pillows in the master bedroom, and they both agreed on the fragrance. It was a woman's perfume, for sure.

They went around smelling other linens, curtains, sofas, and even the closet. They identified the same smell all over the house. They now realized Lucky had a female sidekick. This was the break they were looking for. Until now, they'd thought Lucky was a loner. Speedy was really impressed with how quickly they figured out he had a female sidekick.

Speedy went outside to speak to some of Lucky's neighbors, while Ace and Country kept searching. When they reached the basement, they triggered the alarm.

Meanwhile Lucky was watching these new faces rumble through his basement. He was puzzled, but it quickly hit him. His old partners were desperate and had hired more outside help.

As Ace and Country looked through the basement, Speedy was yelling their name out loud. They quickly ran upstairs to see what Speedy found or wanted.

"Wait a second. Before I tell you what I just heard, let me ask you a question first. Did you just come up from the basement?"

"Yes, we did."

"Shit! Fuck!" Speedy yelled.

"What happened? We weren't supposed to enter his basement?" Country asked.

"No, but it's my fault for not mentioning it. We believe Lucky has a camera set up in the basement, so if you guys went down there, he now knows how you look. If I know him like I think I do, he's on the Bureau's database right now trying to type-match your identity."

"Aw, man, we didn't know," Ace replied. "But seeing our faces may bring him out of the dark."

"Yeah, maybe, but anyway, I was calling you guys because one of his neighbors spilled the beans on his female friend. He said he knew there was foul play involved. She seemed so young, young enough to be his daughter. He said she went to the same diner every day to pick up lunch. He gave me the name of the diner, which is right up the street."

"Well, let's go over there and see if they have any kind of surveillance that may help us identify this mysterious, good-smelling female. Country, you stay here and see what else you can find. Check their garbage too," Ace said.

When they reached the diner, they went in and noticed a security camera. They smiled. The Italian restaurant was full of customers, so they didn't want to make a scene.

Speedy approached the hostess, flashed his badge, and requested the manager. When the manager introduced himself, Speedy asked him to step outside.

"Okay, what's going on here? Why are we outside? And who's that?" the manager asked, pointing at Ace.

"Okay, listen," Speedy said, "you are not in trouble. What's your name?"

"Sergio."

"Look, Sergio, we just have a few questions. I know you watch the news. Two blocks from here lives a very dangerous man, and I'm stunned that no one has seen his face around here. So let me ask you. Has he ever eaten at this diner?" he asked, holding up a picture of Lucky.

"Yes, he has, but a long time ago. Maybe two years before all this media frenzy."

"Two years ago. Are you sure?"

"Yes, I'm positive."

"What about this pretty little lady, about five, three? From what I hear, she has an awesome body. She came in here every day for lunch. Do you know who I'm referring to? Do you know her?"

"You mean, Chanel. Yes, I know her. What about her?"

"We think she was connected to the rogue cop we're after."

"Are you sure? She said the lunch was for her ill father."

"Well, I'm sorry to break the news to you, buddy.

Pretty lady is a criminal. Anyway, we noticed you have a camera. I'm going to need some footage with . . . What's her name again? Chanel, right?"

"I don't know her name. I just always called her Chanel because that's the name of the perfume she wears. As far as the tapes, I'm going to have to wait until the owner gets here."

Ace removed his sunglasses and removed the toothpick from his mouth. He walked up to Sergio and got about eight to ten inches from his face. "Listen, unlike my partner, I don't have the fuckin' patience. You have about three minutes before I whip my gun out and turn your brain into fuckin' meatballs."

Sergio froze when he saw Ace reach under his shirt and grab his shiny chrome 9mm.

Speedy gave Ace a small shove and got in between Ace and Sergio. "Sergio, please hurry up with the tapes. Don't make my partner upset. You don't want to see him upset."

Sergio was already shitting in his pants, so he didn't even need Speedy to convince him. "I will be right back with those tapes. Give me two minutes."

Speedy and Ace were laughing their asses off when Sergio walked away. They couldn't believe he fell for that old good cop, bad cop trick.

A few minutes later, Sergio walked out and handed them a DVD.

"What the fuck is this?" Speedy asked.

"It's a DVD. I downloaded about six months' worth of surveillance."

"You better not be fuckin' with us. I have a laptop right in the car. I hope I don't have to come back."

Sergio ran back in the restaurant, happy to be alive.

Speedy and Ace walked back to Lucky's house. They both went straight to the car and popped in the DVD, and Sergio was on the money. He gave them six months worth of footage, and the DVD program was user-friendly. All they had to do was type in a date and time, and the clip would pop up. Every time they punched in 12:30 on a weekday, the same pretty girl everyone kept talking about appeared. The only bad thing was, she always had on shades and a big hat, so she didn't give them much to work with. They knew that was Lucky's sidekick.

Speedy called out, "Captain, I finally got some good news."

"Speedy, spit it out."

"We found his sidekick, and she's a girl."

"That's perfect. Bring that bitch over to the apartment right now."

"No, Captain, not in the physical form, but we have some footage on her."

"Just bring what you have. How are the new boys working out?"

"They are perfect. Nothing fake about them. I will be there in thirty minutes or so."

The captain got off the phone and continued the party.

Speedy and Ace walked back in the house to look for Country. When they found him, they asked him if he'd found anything else.

"Yes, I found the camera in the basement. I know where it's located."

"You do? Let's take it down," Ace said.

"No, leave the camera alone. Let's get back to the apartment and re-group."

Speedy grew balls and was calling the shots on this run. While they were walking back to the car, he thought of something.

"Wait, hold up. Ace, grab my laptop, and let's all go back down to the basement. I got a plan."

"I think I already know," Ace said, grabbing the notebook.

They all went back down to the basement, and Speedy opened the laptop.

Lucky jumped off his sofa, curious as to what Speedy was up to. "What are you doing, Speedy? What do you got there?" he said to himself.

Lucky wasn't surprised that they'd found the camera. He was wondering what took them so long to find it in the first place. However, he was on his feet, eyes glued to the monitor, as he waited in anticipation. He knew his former partner wasn't bluffing.

When Speedy flipped the laptop around, Lucky saw video footage with someone in it that resembled Diamond. He sat up, turned his monitor off, and laughed. Instead of getting nervous because of the new footage, he just brushed it off and got ready for his next plan. He calmly called Diamond in the room and made her aware of the footage Speedy sent him.

"Listen, we need to bounce. No, let me rephrase that. I need you to bounce because they are getting too close. This is getting too dangerous, and I'm not trying to lose you, baby."

"Where the fuck is this coming from now?"

"Come here, baby."

Lucky hugged her for two minutes. In that two-minute span, he thought about the first day he'd met her outside the strip club. He would have never thought they would be in this position, where he would actually fall in love with her.

It had started out as some quick head, and now they were living together. It was tough in the beginning, especially not having sex. It took a lot for him to hold back and not touch her beautiful body.

But Lucky thought it was always harder for Diamond. Taking sex away from a prostitute was like taking dope away from a fiend, who'd go through long, sweaty nights of withdrawal. Lucky always felt it was important to gain Diamond's trust and respect. So he reformed her into a new woman, and that's how their bond was forged.

He remembered their first month together. He knew she was sneaking around her old way, looking for her pimp. She was hoping he was still alive and could take her back. He understood her issues, and instead of flipping out on her, he kept it to himself. It took about four months to get her to realize that her old lifestyle was a deadly way to make money.

When she finally realized Lucky's true intentions, she started to fall in love with him as well. At first, what Lucky was doing for her was no different than what any pimp would do, providing shelter, clothing, and food. That was the reason why she didn't feel comfortable at first. She thought Lucky was some pervert looking to turn her into his sex slave.

But as time went by, she began to learn who he was, and his passion for respecting a woman, which Lucky learned from his mother. Their relationship was rocky the first year as they grew to learn each other's ways, but after that, it was smooth sailing.

While Diamond was hugging him back, she also had

some flashbacks about the first time they'd met, and about her family. She wondered if her family ever missed her. She had two younger sisters, and all three were treated horribly.

After she'd made those accusations against her father, everyone turned their back on her. She ran away because she thought they would be happier without her. She'd once read a story in the newspaper about young girls making a good living in New York City by being high-end hookers, so she bought a bus ticket, only packed her sexy garments, and never looked back. Every now and then, she would wonder about them, if they missed her.

When she jumped off the Greyhound bus in Time Square, she had high hopes of being a famous call girl, but she ended up sucking dicks in alleys and fucking in elevators to make a living.

Diamond, to this day, felt like God sent Lucky to save her life. She always thought she was blessed, having such a great man on her side. She had been through hell since birth and thought maybe God sent her an angel.

At first, she didn't trust him. He was too honest. To her, all men were liars and cheaters, but he proved her wrong.

While they were hugging, Diamond was crying and shaking because she knew the day had arrived. Lucky was leaving her behind, and there was a big chance she would never see him again.

"Okay, baby, I'm going to let you get back to work. Call me when you're ready for me to hear the next move, daddy."

"That's my baby. I love that attitude. It's good for

your health to always think positive. I'm going to be as safe as possible and make sure I come back in one piece."

Once Diamond left the room, he turned his monitor back on and saw a piece of paper with a telephone number written on it that Speedy left for him to call. Lucky turned off the monitor and turned on some music to help him relax and think. His next move had to be clever, but he was tired of running. He just wanted to get this over with it and face off with his old partners. He knew in order for him to even think about resting anywhere in peace, they all had to be killed. Lucky wouldn't be satisfied if they each received a life sentence. Death was the only resolution. He was also aware that his former partners felt the same way.

When Speedy and the others returned to the spot and gave Tuna the tape, they were celebrating like they'd found Lucky. All they had was footage, but to them it was a small victory. They'd finally caught him slipping.

Tuna was really excited. He quickly gave The Watcherz the DVD, so they could get to work. "Shit, we need to find this girl," he yelled out loud.

"What about the media?" Floyd suggested.

"What about them?"

"They could show her face on every news channel there is," Floyd added.

"Cap, he's right. What other choice do we have? We need to find Lucky as soon as possible. This girl could lead us right to him," Speedy added.

"I don't want the media involved. It will attract heat for us as well. Let's keep this information to ourselves until we figure out what to do. Maybe by then The Watcherz will find her real identity. I don't even want Lucky to know about this new video."

"It's too late for that, Captain," Speedy added in a low-toned voice.

"What do you mean, it's too late for that?"

"Well, Cap, I thought it would be a good idea to show Lucky we had his girl, so we went down to the basement and showed him footage of his girlfriend through his camera."

"You did what? How stupid can you be, Speedy? You basically showed him our hand. You never reveal your hand."

"I thought maybe by showing him the footage, he would come out of hiding. I'm now realizing it was a dumb idea. I'm sorry."

The captain was pissed. He couldn't believe his most loyal cop disobeyed a direct order of staying away from the basement.

While the captain was chewing Speedy's ass off, his cell phone started ringing. He picked up.

"Hello, Captain. This is the commissioner. What's the latest on this scumbag? Did you locate his whereabouts?"

"No, Mr. Fratt, but we have a lead on his new girlfriend. We only have footage of who she is, but we still haven't identified her. We don't have a clear shot of her face."

"Send me the footage, and I will have the media take care of the rest. Somebody will come forward with some information."

"I don't think that would be a good idea."

The commissioner interrupted Tuna. "I didn't ask you to send me the footage. I'm giving you a direct order. Listen, you are not at liberty to make choices. Do we understand each other?"

"Yes, I will send over the footage as soon as I hang up the phone."

"Okay, listen, I will give you a few days to identify her before I turn the video over to the media."

"That's all I need, a few more days."

"Another thing, Captain, let me remind you that you need to cool down this heat. Hurry up and find this scumbag."

After the captain hung up the phone, he turned to his crew and said, "Listen, fellas, this is my show. I'm sailing the boat. If any of you guys make a decision without consulting with me first, that would be your ass."

The captain was still in fumes about Speedy's decision to show Lucky what they were working with. He'd dodged a bullet when the commissioner gave him a few more days to identify Lucky's female friend, but five minutes after the commissioner got off the phone, he called right back and told the captain he needed the tape ASAP.

"I thought you were giving me a few days," Tuna said.

"I changed my mind. You need help in this case, and the media has always been our friend in tracking down criminals."

"I have everything under control, Mr. Fratt."

"Do you really? Again, have the DVD in my office before the day is over."

The captain was pissed the fuck off. There was nothing he could do to stop the footage from hitting the media. He sent Speedy downtown to meet the commissioner and hand him the footage.

By the ten o'clock news, images of Lucky's sidekick were all over the news and Internet. Since the media had little information to work with, they started getting creative with the title of each story. Some stations called her "The Rogue Cop Lover," others called her, "The Young, Pretty, and Dangerous Girl."

The police department released a statement that she was wanted, though they didn't have any evidence to charge Diamond with a crime, and considered her armed and dangerous.

Once Lucky noticed all the news channels broadcasting the story, he knew it was time to panic. He had to find a way to disconnect Diamond, who walked in the room and asked him about his plans, from all this drama.

"We are in a tough situation here," he said. "The last thing I wanted was for you to get hurt. Now you are wanted by the NYPD. You should hear the names they're calling you."

"But they don't know who I am. Fuck them! They can't find us."

"Listen, Diamond, I think it will be best if we just separate, period, end of discussion."

"What part of 'I'm rolling with you' don't you understand? I'm wanted by the law. You can't leave me now."

"I don't know if you are ready, and for the record, I'm not going to leave you, girl. What's wrong with you? I'm going to try to clean your name up first. I'm going to paint the picture that I kidnapped you. Once they learn that you're a runaway girl, they will believe our story, and you should be good after that. The only bad thing about my plan is, they will try to reunite you with your family."

"No! I won't be good after that. I will be good right here with you. But, whatever, you are the shot caller. I just want you to know that I hate your plan," she said right before walking away from him.

Lucky called Diamond at least three times, but she never acknowledged him or came back in the room. He could hear her crying in the other room, so he just left her alone. This decision was hard on him as well, but he felt like it was the best decision because he didn't want her to get hurt. The burden would be too much for him to handle. A little leery about his plan, he was, hoping Diamond didn't fold on him.

Lucky made an anonymous call to the 28th Precinct on 124th Street and Eighth Avenue and informed them that the girl all over TV would turn herself in tomorrow morning. He also called one of his old contacts from the local newspaper and told him the made-up story, knowing the reporter would run his mouth.

By the time the morning came around, the story was all over the city paper that "The Rogue Cop Lover" was turning herself in. The story mentioned that Diamond was being held against her will.

Now, the pressure to capture Lucky was high on the police department's list. The media was doing a good job in creating this hate against Lucky. Already considered a rogue cop, Lucky was going to face additional charges of kidnapping and, because it was believed he had snatched her before she was eighteen years old, endangering the life of a minor.

Lucky called the 28th Precinct around one thirty and told them the girl would arrive at two o'clock in the afternoon.

* * *

The Watcherz heard the call on the police scanner and notified Tuna. He thought Lucky was smart by having her dropped on the same day the Colemans had a protest march taking place downtown, putting a strain on limited police resources. There wouldn't be enough cops around to capture him.

"I got your ass now," Tuna said to himself. "You can't fool us."

Tuna quickly got the boys together and set up a surveillance watch all around 123rd and 124th streets, waiting for Lucky to show up. They figured this would be a perfect opportunity to get close to him.

It was now going on two o'clock in the afternoon, and still no signs of him or the girl. They weren't buying the whole kidnapping theory, but they didn't care. He was their target, not the girl.

Lucky was present but watching from 122nd Street, from the inside of an abandoned building. He knew his former partners were hiding and watching as well.

"Captain, I believe that's her walking up to the front now," Speedy radioed in.

"I see her. Black shirt and white pants, right?"

"Affirmative."

Speedy, Ace, and Tuna kept their eyes on the girl, while Loose, Country, Chucky, and Floyd were searching the perimeter for Lucky. Ace and Speedy were on the roof with sniper rifles, waiting on the signal that Lucky had been spotted, so they could take him out, but they couldn't find him.

The captain was getting a bit overzealous looking at the girl. He yelled into his radio, "C'mon, fellas, find this muthafucka! I know he's out here somewhere. The bitch is standing right outside the precinct for a reason. It must be a signal she's giving him. Please, someone find this nigger, and do something before it's too late."

A few seconds later, two loud shots were fired, both hitting Diamond. One hit her in the head, and the other, in her chest, slamming her beautiful body against a parked police cruiser. The gunfire sent the streets of Harlem into chaos, with people running and screaming all over the streets.

Ever since the 9/11 terrorist attacks, New Yorkers have been real sensitive to any type of loud noises. When the people heard the loud shots and saw a body on the ground, they didn't know what to think. Not to mention, it was right in front of a police station. Some thought there was a maniac inside the station killing people, or maybe another cop went crazy and shot an innocent bystander.

The captain was furious about what just took place. He radioed his troops. "Who just took that shot?"

No one answered him.

"Didn't I make myself clear about making decisions without me? Who in the fuck took that shot?"

Everyone radioed back in and confirmed they didn't take the shot, but the captain didn't believe them. They all re-grouped and went back to the apartment.

Ace and Speedy were being blamed because they were the ones with the sniper guns, but Loose Cannon and Chucky were also nearby and didn't need a rifle to take her out.

Everyone in the van was blaming each other. The friction got so bad, even Tuna and Floyd got into it.

"Floyd, I hope one of your boys didn't cross the line."

"It sounds more like one of your boys. You need better control of your team, Tuna."

"The hell, I do. Well, once the autopsy is done, we will know who shot her. Till then, I don't trust anyone in this van. I cannot fuckin' believe it. This will bring more heat our way. Why in the world would I want to kill her in front of the police station?"

As they drove home, you could tell everyone was scared about what could happen next. Everyone started looking at each other, looking for the smallest clues, so they could blame the individual.

The only one who wasn't scared was Loose Cannon, who actually had a smirk on his face the whole ride back. The captain feared he was the only one who could have pulled the trigger but didn't want to pull his card in front of the team. He planned to pull him to the side, once they got back to the apartment.

The captain's only fear was the local newspaper. He knew Lucky had already contacted them and spread the word he was going to turn her in, but once they found out she got shot in front of the police station, the accusations would start flying all over, and of course, Tuna and his team would get blamed. He couldn't afford any more charges or complaints against him, especially since they were all suspended. He also knew once the organizers for the Colemans' protest heard about the shooting, they would use it as fuel for their movement.

Chapter Ten

The Protest Rally

It was going on three o'clock, and City Hall was jam-packed with protesters eager to vent their frustrations. The rumors were correct. Minister Muhammad had arranged a huge rally in support of the Colemans and their tragedy.

Everyone was gathered around One Police Plaza, and they were going to march all the way to City Hall. A small stage with six seats was set up right in front of the police plaza, four for the Colemans, one for Minister Muhammad, and one for their civil lawyer, Joseph Anderson.

As three o'clock approached, the stage was still empty. People were too busy shouting out rants to notice the time. The city already knew that the girl Lucky had kidnapped was supposed to turn herself in. Now word started spreading through the crowd that she was shot dead in front of the police station.

Around three fifteen, the Colemans, Muhammad, and Joseph finally reached the stage. The protesters exploded in cheers. The city really wanted to show them how supportive they were of them. There were at least 6,500 people out there ready to protest and singing as loud as they could the words of the late great Bob Marley's "No Justice, No Peace."

Minister Muhammad approached the mic and raised both hands, signaling the crowd to calm down. "Good afternoon, New Yorkers. Today we show the unity of this great city. Today we show we've had enough, and that we won't take it anymore."

The crowd erupted in cheers.

"Today marks a day of change. As I stand before you and I look among you, I see a nation of all colors. I see a city of all ethnicities, which means we as a city stand as one. Today is the day we destroy racism and sexism. I hope the world is watching because, America, this is how you begin a change . . . by uniting as one."

There was more applause from the crowd.

"Behind me, I have a family who's living in a twenty-four-hour nightmare. A family who has been hit with a tragedy that destroyed their peace of mind. This family . . . Laura, can you please step forward?"

The crowd exploded in support of Laura because of the strength she had shown throughout the ordeal.

"Laura, can you please stand next to me and bear witness to this beautiful sight? These New Yorkers, most of whom are strangers, have now become your new family. They are here to fight the war with you. Am I right, New York?"

Once again, the protesters went nuts and started singing again.

Laura, amazed at the amount of people who came out to support her only child, couldn't stop the tears from running down her face. It took her a few minutes to speak, and while she stood there mesmerized, the crowd's roar grew louder by the second.

"Good afternoon, everyone," she said, her voice cracking. "I first want to thank all of you who showed up today looking for answers to a better way of life. As we all know, we are here because three police officers opened fire on my son, killing him for no apparent reason. They destroyed not only our lives, but the future life of his son." Laura pointed at little Perry, who was sitting on his mother's lap. "These police officers got a slap on the wrist for their crimes. But they have the opportunity to go home and kiss their wives and play with their children, not my son. I'm not blaming the entire police department, but when you have the police commissioner and the mayor saying this shooting was justified, it leaves me no choice but to attack the department as a whole.

"My son"—Laura paused and let a few more tears out—"my son was a great husband and father. He didn't deserve this. My son was an innocent city taxpayer who woke up every day to earn his living and provide for his family. I will no longer get the opportunity to speak to, or even touch him. I understand he committed one little error as a juvenile, but who among us is perfect?

"My husband and I worked hard to buy our first home. We worked hard and prayed every day that we would have a normal life. When Perry was six years old, he always talked about joining the army to fight for this country, like his grandfather and two uncles. Perry always dreamed big. Throughout his school years, he maintained a 3.7 grade point average. He loved playing sports and his band. Oh boy, I could still hear those drums. He played his drums every night for about a good six years. He drove us crazy, but that was his drive, and we never discouraged him. I can't recall ever having to attend his school and hear negative things about him, even after he was arrested. Mostly, all his high school teachers were there to support him, because they all knew he made a silly mistake.

"I remember I used to go to bed happy every night because I felt confident that I raised a great young man. That was until I received that awful phone call that I can't seem to erase from my head. When I first heard that my son was shot and killed because he pulled a gun out on undercover cops, I knew for sure they were lying and were trying to cover another unjustifiable police shooting. That's why I was relieved to hear that my son never had a gun on him and he was indeed murdered by racist cops.

"If we continue to let these trigger-happy cops run our streets, soon all of our babies will be dead. This could have happened to anyone of us. I won't stop until justice is served. I won't stop until those police officers are stripped of their badges and thrown in jail. I won't stop until I receive an apology from the mayor. I want to thank everyone who came out." Laura threw her fist up in the air and yelled, "No justice, no peace!"

The protesters all joined Laura and sang those famous words. Laura's speech had angered a few protesters because they felt her pain, and they began fighting with a few cops there to keep the peace. They were quickly arrested, but the message was clear—New Yorkers had had enough.

Minister Muhammad walked back to the mic. "Listen," he said, "I have some bad news to report. Today, while we are here in downtown Manhattan fighting for our rights, I have just been informed that a young female has been shot in front of a police precinct in Harlem. I can't confirm who killed her, and at this moment the police doesn't have any suspect or leads. Today, Officer Donald Gibson was turning her in, and she gets assassinated on the doorsteps of a police precinct. Something doesn't smell right. And that's why we are here today, because we are tired of it."

The minister didn't know his words would ignite a riot. Protesters started picking fights with all the officers present.

The officers .were already looking for an excuse to shut down the rally, and now the people were providing one for them. They began pepper-spraying as many protesters as they could.

Meanwhile, Minister Muhammad was yelling on the mic, trying to restore order. He knew the rally would get shut down if they continued to act in this manner. "Please, calm down. Don't give the police a reason to shut us down. This is exactly what they want us to do. Please, calm down!"

Most of the crowd listened to the minister and stopped, but others kept fighting with the officers.

Ten minutes into the melee, about one hundred more cops showed up to the scene. They restored order amongst the wild bunch, handcuffing every idiot who was causing a disturbance. A few police officers were hurt in the process, but there was no way the NYPD was going to lose control of the situation.

Twenty minutes later, after order was restored, the crowd turned its attention back to the podium, because Kim had made her way toward the mic to address the supporters. She was the only one who had been silent throughout the ordeal. Everyone was eager to finally hear her voice and feel her pain.

"Hello, everyone," she said nervously. "I want to thank everyone who showed up today, and please stop the fighting. Please, no more violence. This is why we are all here today. To stop the violence. We need to lead by example. I know my silence has shocked certain individuals, but I can't explain how I'm feeling. I know I'm supposed to be strong, but how strong can I be when little Perry keeps asking for his"—All of a sudden, Kim fainted right in the middle of her speech.

Laura quickly ran to her aid and began fanning her face. Since there were ambulances present, attending to some of the officers and protesters who were hurt during the melee, Kim quickly received medical attention. She was rushed to a nearby hospital, the Colemans and little Perry accompanying her.

The crowd was stunned. Some were in tears because they could relate to her. Minister Muhammad approached the mic, at a loss for words himself. He'd never used words like *quitting* or *giving up*, but for the first time ever, he had to cancel his protest.

"I guess we were too concerned with making a stand that we forgot to help the one who really needed our support. However, on a positive note, I want to let everyone know that Kim is conscious in the ambulance, so that's a good sign. We are going to have to cancel this rally, but the battle is not over. I hope America is listening. We the people declare war on the government. No justice, no peace!"

As the minister walked away from the podium, some cheered, but others, a lot of frustration built up inside, were upset because they still wanted to march. But without the minister or the Colemans present, it felt like a lost cause.

About an hour after the ambulance left with Kim

and the Colemans, the streets were cleared, and everyone rushed back home to watch the news, eager to catch up on the latest events in Harlem.

The police department was puzzled, because Lucky was supposed to turn her in. So how could she get shot right in front of the police station? The media wanted to blame Lucky but didn't have proof. The autopsy would give them a better idea, but everyone had to wait a few days for that.

It was a circus outside the police station. Mayor Gulliano and Commissioner Fratt were slow to respond to the shooting, only because they were downtown, overlooking the rally. Once they arrived at the police station in Harlem, the small crowd outside started shouting out negative remarks toward the both of them.

"Take control of the city, you coward!"

"Stop letting the trigger-happy cops run through our city!"

A White male yelled, "Once the pigs start killing White people, then you will care!"

Both the mayor and commissioner, ignoring every comment thrown their way, made it through the hostile crowd. Their facial expressions said it all. They were hurt by what the people of the city were saying. The small crowd outside consisted of not just African-Americans and Latinos, but White people as well.

When the mayor finally made it inside, he quickly demanded a meeting with both the sergeant and the captain on duty. They entered one of the interrogation rooms, along with the commissioner.

The mayor was upset and didn't waste any time letting it be known. "Before I start, please state both your names."

"My name is Sergeant Michael Spinks."

"And I'm Captain Brett Roots. I've been in the force for—"

"Did I fuckin' ask how long you have been a cop? I just asked for your name. Now, listen carefully. I'm going to ask another question and please just answer it. I'm not interested in your favorite color. I didn't come here to spark a friendly conversation. Got it?"

Both officers nodded in agreement, too scared to even say yes.

"What the fuck happened today? Who shot this poor girl?" The mayor pointed at Sergeant Spinks.

"We still don't know. We're one hundred percent sure it didn't come from inside this precinct. We are waiting on the autopsy report, and we are hoping the ballistics will provide us with a lead."

"Let me get this clear. She was supposed to be turned in today, right?" the mayor asked.

"Correct."

"So who shot the girl? If you had to give me an answer, whether right or wrong, who do you think shot the girl?"

"Honestly, Mr. Mayor, I don't know," Spinks said.

"How about you, talk a lot?" he asked Captain Roots.

"Whoever did it wanted to bring more negative attention to our city and department. If you ask me, one of the thousands of supporters for the Coleman family could have pulled the trigger, just to add fuel to the fire."

"We have a serious situation on our hands. I will expedite the autopsy report and have it up in an hour or two. Meanwhile, I have to go back outside and face these reporters and get my ass chewed in front of these live cameras. I want you two to interview each uniform in here privately and find out what they know."

The mayor went outside alone and faced the wrath, answering every question as best he could, making it clear that, to his knowledge, it wasn't a police shooting, and that the investigation was still ongoing.

"Today, not far from where I'm standing, a young lady was shot. This young lady was allegedly kidnapped by a former detective named Donald Gibson. There are still a lot of unanswered questions, and at this moment, we don't have any leads or suspects. We are trying to iron out all the facts about this case."

"Mr. Mayor, was she killed by a police officer?"

"I can't confirm nor deny that at this moment."

"Mr. Mayor, then who shot her?"

"Again, we are investigating the situation as we speak. We are waiting for an autopsy and a ballistics test on some fragments left behind from the two bullets that entered her body."

"But an autopsy could take a few days," another reporter commented.

"Because of the magnitude of the situation and how this could somehow be connected to another high-profile case, we are making a few exceptions. We should have one in a few hours."

"This other case you are referring to, is it the one involving Perry Coleman who was gunned down by police officers?"

"Well, at this moment, we are focusing our attention on the death of a young lady. We are looking for answers, and I'm confident those answers will arrive quite rapidly. I stand behind this great city, and also the brave men who risk their lives every day and night. Police officers are not bad people. In fact, wearing the badge is one of the greatest honors."

The mayor was getting annoyed by the questions being asked. Right before another reporter was about to ask a question, he noticed Richard Claiborne, a spokesperson for his office. To quickly get out of the situation, he said, "Well, if you guys need more answers, Mr. Richard Claiborne is the guy to ask."

As the reporters all rushed him, the mayor was able to get back inside.

Forty-five minutes later the autopsy was done, and the information was related to the mayor. The two bullets matched a unique rifle that wasn't due to hit the market for another two years. The FNAR .308 rifle guaranteed at least a mile of accuracy.

No one in the police station had ever heard of such a weapon, except the commissioner. He knew he'd heard of that gun before but couldn't remember from where. They put a call out on the radio asking for help.

The Watcherz heard it and quickly contacted Tuna.

When Tuna got the call, he gathered all the troops back in the apartment and related the news.

"Listen, fellas, we just got word what kind of rifle was used to kill the girl. I know it wasn't one of ours, so I apologize."

Everyone looked relieved, no one wanting friction among the team, usually the first sign of a sinking ship.

"I know everyone is happy to hear the good news," Tuna said. "But now it really throws a wrench in it. If we didn't kill that girl, and Lucky didn't, then who shot her?"

"How we know Lucky didn't kill her himself?" Floyd asked.

"That's not his style. I think maybe there's a third party involved," Tuna replied.

That was the question of the day. Who shot Diamond?

As Tuna was about to talk to the crew about a new plan, The Watcherz called him upstairs to take a call.

Tuna went upstairs, grabbed the phone, and didn't bother to ask who it was. He already knew the commissioner was on the other line. "Hello, Mr. Commissioner."

"Oh, it's not the commissioner, you bitch! Surprise! It's your worst nightmare."

"Lucky, you got some nerve calling me here." Tuna snapped his fingers at The Watcherz, so they could start a trace.

"I see you got yourself some hired guns from out of town. You think I don't remember you mentioning your cousin Floyd from Florida? He's one of the best bounty hunters in the state, so you say. How the fuck is he the best, and you still don't know where I am?"

"Don't worry about me. You need to worry about yourself, and what will happen when we do catch you. Trust me, one day you will run out of luck, Lucky."

"Ha! Ha! I know that's what you're wishing for."

"You will slip up. Just like we found your little girlfriend, we will find you. Talking about your little girlfriend, whatever happened to her? I heard she never turned herself in. What a shame."

"Fuck you! This will come back to haunt you. Remember the Jersey job? And, for the record, I know you didn't pull the trigger—You don't have the balls."

“You know I have the balls to pull the trigger. I don’t even know why you would question my actions.”

“I know you didn’t shoot her.”

“How you know, Lucky? Please enlighten me,” he said, looking at The Watcherz, wondering why they hadn’t located Lucky’s signal yet.

“Because I killed her. I couldn’t take the risk of her talking. I pulled the fuckin’ trigger, and I’m coming after you next, bitch!” Lucky slammed the phone down.

Tuna pulled the phone away from his ear and looked at it in disbelief. Lucky had caught him off guard with the call. He didn’t understand why he would kill her. That was out of character for him, but it made sense. What really puzzled him was the mentioning of the Jersey job. He didn’t see the connection.

As the captain was about to leave the apartment, the phone rang again. He turned around, ran back, and answered the phone.

“Listen, when I catch you, fuckin’ little rat, I’m going to rip your fuckin’ heart out!”

“This is not one of your little playmates on the line.”

Tuna tried to clear up his voice when he realized it wasn’t Lucky on the line. “This is Captain Youngstown. How can I help you?”

“Please, Tuna, cut the crap. It’s the commissioner. Is this line secure?”

“Yes, sir.”

“Remember that job I wanted you to take care of for me in New Jersey?”

“Which job?” Tuna asked, playing dumb.

“You know, when we hit those gunrunners and we kept five assault rifles for ourselves. Remember those weapons? I can’t recall the names.”

"I think I remember that job. But, boss, why are we talking about the Jersey job, anyway?"

"The girl that got killed in Harlem today was assassinated by slugs that were fired by one of those rifles."

Tuna went silent on the line, finally figuring out why Lucky had said this would haunt him.

"Tuna, please explain how that could happen when I specifically told you to destroy those weapons. This could land us in some serious boiling water, and if my name comes up even as a rumor, I'm throwing you under the bus. Got it?"

"I understand, but let me explain. Lucky is behind this. He killed the girl in Harlem. It's a ploy to set up my unit. He must have kept one of the rifles."

"Lucky killed the girl? It makes sense, but I'm going to need proof he pulled the trigger. But how in the world can he have kept one of those when I asked them to be destroyed?"

"I thought they were. He's usually the guy who destroyed all the evidence. I didn't know he kept one. Let me ask you this. Why do I need to prove it? I know no one from my squad pulled the trigger."

"Please, Captain . . . just like you told me all five rifles were destroyed. I'm not taking anymore chances with your reckless unit. I need proof. You better hurry up and get this Lucky situation under control ASAP. Your career and life depend on it."

"How easy we forget. You hired my reckless unit on many occasions to handle your dirty deeds. Now you can't believe a word coming out of my mouth. I know for a fact he killed the girl. I have him on tape, confessing the murder."

"If you have him confessing on tape, that's perfect. Let's release it to the press."

"Didn't you say you don't want your name to surface near this case? If we release the tape, it will open the possibility."

"You're right. Just handle the situation. Remember, you owe it to us. We're doing everything possible on our end to make the Coleman case disappear. Goodbye. I'm hanging up."

Tuna walked back downstairs and gave a brief update on what just took place. The team couldn't believe Lucky was responsible for pulling the trigger, but they weren't surprised.

Floyd, for the first time, realized why his cousin was having such a hard time with Lucky. "I see why you need help catching this son of a bitch. He's a monster, for him to kill that girl in front of a police station, with a gun that could implicate the police commissioner of this city. This is one slick animal. We need to take him down like the dog he is."

"I couldn't agree more. That's why we need to be a lot better at whatever we are doing. We need to pay attention to every little detail, go with your hunches," the captain pleaded.

After Lucky got off the phone with Tuna, he sat on his chair and leaned back, mentally exhausted. His thoughts were getting him dizzy. These last few weeks had been the most intense in his whole life. He needed a few minutes of quiet time, so he sat there for a good seven to eight minutes in complete silence. You would have thought he knew yoga and was meditating.

Lucky snapped out of his daze when he heard the sound of a flushing toilet. He sat up.

Diamond came out of the bathroom. "So what happened, baby? Did they buy your story?" she asked.

"Yeah, I know they did. The plan is now in motion. In tomorrow's headline, I will be wanted for murder. They will find a way to blame me. But at least this time I really did commit the crime. You were in that bathroom a long time. Did you wash your hands, stinky?"

"Don't play with me. You know I did."

Lucky was trying to soften her up before he dropped the bomb on her. It was time for them to separate. It was time for her to disappear.

"Baby girl, we need to talk. You definitely have to skip town. There is no way we can be seen together. This shit here is way past dangerous."

"Trust me, daddy, I'll never question your word again. After what you pulled off today, I'm amazed. I don't know how you think of shit like this. You are a fuckin' genius."

"What do you mean, girl?"

"This whole setup thing between you and Sergio. You have been working on this for a long time. How did you know they would go in the restaurant and ask about me?"

"That's why I became a cop. It's a gift of mine. They fell into a trap. It's like I'm psychic. I'm always thinking of a way to outsmart my opponent. Anyway, I know the heat will be getting closer. I need you gone by the morning. Pick up a hundred thousand dollars from the storage spot. Your Honda Accord is still parked there, so take your keys. While you are in there, look for a shoebox that has the word *cemetery* written across it."

"Cemetery?"

"That's right, *cemetery*. Pay attention. Inside, you will find a red envelope with an address written on a piece of paper, and keys to a town house I own in Glen Burnie, Maryland."

"Glen what? Come on, Maryland? Are you serious?"

"Didn't you just say you wouldn't question my words?"

"Okay, okay, I've just never heard of it before."

"It's nice and quiet. Trust me, you will love it. When you arrive there, get familiar with the area. That will be our new home. There's a telephone number on there. The person on the other line, he will take care of all your paperwork."

"Paperwork?"

"Yes, baby girl. You know, a driver's license, social security card, and a job if you want one. You will have a new life and identity. You get a chance to start all over."

"A new job and identity, huh. I see what you're doing. Lucky, you are never coming back. You think I'm stupid?"

"C'mon, baby, you can't think like that. Honestly, the chances of me surviving are real slim."

"So then leave with me. We have enough money to disappear. You must have over two million dollars in that storage. Please say yes. Let's just go."

"I can't. If I don't kill them, I will be running forever. They won't rest until I'm dead, either. I'm coming down there, baby. Don't worry. Let me take care of business and eliminate these fools. The folders haven't even hit the fan yet. It sounds like fun, but—"

"I know, I know. It's too dangerous."

"Oh, you're being smart? Come here, girl," Lucky said as he grabbed her. "You know I love you, right? I just want you to go down there and become a free woman. It's time for you to shine."

Lucky hugged her for a few minutes. He knew she was crying.

Diamond was so in love with Lucky, he probably didn't realize how much. They got in bed, and she quickly started to please her man.

After hours of sex, Lucky was still up thinking about his next move. He'd already sent out all the packages. All he could do now was fall back. Lucky expected the federal government to get involved. He was lying in his bed, playing his plan over and over in his head, while Diamond rested on his chest.

He kissed her on the forehead and whispered, "Don't worry, baby. Soon all this will be over."

"I'm more worried about you, daddy."

The next morning they both jumped in the shower. Diamond was trying to enjoy every last moment with him. While in the shower, she decided to fuck her man one last time. She moved the shower head toward the wall because she didn't want to get her hair wet. She dropped to her knees and began to slowly kiss on Lucky's balls, jerking him off with one hand, and rubbing his buffed chest with the other. Once Lucky was hard like a rock, she began to jerk him a little faster.

Lucky leaned back against the wall and enjoyed the show. Diamond then started to suck and kiss the tip of his dick while she looked up at him. Her eyes alone almost made him come.

He looked down at her and placed his hands on her face, one on either side, and slowly pushed his dick in and out of her mouth. Every five or six strokes, he would go deeper and deeper.

After a good five minutes of mouth-fucking, Diamond broke loose and started to suck him off exactly the way he liked it. She would go as deep as she could while jerking it then switch to no-hands and begin her deep-throat magic.

Lucky's knees buckled, ass cheeks got tight, and he wasn't even about to climax. That's how good she could blow. Diamond never gave him head without swallowing his cream, which never took long. She was Lucky's personal "Superhead."

After he came, he flipped around and started finger-popping her to get the pussy ready. He always started slow, ignoring her cries about fucking her hard.

Diamond spread her ass cheeks apart with her hands and said, "Fuck me, baby. I want it right now. Kill this pussy!"

Lucky granted Diamond her wish, placing the tip in her pussy, enough to get her excited. Right before she opened her mouth to ask him to fuck her, he rammed his dick in her, and she let out a scream that almost burst his eardrum. He ignored her yells and continued ramming her pussyhole. Diamond was screaming for more, and that's what she received. Lucky knew he was going to miss her great pussy, so he was up for the challenge of killing it.

They got out the shower and moved the party back to the bed. Diamond got on top and started riding his dick slowly. Every eight to ten strokes, she would jump off and suck his dick then jump back on. She was riding so hard, she was making her ass clap. Then she started shaking and squeezing her tits. She was climaxing, multiple times too, her eyes rolling to the back of her head. After she came, she jumped off and sucked all her pussy juices off his dick.

Lucky then flipped her on the bed and got on top. He bent back both her legs around her neck and began to eat her out.

Diamond always thought he did tongue exercises well. He had one strong tongue. He would press it against her clit and move it side to side, up and down, as quickly as he could. He always drove her crazy when he did that, and she climaxed a few more times.

She grabbed him by his head, pulled him up, and started kissing and licking all her juices from around his lips and chin. She whispered in his ear, "Daddy, I got my legs cocked back, what are you waiting for? Break this pussy in half."

Diamond dirty talk was his Red Bull. He slid his dick back in her wet pussy and started to pound her out.

A good thirty minutes later, they were both laying across the bed out of breath.

"I'm going to miss you, daddy."

"I will, too, baby girl."

"Let me jump back in the shower. I need to hit the road."

As she jumped back in the shower, he quickly turned on the news and logged on the Internet. He wanted to see if any new developing stories hit the press.

Lucky was laughing at some of the articles he was reading online. He said to himself, "You think the shooting shook up the city? Wait until these envelopes hit the press."

Fifteen minutes later, Diamond came out the shower. While she got dressed, Lucky called up a taxi to take her to the storage facility. They hugged and kissed each other for a few moments.

Lucky wiped her tears and told her, "No worries. I will make it back safe. Stop crying. You have a long day ahead of you. Stay focused. Now is the time to be strong. Remember your training. This is the time when you need to apply your skills and survive. You feel me, baby girl?"

"I guess so. I know I will be all right. I just hope I see you again," she said as she walked out the door.

Lucky stood by the front door and watched her walk down the hallway and catch the elevator. He felt bad about lying to her. He closed his front door and leaned against it, thinking about all the good times he'd had with her. He wanted to open the door and chase after her, but he couldn't find the strength to go against his ego, his pride.

He didn't have any plans of heading down to Glen Burnie and reuniting with Diamond. The house and the money he gave her were his buyout. He could only hope she didn't break down when she realized the truth. In his heart, he knew it was better for her to start a new life without him. He didn't want to keep holding her back. She was beautiful, young, smart, and a perfect female to marry. He didn't want to ruin her future.

What really made him change his mind was when he looked through the scope and killed that girl in front of the precinct. Right before he'd pulled the trigger, he envisioned Diamond's face. That scared him, and it was the sign he needed.

He leaned off the door and walked to his bedroom. The guilt was starting to wear off. He knew he did the right thing and wasn't about to beat himself over his decision. Plus, Lucky thought it would be a better idea to hide and live with his baby mother and daughter. He would always love Diamond, but when it came to his daughter, it was a no-brainer. He decided to work out and then rest, which usually helped to ease his mind.

A day later, Lucky was still depressed. He felt bad about sending Diamond away, but under the circumstances, he had no choice. He sat on the edge of his bed, and for the first time since the night Perry got killed, he caught an itch. An itch to snort cocaine.

Lucky quickly jumped off his bed and began to slap his head with both hands. He was trying to prevent those demons from recurring. This was the mental war the addicts talked about all the time. The war on drugs was a lifelong battle. The itch to relapse would come again and again.

Lucky was going through one of his withdrawals. He wanted to find a quick solution to help the pain fade away, and coke used to be that quick fix. He paced back and forth in his living room for about two hours, sweat pouring down his face. The only thing that saved him from snorting was, there wasn't any cocaine in his presence. For the moment, he won the battle and was able to refocus on the task at hand. It wasn't an easy recovery, but at least he was able to snap out of the hypnosis.

He went in the kitchen, grabbed a box of Apple Jacks cereal, milk, a spoon, and a bowl. He went back to his room and turned on the TV. He didn't get a chance to pour the milk in the bowl before the TV got his attention. It seemed those envelopes were starting to hit their destinations. The news was reporting that there were numerous reports that lawyers defending different high-profile cases were receiving new evidence that could clear their clients of all charges.

Chapter Eleven

The Shake-up

"Good morning, everyone. This is Angela Stile, for BETV Channel 20 News. This morning, we are receiving numerous reports about different lawyers receiving packages through the mail with evidence that will prove their clients' innocence. We are hearing that some of the evidence will prove their clients were set up by the NYPD. Unconfirmed reports are implicating the same officers involved in the shooting that killed Perry Coleman. We will have more on this story as it develops. Again, we have, I believe, three envelopes sent in total. This is Angela Stile, for BETV Channel 20 News."

Lucky forgot all about his Apple Jacks and began to get dressed. His next plan was in motion, and he had a lot of work ahead of him. He had to stop thinking about Diamond and get focused before he became the next murder victim.

* * *

While Lucky was getting dressed, his old partners were shitting bricks. All stunned and shocked, they couldn't believe what they'd just heard on the TV. The captain and Loose looked at each other because they knew all the foul activities they'd done. If only 10 percent of their dirt was publicized, they could ruin the NYPD's image forever.

"This son of a bitch, who in the hell does he think he is?" Tuna yelled.

"Captain, I know Lucky is behind this. This muthafucka never destroyed any of the evidence. What are we going to do now?"

Loose didn't like the look in his captain's eyes. He hadn't seen that look in years. The captain quietly escorted everyone out and sent them down to the fourth floor, everyone except Loose. And, of course, The Watcherz, they were always on the computer.

"What's up, boss? Why you kicked them out? What's going on? I don't like that look. Talk to me."

"Loose, I'm getting sick and tired of me finding out new information via the news, radio, or third party, but never from my own goddamn team." Tuna turned toward The Watcherz. "Why in the fuck am I paying you guys all this money and you are never close to providing anything? You guys can't find your own dicks!"

Loose tried to calm Tuna down because he knew where it was leading. He was about to take out his frustrations on the two brothers. He pushed Tuna away from the brothers, but he didn't realize Tuna walked in the kitchen and grabbed a Louisville Slugger he kept by the refrigerator.

The Watcherz turned back around and went back to

work. They never once noticed where Tuna went, and never saw him creeping.

Loose noticed, but he did nothing. He wasn't the type to stop too many fights.

Tuna got in a Barry Bonds stance and swung the bat as hard as he could. He hit Hack first, and as he was falling on the floor unconscious, Little Hack turned to his left to try to grab his brother before hitting the floor. When Little Hack looked up to Tuna to ask why he hit his brother, Tuna hit him across his face, breaking his nose and knocking out all his front teeth. As they both were on the floor bleeding, Tuna kicked both brothers across the face and head.

"You two muthafuckas think I'm stupid! I'm paying all this money for shit! How you like me now, bitch?" Tuna yelled as he kept hitting both brothers.

After three or four more hits, Loose finally decided to grab Tuna and take the bat away. He looked over at The Watcherz. He knew one of them was dead. The other one was shaking like he'd caught a seizure. Loose walked over and gave him one more shot over his head. He hit him so hard, blood spattered all over his clothing. It looked like a scene out of the movie *Saw*.

After he made sure both brothers were dead, he kicked one of them in the ass and said, "Ha! Ha! You should have done your job, asshole!"

Speedy grew suspicious when Tuna asked everyone to leave. That only meant his partners were plotting on deadly violence. He didn't wait downstairs like the others. He didn't like being left out. He headed upstairs to see what was taking them so long to come downstairs. When he opened the door, he expected to seen Tuna and Loose working on new tactics, but he saw The Watcherz lying in a pool of blood.

"What in the world happened here?" Speedy yelled. "Please tell me they are not fuckin' dead, please."

"I'm sorry, Speedy. The captain lost it and took it out on them. They took too long in finding Lucky. The captain is in the bathroom. If I was you, I wouldn't go in there. Well, at least not right now."

"You know what? You are one crazy, psycho cop. How the fuck you let this happen?"

"Watch yourself there, Speedy boy."

"I don't have to watch shit. I can't believe you guys. Right now, we have all this heat on our backs, and you want to add two more murders? We are so fucked! I'm out of here. I'm not going down for this bullshit."

"Wait a second. What the fuck you mean, you are not going down for this shit?" Loose got in front of Speedy and blocked his way. "You starting to sound like Lucky. What are you trying to imply?"

Speedy pushed Loose out the way so hard, it caused him to bump the back of his head against the wall.

Loose rushed Speedy, tackling him to the floor. He stood over him and began to punch him, hitting him across his face.

Floyd got in between them. Curious like Speedy, he had come up to find out the latest updates. He was also shocked to see all the blood in that room.

"What the fuck is going on here? You two are partners. Why in the hell would you want to hurt each other? What the fuck is wrong with you two? Where is Tuna? And can someone explain why there are two dead bodies in this apartment that were not here just twenty minutes ago?"

Tuna came out the bathroom, dazed out in his own world. He didn't know about the fight.

"Tuna, wake the fuck up and snap out of it! Someone, anybody, please talk and explain what is going on."

Tuna didn't respond, and Loose was too frustrated to talk. He still wanted to fight.

"I will explain what the fuck is going on." Speedy wiped the blood coming down his nose. "We are all going to jail, what's going on. My captain and his sidekick just bought us a first-class ticket to the big house."

"Shut the fuck up, Speedy!"

Floyd held Loose as he tried to rush Speedy. "Hey, cousin, speak up. What the fuck is going on?"

Tuna finally broke his silence. He looked at his cousin and said, "We are all fucked. What can I say? This muthafuckin' nigger beat us at our own game."

"C'mon, cousin, I never heard of you quitting before. What is wrong with you? Get a grip. We could find a way to still catch this son of a bitch. I will have Ace and Country clean up this mess in here, and no one will ever know The Watcherz were ever in this apartment. But let's not give up."

"Floyd, didn't you see what we saw on TV? Lucky sent evidence to lawyers that will prove we framed their clients. I could see the headlines now. They will eat us alive. We'll need a miracle to get out of this one," Speedy said.

While Tuna and Floyd moved over to a corner of the apartment to have a private conversation, the rest of the crew began cleaning up the mess.

Ace and Country picked up the bodies and threw them in the tub. Within an hour, both bodies were chopped up in little pieces, and all the blood drained.

Chucky and Loose began cleaning up the blood and wiping down all the computers. Speedy locked himself in the bathroom and was cleaning his face.

Loose knocked on the bathroom door. "Speedy, open up. We need to talk."

Speedy wanted to blow him off, but he opened the door. "What's up, Loose?"

"Hey, listen, my bad. I didn't mean to call you a snitch. Right now, my state of mind is all fucked up. I hope you could accept my apology."

Speedy thought, *What apology?* But coming from Loose, the most stubborn human on this planet, it meant a lot to him.

"Don't sweat it, bro. Brothers fight all the time. We need to get back to business and figure out how we're going to avoid jail," he said, embracing his partner.

It was only 10:30 in the morning, and the day was just beginning to unfold, but there was already so much drama for one day.

Floyd took his crew back down to the fourth floor while Tuna spoke to Loose and Speedy about their next move.

"Okay, we are in deep shit, and I'm sure I will get a call in a few minutes to come in the office and explain these recent events. The commissioner already came down my throat about not getting rid of those guns from the New Jersey job, so I'm sure he will chew me a new asshole. Do you guys have any suggestion or ideas?"

No one answered, a clear signal they were all clueless about their next move, or maybe they didn't believe in their boss anymore. They both saw how dazed Tuna was through the drama.

Tuna picked up on their lack of enthusiasm. "Don't

tell me you two are losing your faith in this team. C'mon, we're in this together. This will be the worst time to fuckin' quit on me."

"Boss, things are not looking good, and I can't go to jail. My wife and kids, they need me."

"I have to agree with Speedy on this one. I'm not going to jail. They will have to kill me first. Another thing, boss, I never saw you freeze up until today."

"What the fuck you mean? C'mon, Loose, you know me better than that. I'm just in a state of shock. I don't want to go to jail, either. We should have killed him, like Tango."

"What do you mean, you should have killed him as well? Are you saying Tango's murder was our call?"

Tuna tried to downplay his comment, but it was too late.

Speedy started to yell at both Tuna and Loose. "How in the world can you guys kill your own brother? I could understand why we want to erase Lucky. But Tango, why?"

"Tango was working with Internal Affairs. We got word from an insider over at IA. You know our source over at IA is legit. We had to take care of him quickly," Tuna explained.

"I still can't believe it. Tango was a snitch? C'mon, did you guys ever confront him about it? I don't understand why you guys kept a secret from me, but we call ourselves brothers. I'm out of here. I'll call you guys later. I'm going home to play with my kids. Given the current events, I don't have a lot of time on my side."

Speedy caught them off guard, wanting to leave, but Tuna allowed him to leave without any argument.

Loose Cannon wasn't happy. "Speedy, remember, we are in this together."

Speedy didn't look back. He just walked out the front door and went home. He was disgusted with his partners and didn't feel comfortable around them anymore.

The first thing that came out of Tuna's mouth when Speedy left was, "I hope we don't have to get rid of him too."

"Just give me the word, Captain, and he's a goner."

"Let's just watch him for a few days and let's make sure he doesn't do anything stupid," Tuna said.

Tuna and Loose joined the rest of the crew down on the fourth floor. They told everyone that Speedy left to take care of some personal family issues.

Going on noon, they decided to watch the news and see the latest on the envelopes Lucky was sending out. When they turned on the news, a reporter was talking about an alleged report of the commissioner's involvement in corruption.

Before the reporter finished her story, Tuna's cell started ringing.

"Hello?" a dumbfounded Tuna said, knowing it was Commissioner Fratt on the other line.

"Hello? That's all you have to say. I know you are watching the news. I need to see you ASAP. Meet me at the village. Do you still remember the apartment?"

"Yes, I do."

"And hurry up and get here, and come alone."

Before Tuna could answer, Fratt hung up the phone on him. Tuna told everybody he would be back in a few hours.

Before he left by the front door, Floyd said to him, "Hey, listen, cousin, I was talking to my crew, and we all decided that this will be the end of the road for us."

"What the fuck do you mean, the end of the road?"

"We are all going back to Florida. We were under the impression you had this situation under control, and you don't. We are out of territory, and it looks like the heat is about to broil. I can't continue to risk my crew's freedom with unorganized tactics."

"Hey, coward, if you want to leave then go ahead. I thought blood was thicker than water, but I see you have your new family to worry about. Thanks for coming, and fuck you very much!"

Tuna left furious. His team was falling apart like a music group, and now family was moving away as far as they could from him.

After Tuna left, Loose Cannon tried to explain what was happening.

But Floyd didn't want to hear it. "Save it," he said. "We're all leaving."

They all drank a few beers and continued watching the different reports surfacing on the local news channel.

Lucky was also watching from a local coffee house. With his disguise, he blended in perfectly with everybody else in New Jersey. No one knew they were sitting right next to the most wanted person in New York's history. He wanted to catch Destine's report because he'd mailed her a package as well, with graphic pictures of a priest sexually molesting teenage boys.

"Good afternoon. This is Destine Diaz for Channel 5 News. We are here to bring the latest on these mysterious packages. We believe there are a total of five. Four were mailed to lawyers, and one was

mailed to me. I have specifics, but they are sickening, graphic pictures of little boys getting sexually molested.

We have unconfirmed reports that the man in those pictures is none other than Cardinal Joseph King III, the same priest who performed the marriage vows for the mayor and his wife. According to the letter I received along with the pictures, this mysterious informant is indicating that Joseph King III was never prosecuted because of his political friends. Again, these are unconfirmed reports. We are waiting on official word from Police Plaza and the district attorney's office."

Lucky was smiling from cheek to cheek, happy to hear Destine speak about the envelopes. He knew he'd picked the right reporter. She wasn't scared of the controversy. He ordered another cup of coffee and continued to listen to her report.

Lucky wasn't the only one listening. The people in New Jersey were also eager to hear the story, being closest to all the madness.

The Colemans were hoping some new evidence would pop up to help their son's case against the city. Laura was sitting on the edge of her seat, watching the news.

"Laura, sweetheart, sit back please. Let's just hear what the young lady has to say," Perry Sr. said.

"I'm just praying for a little help from God. I think we deserve it, baby. We need the help."

"I agree, but let's just watch the news and see what else they got. If the same cops are involved, this will help our case to some degree. It will prove how corrupt those officers are."

"You are right, baby. Oh, the commercials are over. Be quiet. Let's see what else she has to say," Laura was on the edge of her seat again.

"Welcome back. This is Destine Diaz, Channel 5 News. We have new information on those other four folders. I don't know if some of you guys remember, but about seven years ago Rell Davis was charged and convicted of double murder. He was sentenced to double life sentences without the possibility of parole. Rell pleaded innocence throughout the whole trial, claiming he was framed. Rell has also had two appeals denied. Well, today his lawyer, Nicholas McCarthy, confirmed he received a package with evidence that Rell Davis was not the shooter the night Connie and Rodger Newton were gunned down while they slept in their Hampton mansion. We will have more information on this one as it develops.

"The other package was sent to the lawyer of Juan "Pito" Medina, a convicted drug kingpin who was sentenced to life in prison without parole. His lawyer, Edwin Gustavo, has stated he also has concrete evidence, which includes photos and conversations, proving his client was set up as well.

"Then there is the case involving a family in the Bronx, where a father was gunned down when police mistakenly raided the wrong house.

"And finally I remind viewers of our earlier report this morning about Police Commissioner Brandon Fratt. These stories have the whole city disturbed and disappointed.

"This is Destine Diaz. We now turn it over to traffic."

Laura and her husband were sitting with their mouths open. They couldn't believe the reports they'd just heard.

While they were discussing the latest news report, Kim walked in the living room and was asking what all the fuss was about, and they told her what they'd just heard.

She thought it was time to tell them about the package Lucky left behind. "Well, I have a confession of my own. Remember the day Lucky came by the house?"

"Yes," they both said.

"Well, he left a package behind as well."

"What? Why did you take so long in telling us? I'm surprised at you," Laura said.

"I'm sorry, but I was told not to say anything until the trial was over. I'm sorry, Laura. I hope you can forgive me."

"It's okay, baby. I just don't know why he wouldn't want us to see it until after the trial."

"He said, if we bring it up during the trial, the evidence would disappear. He wanted us to wait until the civil case was in progress. I think he was just looking out for us and making sure the City pays for what they did to Perry."

"Honey, I think I understand his logic behind keeping this a secret from us. Let's not come down hard on her. Let's just see what he left behind and take it from there. Kim, please bring us the package."

While Kim went to get the package, Laura and Perry Sr. waited in suspense. They wanted to know what he'd left behind, but they were also scared. When

Kim returned and placed the package on the coffee table, they all stared at it. They knew whatever was inside could place their lives in even more danger.

Laura reached for it and began to rip it open.

There was a computer disc along with a note. The note said that the CD contained a conversation between his former partners the night after Perry was gunned down. The CD was sufficient evidence to implicate Loose Cannon and Speedy.

They placed the CD in their computer and turned up the speakers. They heard the cops discuss how it was a brilliant idea to get the gun out the car, shoot out the windows, and place it on her son.

They all began to cry when they heard the captain say, *"Good thing we keep that gun with us at all times. The press bought the story about that little nigger carrying a gun and shooting at us first."*

Laura stopped the CD from playing and asked her husband, "What are we going to do now? Should we call Minister Muhammad?" She had to pinch him to get his attention. "Honey, I'm talking to you. What are we going to do?"

"I don't know, baby. I just heard a trigger-happy cop make a racist remark about my son and also implicate himself. So Lucky was telling the truth. Not that I didn't believe him, but this certifies his side of the story."

"So, Who should we call? is my question, babe."

"I don't know. Kim said Lucky didn't want us to bring this evidence up in court, he wanted us to wait until the civil case. I don't know, baby. I really don't know who to trust. Remember how they pulled the plug last time we went public?"

* * *

While the Colemans contemplated their next move, city officials were scratching their heads over a way to respond. Lucky not only blew the whistle on his former partner, he blew the whistle on the city that never sleeps, the mecca of entertainment. New York City had earned a new name, "Corrupt City."

Donald "Lucky" Gibson was now officially the number one enemy, but not to the people, because they loved the fact that he had the guts to come forward and expose the truth. The City was real concerned about the allegations against the commissioner and Cardinal Joseph King III had caught the attention of both the Republican and Democratic parties, and there was going to be a discussion on it in a City Hall meeting in two days.

Even the President of the United States of America made a comment on his weekly radio show, stating, *"It saddens me to hear the negative attention the great city of New York is getting. I don't know all the facts, but I'm gathering there are allegations of corruption and murder. I will be visiting the city soon, meet with both parties, and address exactly what's going on. I could understand the concerns my fellow New Yorkers are expressing about police brutality, but also as the President of this nation, I must also listen and see all the facts before I make judgment. We all know I cleaned up corruption in the White House, so if we indeed are experiencing corruption, we will clean it up and return the glory back to the City of New York."*

When Lucky heard the playback audio on the news about the president coming to New York, that really shook him up. He knew he was going to shock the city, but he had no idea the whole country was also going to pay attention to all the drama.

He quickly headed to the supermarket and spent close to five hundred dollars on groceries. He figured the next few weeks he would have to stay indoors because soon the FBI would also be looking for him.

When Captain Tuna met up with the commissioner, he was shocked to see two gentlemen in suits there with him. He thought for a second the commissioner had called Internal Affairs on him. He was wrong.

"I'm glad you finally joined us. Please have a seat."

"I didn't know you were having company over. What's this all about, Brandon?"

"Well, first it's *Commissioner* Brandon. Address me correctly. I took the liberty of inviting two of my friends from the Bureau. Please meet federal agents William Kuntz and John Pillar."

"What the fuck are they doing here? You know we don't deal with the feds. I'm surprised, Commissioner Brandon. Don't set me up like this. At least give me a warning first."

"You mean like you warned me about all this shit coming out through the media?"

"You know I didn't know what was coming. I was also surprised."

"You shouldn't be. I specifically told you to personally destroy all the evidence, not let some fuckin' monkey do it. You no longer have the situation under control. Agents Kuntz and Pillar will help you find Lucky."

"Fuck you! And fuck both of these pigs! Working with the feds is like working with Internal Affairs. I'm not doing it. We will find Lucky and shut his mouth up once and for all." Tuna got up and headed for the door.

Tuna didn't like that the commissioner tried to corner him like a fucking rat. He was going to leave without shaking his friend's hand. He'd just about had it with all his friends trying to turn on him now that the heat was on. He wasn't an idiot. He knew the commissioner was trying to figure out a way to escape the allegations, which meant Tuna and his team would have to take the fall.

Right before Tuna reached the front door of the apartment, Kuntz said, "Tuna, we know where Lucky's daughter lives."

Tuna stopped, turned around, and looked at him up and down, trying to make sure Kuntz wasn't pulling his tail. "You do. Where?"

"We will share this information with you if you let us help you catch him. And, for the record, our Bureau is not aware we are here to help. We're here because our good friend Brandon, excuse me, *Commissioner* Brandon, asked for our help."

That changed the whole ballgame. Tuna knew those agents were there to help find Lucky and kill him. He agreed and told them to drive back with him to meet Speedy and Loose Cannon. He said, "I need to warn both of you guys now. They won't accept this new partnership peacefully, but once they hear you guys know where his daughter is located, they'll change their minds."

Chapter Twelve

www.thesmokygun.com

The next day, after those mysterious envelopes hit the media, more concrete evidence was starting to surface via the Internet. The public had a better idea of what was going on and so far, the rumors were turning out to be true. Also, according to a few reliable sources, those envelopes came from Donald "Lucky" Gibson himself. In total, five envelopes were sent, and all five, along with a few pictures, were posted on a Web site called www.thesmokygun.com.

This Web site specialized in exposing high-profile cases. They were the first ones to post the video of an R&B singer pissing on little girls. They'd also posted all the mugshots of every time a celebrity was arrested. The Web site had a breakdown of each envelope.

Envelope #1: *The State vs. Rell Davis*: Rell was charged and sentenced for a double murder and received a life sentence for each murder. Rell has maintained his innocence since day one. He was convicted of killing Rodger and Connie Newton.

Rodger ran one of the most successful realty companies in Manhattan. His estate was worth over three hundred and fifty million dollars. He and his wife had a major gambling problem, and according to the information received from Lucky, he lost his life over a major horse bet. Rodger had reportedly received a few tips on the Belmont race and he sold his information to numerous high rollers, including the Italian mob.

After the race was over, Rodger's tips were off, and he owed millions, not to mention the five million he personally bet as well. Rodger took his time paying his debt, and that's when the mob hired Captain Tuna and his crew to kill him and his wife.

Documents show Speedy found Rell's profile and noticed he was just released from prison after serving four years out of a six-year bid for attempted murder after a robbery went wrong. What attracted Speedy to Rell's profile was, he was charged for entering someone's home and shooting the victim while they slept.

Rell was a perfect scapegoat for the job Captain Tuna wanted to pull. Lucky provided pictures and written documents supporting the allegations that Rell was watched for a few days before he was framed. Lucky also provided pictures and audio tapes supporting his claim that he and his former partners were the ones who pulled the trigger and killed both Rodger and Connie. In one of those tapes, you could hear these crooked cops laughing about sending Rell back to jail for their crime.

The night they killed both Rodger and Connie, they made sure it was the same night Rell was home alone and had no alibi. Captain Tuna made up a bogus witness report about an old lady seeing a young Black man matching Rell's description running from the house and jumping in a black Maxima, which of course also matched Rell's black car.

Two days later, at 2:00 a.m., Captain Tuna was able to get a warrant, and they raided his house while Rell was asleep. They forced Rell into touching the murder weapon and leaving his fingerprints on it. This case received a lot of media attention because Rodger wasn't only a millionaire, he was also a well-respected man, who ran one of the biggest real estate companies in Manhattan.

Rell, a convicted felon, lost his case before the trial even started. The DA's job was easy on this one because of all the bogus evidence pointing at Rell. Nicholas McCarthy, his lawyer, held a press conference and stated that Rell was expected to be released from jail within days and he said his client is 100 percent certain he will sue the City and police department for the injustice against him. There were already rumors circulating that the City, not wanting to drag out this embarrassment in court has already reached out to Nicholas McCarthy about a settlement.

Envelope #2: *The State vs. Juan "Pito" Medina.* He was charged with kingpin charges and received life without possibility of parole. Pito's case played with heavy rotation in the media as well. A high-profile gangster who partied with all the major superstars and politicians, you would always find him in the front row of any sports arena, concert, or award show. Pito had it all—good looks, money, and power.

If he didn't have felonies on his record, he could easily run for a Senate seat. There were rumors for years that he had cops on his payroll. Pito also claimed those drugs found in his backyard were not his.

Pito was born and raised in the Dominican Republic. He first came to the United States when he was nine years old. His father was also a major drug dealer. Pito's father risked both their lives in order to live in the United States. He jumped on an airplane with over two kilos of heroin in his stomach, and also made little Pito swallow a few balloons.

At nine, he was already trafficking drugs. That is one of the few memories Pito had of his father. Two days after arriving in New York, Pito's father was killed by the same people who'd hired him to bring the drugs in.

Pito lived with relatives until he was old enough to run his own drug corner in Washington Heights. One corner led to another, and before you knew it, Pito ran a twenty-block radius in Washington Heights.

They nicknamed him, Mr. Broadway. The blocks he didn't run were still his, because those dealers were buying off him anyway. One summer night while Pito was at his Rockland County home with his wife and kids, the ATF raided it. After a two-hour search, they found ten kilos of cocaine buried in a 20 x 10 hole underneath a shed in his backyard. This tunnel, which included electricity and a phone line, cost over a million dollars to build, and was large enough to store close to two hundred kilos of cocaine. It was also designed to keep the drugs fresh and contain the smell.

When Pito first built the underground stash, it was for drugs and guns. As his empire grew, he built a few stash houses, so he didn't need to store his own drugs. Instead, he used it to keep his money. It was basically a giant safe that stood full at all times. Pito claimed those drugs were not his, and that the underground safe was actually a panic room for his family, just in case his family was in danger of a fire or intruders.

He also claimed over three million dollars was stolen by the police, but those allegations were dismissed in trial. Pito also accused the cops of extortion for all the protection money he was forced to pay over the years. In fact, he was the first one to go public about Captain Tuna and his rogue team terrorizing the city. Those allegations of corruption were also dismissed at his trial. No one believed a two-time felon, whose nine-to-five was to run a drug cartel in Harlem.

Edwin Gustavo, Pito's attorney, received new evidence from Lucky proving Pito had paid for protection and providing information. Lucky had sent audio conversations between him and his old partners talking about who was driving to pick up the money from Pito. They each took turns.

Lucky also sent Captain Tuna cell phone records, which showed a total of over three hundred calls to Pito's cell number.

There was also a recording of Tuna saying he was going to turn Pito over to the ATF squad as a favor to the commissioner. Tuna said the police department was looking for a way to bounce back and clear up their image after they went through an ugly trial about shooting an unarmed African immigrant forty-one times in the Bronx. That's when Captain Tuna decided to raid Pito's house, enter the underground safe, and plant the five kilos of cocaine. Those recordings would justify Pito's claim of corruption.

Attorney Edwin Gustavo had his hands full. Getting Pito out of jail wasn't an easy task. He had two felonies on his record and was a known criminal who ran one of the largest drug operations in Washington Heights. Edwin Gustavo was just hoping to at least get Pito a new trial and revisit his bail status.

With a little bit of luck, Pito could walk free from jail or receive a new reduced sentence. He'd already served five years. Though no new evidence had surfaced clearing him of the drugs found in his basement, he still maintained they were planted. With a new trial, Edwin could hopefully swing the jury on his side and have all charges dropped. But there was still a lot of cash and a few guns found that did belong to Pito.

His attorney was hoping to get the jury to buy the "illegal search warrant" theory. Pito knew Tuna must have snitched on him, because they were the only two who knew about the underground stash, so he decided to blow the whistle on Tuna. At first no one believed Pito. In fact, the press and the public barely paid attention. But with all the new evidence, everyone was eager to hear the truth. Pito's lawyer knew, if he played the right cards, his client would be in the streets pretty soon.

Envelope #3: *The State vs. The Wiggins Family*. In 1999, the Street Crime Unit was working on an anonymous tip about a two-family house in the Bronx that was selling guns at wholesale prices. At the time, Officer Tuna only had two years' experience with S.C.U. They raided this house at four o'clock in the morning.

Inside lived an African American family of six, two parents, three kids, and an uncle that lived in the basement. Instead of staking out the house to make sure there were guns inside, they pressured the judge to sign off on a search warrant without any concrete evidence. Only thirty-six hours went by between receiving the tip and the actual raid.

When the front door of the Wiggins' house flew open and the agents marched in yelling, "Get on the floor," with their guns drawn, all hell broke loose.

The Wiggins were caught off guard, so of course the father, Joe Wiggins, and his brother Jonathan put up a fight. Joe didn't know what was going on, and he briefly fought off two agents, knocking them down to the ground. Once Joe heard his wife and kids yelling, he stopped throwing punches and ran toward them.

The agents didn't allow him to reach his family. Joe ignored the officers' plea to freeze, so they shot him three times in the back, killing him in front of his family. The officer claimed Joe was running to retrieve a weapon, which was never found.

Meanwhile, Uncle Jonathan was still fighting, even after he realized they were agents. Two minutes into the struggle and one minute after Joe was shot, Jonathan was shot as well in his lower abdomen, the bullet rupturing his spine, and paralyzing him for life.

After the smoke cleared, they realized they must have raided the wrong house, because they didn't find any drugs or guns. This case went under the radar for years. No one had ever heard of this incident before, not until Lucky brought it to the media's attention. The reason for the silence was because the City of New York had paid an undisclosed seven-figure settlement to the Wiggins.

A reporter tried to reach out to the Wiggins after he read thesmokygun.com report, but they refused to talk about the raid or settlement. But not Lucky. He revealed some insight as to why the Wiggins were reluctant to speak to the press. When they received their settlement, the City gave them additional money to keep their mouth shut forever. They even made the Wiggins sign an agreement that if they ever leaked any information, they would get sued and would have to return the settlement, plus interest. Lucky sent in documents highlighting the parts of the settlement that threatened the Wiggins.

Lucky didn't have much information on this case because he wasn't around in 1999, but he was able to steal documents off Tuna's computer. Lucky knew the press would jump all over this story, because they'd missed it in 1999.

Envelope #4: *The State vs. Cardinal Joseph King III*. This case was sensitive and went under the radar just like the Wiggins' case. The cardinal was the same priest who'd married the mayor and his wife, and the one, after the 9/11 attacks, to organize so many relief programs, generating millions in funds for those financially handicapped after the attacks.

Joseph, in many New Yorkers' eyes, was considered a hero. People kept saying he should be the next pope. He didn't hesitate to get involved in community-related issues, and he loved the spotlight. Being on TV so much, Joseph was considered a celebrity and received rock-star treatment everywhere he went. But he kept a very large basket of dirty laundry.

Lucky and Tango were investigating this high-profile escort service based in Queens, but servicing the entire city of New York. One night, they followed this limo when they saw two girls jump in. The limo drove for about twenty-five minutes and stopped at the Holiday Inn off the Long Island Expressway, a few minutes into Long Island. The limo was parked in the parking lot for a few minutes.

While Lucky and Tango watched from the bushes, they didn't see anyone jump in, so they thought the girls were doing the limo driver. Right before Lucky was about to get a closer look and snap pictures, he noticed headlights pulling into the parking lot, so he jumped back in the bushes.

Once the headlights got closer, they noticed it was an expensive luxury car pulling up next to the limo. Someone from the backseat jumped out and got in the limo. Lucky and Tango quickly recognized his face and were both shocked to see him jump in the limo. That someone was the cardinal Joseph King III. Because he loved the spotlight so much, everyone knew his face. That was why he was picking hotels in deserted areas where truckers rested, to avoid any identity surprises.

Five minutes later, the doors from the limo swung open, and both the girls and Joseph got out the limo and headed toward a room. While walking to the room, Joseph was holding a bottle of vodka in one hand and squeezing the ass of one of the girls with the other.

Lucky and Tango were still shocked, but it didn't stop them from taking pictures, and continuing to do their jobs.

Four and a half hours later, they finally exited the rented room. All three of them appeared drunk as they stumbled out. Joseph's driver had to help him get in the car.

As soon as the cardinal left with the limo, Lucky went up to their room, while Tango kept watch, looking for extra evidence like saliva, fingerprints, and sperm, anything to ensure Joseph couldn't lie his way out of the situation.

Lucky was collecting towels and sheets. Then he looked in the garbage and saw two condoms, which still had sperm in them. He put the towels and sheets down and just left with the condoms. He couldn't believe the cardinal was that stupid.

When the cardinal fell into their lap, the captain made a decision to blackmail Joseph instead of pressing charges and embarrassing him. Tuna and his team weren't called elite for nothing. They started gathering evidence. That way they could demand a seven-figure payout. Within days, Tuna and Speedy were inside of Joseph's mansion at the Hamptons. Speedy downloaded everything off his computer, and they left.

The next day was when they made the discovery of Joseph's true identity. He wasn't just into escort services; he ran a film company that produced child pornography. There were video clips of the cardinal performing sexual acts with little boys who appeared to be no more than nine and ten years old. Grown men were penetrating the rectums of little boys and recording everything. They went through about twenty-five videos and witnessed about thirty-five different kids being molested.

In some videos, the cardinal was seen with two boys at the same time. Captain Tuna and his crew were not about to protect a child molester, so they decided to expose the cardinal, instead of extorting him. They arrested him and pressed charges. A week after pressing charges against the cardinal, he was out on only $30,000 bail.

The city was shocked, but they didn't rush to judge.

In fact, a lot of the city papers had quotes with New Yorkers wanting more proof that he indeed molested younger boys. The public had only heard of these videos. They wanted to see them before crucifying the cardinal.

The cardinal pleaded not guilty, and a trial date was set. During the trial, he was offered a deal without any evidence presented to the jury. The cardinal was sentenced to twelve months of probation and was stripped of his duties as cardinal while he served his probation time.

After the plea deal was made public, Tuna and his boys were very upset because they could have made a few million blackmailing him.

Lucky turned in all the evidence against the cardinal, the pictures and all the videos. He wanted to make sure, when the cardinal died, his name was remembered as a child molester, not a hero.

After the new reports had surfaced, the FBI started to investigate some of Lucky's claims, especially the kiddy porn business Joseph was running. The FBI figured if his claims were accurate, then many more high-profile individuals like him were involved.

Envelope #5: This package was the most dangerous one because now he was implicating the top cop in New York. Commissioner Brandon Fratt had started out as a trooper in New Jersey, where he learned to profile African-Americans. When he worked the New Jersey Turnpike, that's all he pulled over, African-American drivers. Years later, he transferred to the NYPD when his uncle became a chief.

Brandon, at twenty-seven, was made one of the youngest captains in the force. Five years later, he was running an elite squad called "Operation DG," which stood for drugs and guns. Their job was to lock up drug dealers and get the guns off the streets. Brandon handpicked his squad, and his first choice was then Officer William "Tuna" Youngstown.

Operation DG didn't help reduce crime and murder, they helped increase the numbers. That's how dirty this unit was. They were working with drug dealers like Pito, helping them move kilos of cocaine all around New York City. When Operation DG made arrests, they usually would lock up low-end criminals and then frame them with bigger crimes. This process kept the heat off their back from the mayor, and more money coming in from the criminals who paid for protection.

Since Lucky wasn't around at that time, the only evidence he had was recorded conversations between Tuna and Brandon.

Tuna had always credited Brandon for showing him the ropes and how to make millions of untaxed money. Lucky was able to provide certain files to the media, showing Brandon's signature on at least five different house deeds, two of them million-dollar condos. This was excluding the $1.2 million house he currently lived in with his wife and children. Commissioner Brandon also ran a non-profit organization called "The Future Is Now," a non-profit venture to help kids with special needs.

In the three years the company has been in existence, he has raised over fifteen million dollars. Lucky provided documents of an overseas account with Brandon Fratt's signatures on deposit slips. There were over ten deposits totaling fifteen millions dollars. The documents also showed a history of withdrawals, and for the past five years, he had spent over seven million dollars in houses, cars, and lucrative vacations. In 1994, he co-owned a construction company that did all the major projects in Brooklyn.

His company was given a hundred-million-dollar contract to renovate public schools in Brooklyn.

Out of more than sixty public schools, only about twenty were renovated, while another fifteen or so received new computers and books. In total, maybe forty million was used for the schools. The rest of the money was used to buy residents out of their home in order to start building these big department stores in the neighborhood and build big hotels in downtown Brooklyn.

According to Lucky, Brandon Fratt was the mastermind behind their unit. Captain Tuna ran everything through him first, and the commissioner was always the first one to get paid. The commissioner has already gone on record and denied all accusations.

Thesmokygun.com would like to thank everyone who read this article about the five envelopes. Our information comes from a reliable source down in City Hall. We are not responsible or liable for any suit, due to this third party information we received.

Chapter Thirteen

Lucky's Daughter

Tuna arrived with both agents at the apartment, so he could introduce them to his partners. Loose and Speedy didn't overreact like he thought they would. They understood that if Tuna was introducing them, they were legit and in it for the same reasons.

"Fellas, these two brothers are law enforcement, but they are feds. They are here to help us. The commissioner recommended them. They know where Lucky's daughter lives."

"For real?" Loose said. "So what are we waiting for. Let's go find her."

"I agree with Loose. Let's go find her. If they are working with us, then let's do it. Floyd and his boys already left. We need all the help we can get," Speedy added.

They gathered around the living room and listened to the information the agents had to share. They knew, by finding Lucky's daughter, this nightmare would go away. They would force Lucky to get in front of a camera and tell all of New York and America that he basically made up everything to frame his former employers because he was upset over his salary.

"Okay. So, Agent Kuntz, where is Lucky hiding his daughter?" Tuna asked.

"We have a P.O. box address up in Cape Cod, Massachusetts. This is the address that came up on some old hospital document. We ran Donald Gibson's name through the hospital database for the entire United States of America."

"But how do we know this is Lucky's daughter? There could be hundreds of Donald Gibsons," Speedy added.

"You are right, but there were only three Donald Gibsons in the force, and only one of them is African-American. Donald used his police medical insurance to pay for the birth of his daughter. The birth certificate also gives us the name of both his daughter and the mother. His daughter's name is Tamika Freefall, and the mother's name is Tasha Freefall. Their last known address is a P.O. box in Cape Cod."

"Wow! That's some slick shit. I would have never thought about searching birth certificates and shit. I guess we are heading up to Cape Cod, right, boss?" Loose Cannon asked.

"Yes, we are, but we have to be smart. Loose, you and one of the agents go check this address out and bring back the little bitch. I'm sure they're still up there hiding."

"We have to be extremely smart. Tasha must be an expert in hiding because, besides the P.O. box address, we can't find anything else on them. It's possible they changed their names and their looks as well," Agent Kuntz added.

"You are right, but at least we know where to search. It shouldn't be hard to find a nigger in Cape Cod," Tuna added.

They all laughed.

"Boss, I think we should let Lucky know we're heading to Cape Cod. This will put fear in his heart and make him go out there as well. We could kill two birds with one stone."

They all thought it was a great idea.

About an hour later, after getting all the details worked out for their mission, Commissioner Brandon called Tuna's cell to express his frustrations.

"We are running out of fuckin' time. Find this nigger, and end it before we all go to jail for life. Now I have to get the feds off my ass. The DA is still gathering evidence, so we might have a slim chance of getting away clean from this mess. But you need to kill this son of a bitch. Got it?" He ended the call without letting him respond.

"Listen, Speedy, call our people down at the newspaper and make up a tip," Tuna ordered.

"What kind of a tip?"

"Come up with a story about how you received a call from a hotel employee and that those three police officers accused of killing that Black kid just checked in. Tell them that they can't name the hotel, but it's located in Cape Cod. Tell them to make sure they mention that all three police officers checked in, even though only Loose is going out there."

"That's a smart idea. You know Lucky will be watching the news, once he hears about us being in Cape Cod, he will shit in his pants. He will know we know about his daughter's whereabouts," Speedy added.

* * *

When the six o'clock news came on, the first story were those five envelopes. They were still the hot topic, and everyone had an opinion about the whole ordeal.

"Good evening. My name is Barbara Water, Channel 5 News. Tonight, we have more details about those five envelopes. We all know they came from former police officer, Donald Gibson, who not long ago took the stand against his former partners for the murder of Perry Coleman. These allegations are not only shaking the streets, but they also have members of Congress scratching their heads. Every criminal from every corner is supporting Rell Davis and Juan "Pito" Medina. The city streets are feeling their pain about being wrongfully accused and imprisoned. Let's go to Destine Diaz, live from 125th Street in Harlem."

"Thank you, Barbara. I'm here in front of the State Office Building on 125th Street, speaking to the real New Yorkers, asking them how they feel about the recent allegations of corruption. I'm going to run you this clip I recorded an hour ago, this is what people on the streets of New York are saying."

"Hi, my name is Tim, and I've lived in New York all my life. These allegations don't surprise me because I see it every day. These crooked cops are not here to protect us, they protect the shield. If it wasn't for that Black cop testifying, those other three officers would have gotten off. "

"Hello, my name is Sophia, and I think it's sad when we have the highest-ranking officer and the most respected priest committing these criminal acts. I don't know what else to say. I'm still waiting

to hear from the mayor. He's been silent throughout this ordeal. The longer he stays quiet, the more I'm going to wonder." Sophia looked straight into the camera and said, "I voted for your—Beep!—you better say something."

"Wat's good? I hope dis goin' to be on TV, yo. I think iz foul how peoples keep sayin'—What's dat word again?—alle-what, oh yea, yea, allegation, when they got pictures and have you on cam cordas wid li'l kids. Dat's sick, fam."

"It's scary. I'm already working on a plan to move down South. I was born and raised here in Harlem. I don't want to leave, but if I can't trust the police or my mayor, then it's time to leave and start somewhere fresh."

"My name is Moses Williams. I have three sons who I raised well, just like the Colemans raised Perry. Their son was murdered by police officers who were high off cocaine, and they have these officers on a paid vacation. It's sad, and it sends the wrong message. But I tell you what, we are not surprised. This kind of thing has been going on for a long time. I'm just glad the spotlight is now on them. It's going to take a miracle for them to restore the trust of the people. A lot of foul play was involved, and we still don't know how deep it runs. That's the scary part."

"Those are some of the many comments I recorded. Meanwhile, a new trial date has not been set. The DA's office is still deciding whether or not they should move the case to another county. Let's not forget the five bombs that Lucky dropped, and boy, did we receive a wake-up call. This is Destine

Diaz, reporting live from 125th Street in Harlem. Back to you, Barbara."

"Did you hear that, honey?" Laura asked.

"I sure did. They're still undecided about moving the case to another county. I'm sure these recent reports will help us more than hurt us."

Lucky was watching the news as well, smiling. He was looking around the living room, missing Diamond's presence. Usually, around this time, she would feed Lucky whatever he wanted.

He finally got off the sofa and was about to make a sandwich when he heard the breaking news theme song come on. He quickly sat back down to listen.

"This is Barbara Water again. We have breaking news coming out of Queens, New York. The family of Perry Coleman, who was killed by the NYPD, also received what's believed to be a tape. A tape sent by, you guessed it, Lucky. On this tape, the Colemans are saying the three officers are heard talking about shooting, and implicating themselves. They won't allow the media to hear the tape, but they will let the district attorney hear it. They are set to head downtown tomorrow morning for a meeting. This is what Laura Coleman said, the mother of Perry Coleman."

"Good evening. A tape was brought to our attention by detective Donald 'Lucky' Gibson. Bless his heart for caring and making sure justice is served to these animals hiding behind a badge. On this tape, the officers are thanking each other for a

cover-up. They call my son the N-word. At least now I can sleep at night knowing my son never pointed a gun at those officers. That's all for now. I want to thank New York for their continued love and support."

Lucky, at first, was upset that the Colemans went public with the evidence, but then he actually believed it was a perfect move. Due to all the recent allegations against the City, now was the perfect time to hit them where it hurt.

Lucky refocused his attention on the TV when he heard the news reporter say they were attempting to reach the three officers who were on trial, to see if they had any comments about all the allegations.

"We have tried to make several phone calls to their residences, but we've received no answer. However, through a reliable source, we hear the officers are in Cape Cod, fishing, but fishing for what?"

Lucky froze when he heard Barbara Water mention Cape Cod. The first thing that came to his mind was his daughter. "Fuck! They must know where Tamika lives."

He grabbed a few pieces of clothing and packed up his Expedition. Then he drove to his storage on Gun Hill Road in the Bronx.

One of Lucky's best friends, Divine, ran the storage facility, Put-It-Away, and Lucky was a silent partner. They were smart enough to invest their money after the armored truck heist they'd pulled a few years back. He had hired Divine and his two muscles, Pee-Wee and Blood. They made over ten million off the heist, eight million in bonds and two in cash.

The storage facility was really a front. Divine ran a business called Street Secrets. He let high-profile criminals store their money, drugs, and weapons, whatever they wanted. With Lucky's protection and intel, the storage was a successful business. Divine played the roll of banker, offering lockboxes with a 100 percent matching insurance policy. He ran a legit business, too. About 75 percent of the storage units belonged to regular customers, so they were able to keep the IRS and cops off them.

Divine and Lucky had one rule. They only did business with high rollers. There were times they were holding over a hundred million dollars in cash and a few tons of cocaine. They were making a lot of money, so Lucky had a state–of-the-art alarm installed, custom designed for the entire property. They went with technology, instead of armed guards, which would have made customers suspicious.

When Lucky arrived, Divine knew it was war.

"Yo, fam. Wat's good? Everything a'ight? You look like you about to start a war. Let me get my shit, too."

"Not on this one, Dee. I have to go alone. I think these pigs know where Tamika lives. It's going to get ugly. I need you here, just in case."

"Just in case? What you mean, dog?"

"Just in case something happens to me, you could continue running the business."

"C'mon, you sound crazy. I'm ready to die for you, hood. You took me out the streets. I'm still criminal-minded all day, but you got me off the block. I owe you, family. I'm not scared to die, not if I'm riding with you." Divine hugged his childhood friend.

"Damn, nigga! You tryin' to make me cry? Don't worry. I'm coming back. I just want you to hold shit down while I'm gone."

"I got you, but I just wanna let you know I'm not feeling all these moves you're making on your own. You know I'm here, twenty-four/seven for you. You should have came by and scoop me up, my dude."

"My bad, but that's what I been trying to say all along. I need to do this alone. Get the minivan ready."

"And you takin' the minivan? Now I know you about to start a war."

They both laughed as they walked to the back of the business. Lucky headed to his unit, while Divine went to load up the all-white minivan with all kinds of weapons.

Right before Lucky jumped in the van with limo-tint windows, he turned to Divine and said, "Don't worry. God, I will be back."

"You better! Watch your ass out there, and don't sleep on no one, not even baby mom. It's been a while since you seen them," Divine said.

They once again embraced.

Lucky turned the van on and began his trip. He ignored that last comment by Divine. There was no way Tasha could betray him. It was only about a five- to six-hour drive. Lucky figured he could make it four and a half. He started off doing close to ninety miles per hour. He didn't care about any troopers or his own safety. The thought of any harm to his daughter took precedence over common sense.

After three hours of driving like a maniac, he

started to realize he needed to slow down a bit. Long drives always made his mind wander, and he started thinking about Tasha and how they'd met.

He always felt she was a perfect match, a love at first sight for sure. She was also a gym rat, one of the many things they had in common. She loved working out and keeping her body in shape. She worked as a bartender in two of the hottest clubs at the time, Club Limelight and the Palladium. Tasha also took a lot of self-defense courses. Being a female bartender in New York City wasn't an easy task. Every night, she was either cursing or fighting a drunken jerk off her. She had to be on the defense at all times.

Tasha was five-four, caramel complexion with hazel eyes, had a flat stomach, and a nice juicy peach on her backside. No stretch marks or bumps, skin real silky, Lucky always thought she bathed in milk. Customers, both men and women, would always come on to her, looking for one-night stands.

Lucky always partied at the Palladium, and from afar, he had a big crush on her. He would always order from different bartenders because he didn't want her to remember his face and think he was a stalker. He wanted to wait until the perfect moment to make his move and ask her out.

One night, there was a stabbing after the club closed, and Lucky and Tango were two of few officers at the scene trying to calm down the rowdy partygoers. Lucky noticed two drunks harassing a young lady. As he got closer, he noticed it was the bartender. He didn't have to intervene, though. Tasha kicked them both in the nuts and slapped one of them with her purse while she maced the other. Tasha noticed Lucky approaching, and was about to spray him, until she saw the badge hanging from his neck. Lucky always remembered that day. It was the first day Tasha lay in his arms.

They dated for about six months before they moved in together. It didn't take long for her to realize his dirty laundry in the streets. She often asked him to stop before he lost his job or his life, but Lucky didn't take her advice at the time. He was making too much money. Instead of losing his life or job, he lost his first love.

Tasha knew it was over before she got pregnant. They had a long conversation about their next move. She wanted an abortion, he didn't. Tasha thought it was worth believing his words. After Tamika was born, Lucky indeed began slowing down, but was still playing with the devil's cards. Tasha didn't like it, but she didn't complain.

One morning, Tasha found him passed out on the floor of their driveway, car still running. Lucky had cocaine smeared all over his nose and mouth. That morning she decided it was time to leave, and leave him for good. When she went to turn off the car, she found an open box of condoms, two of them missing.

Tasha was more devastated about the drugs than his sleeping around. She had no idea he was snorting cocaine. She left him there on the floor, packed up a few things, and left with Tamika.

When Lucky woke up, he was on the floor with the sun beaming. He went inside and found a letter on the kitchen table. Tasha kept it short and sweet.

Lucky, you are a drug addict, a cheat, and a criminal. I'm moving into the summer house in

Cape Cod. You know how to find us and send money. Don't you dare show up unless that life you are currently living has one hundred percent disappeared out of your system, no ifs, ands, or buts. Tasha

Lucky snapped out of his daze, his eyes watery. He couldn't believe he let Tasha and Tamika walk out of his life. He still didn't know why he'd waited this long to finally reach out to them. All he could hope for was for a new chance. He was ready to settle down and become a real family man.

For the past few years, the only communication he had with his daughter was through a P.O. box address. Every holiday and birthday he would send cards and gifts. Every six months he would send money. Lucky even helped in changing their identities with fake but legit birth certificates and Social Security cards. He even gave Tasha a new driver's license with the new address in Cape Cod.

About two years ago, the last time he actually spoke to Tasha over the phone, she gave him an address at the time and told him, if he ever decided to come up there, to stop by that address first.

When Lucky finally reached his exit, he became real excited. He was about to see his little girl. The long drive was helpful to him because not for one minute did he think about his old partners.

Lucky pulled up to the address and was taken by surprise at the look of the old house. He had to double-check the address a few times. It was the correct house. He just didn't believe someone lived in it. He walked up to the front door and rang the bell three times.

"Why are you ringing my bell this late, Sonny?"

"Tasha gave me this address. She said you have a place for me."

"Oh, yes, yes. You must be her cousin. She told me when the Army discharged you, you would stop by. C'mon in and let me show you to your new room. By the way, my name is Mrs. Rosie. Did you just arrive today?"

"Yes, I did. I really want to thank you for helping. I promise I won't stay long. I just need a few days."

"Don't worry, honey. You can stay as long as you want. Tasha left some things for you about a week ago. I guess she knew you were coming."

After the old lady left the room, Lucky quickly looked through the stuff she left him and found two handguns and pictures of their new looks and names. He laughed out loud when he saw the guns but then refocused his attention to the pictures. They didn't change much. Only their hair looked different. Lucky could tell Tasha had some facial surgery, but she still looked the same.

Tasha's new name was Luz, and Tamika's was Jessica. For a few minutes, he choked up looking at the pictures of Tamika, now twelve years old. The last time he saw her, she was six going on seven. He felt bad about the choice he made. He promised, after all this drama was over with, he was going to build that relationship back with Tamika.

Lucky lay on the bed, backtracking his past, trying to figure out where he slipped up, and how could they have found his girls. He knew he must have made a mistake somewhere, but his mind went blank. He couldn't remember anything.

He got up and looked out the window to help his

mind wander. That didn't help. All he saw was trees and birds. He felt like an inmate looking out his tiny window in a state prison. He wasn't used to the quiet, laid-back atmosphere.

Lucky had to wait until the morning for Mrs. Rosie to notify Tasha. Mrs. Rosie didn't own a phone, so she never asked for anyone's phone number.

Lucky couldn't take the suspense of waiting all night, so he sat on the edge of his bed in frustration and began talking to himself. "Fuck! I feel like a prisoner. I need a drink or two to help my mind relax."

He opened the door to his bedroom and peeked out to see if he saw the old lady. He wanted to ask where the closest liquor store was, or if she had any liquor in the house. He heard what sounded like pots and pans banging against the sink. He figured she must be downstairs washing dishes, so he went downstairs.

He called her name out loud to not surprise her when he approached. "Mrs. Rosie, is you downstairs in the kitchen?"

"Yes, Sonny, I am."

"Do you know where I could purchase some liquor, or even beers?"

"It's almost midnight. Nothing is open this late, but I have a few bottles of whiskey in the basement that belonged to my husband. You could go down there and pick what you like."

"Oh no, I don't want to impose or use your husband's liquor."

"Sonny, you are not imposing. My husband won't mind. He's been dead for eight years. Go on downstairs and pick what you like. I also have some leftovers in the refrigerator."

Lucky couldn't believe how nice this old lady was.

He was wondering how Tasha met her. He figured she must have been Tamika's babysitter when she was younger or something. When he finally reached the basement, there were so many bottles of liquor, he thought Rosie's husband must have died of liver poison. He'd never heard of the whiskey before and figured it was just some Cape Cod brand. He didn't care. He grabbed a bottle and went back upstairs.

Before he went to his room, he asked Mrs. Rosie, "Mrs. Rosie, if you don't mind me asking, what kind of whiskey is this? I have never heard of it before."

"It's homemade whiskey. My husband and his friend used to make it and sell it. I have to warn you, it's very strong. It will burn a hole in your throat," she said, laughing.

"I was wondering why there were so many bottles downstairs, but now it makes sense. Can I ask you another question? How did you and my cousin meet?"

"Actually, your cousin responded to an ad I left in the local grocery store. I was watching her little girl. She's the most precious girl I have ever met. It's a shame her father was never around. After a few years, we became family. She spent a lot of time in this house. She loved the quiet. Well, it's way past my bedtime. I have to get up in a few hours. I'm sorry, Sonny. I'm going to sleep. Make yourself at home."

"Thank you for everything, Mrs. Rosie. Good night."

As Lucky went back to his room, he cracked open that whiskey bottle and put his lips on it faster than a two-dollar hooker. Lucky had been drinking for over twenty years, so he wasn't scared of homemade liquor. He was ready for the challenge.

As soon as he took a big shot of the whiskey, he spat

everything out. He started coughing so hard and loud, Mrs. Rosie was laughing at him.

"I told you, Sonny, it will burn a hole in your throat."

Lucky was on the floor holding his neck, still coughing and tearing up. It took him a good fifteen seconds to regain his composure, but then he caught a head rush for another fifteen seconds.

He wiped the tear off his eyes and looked at the bottle. "What the fuck is this? I can't believe these rednecks drink this shit out here." He closed the bottle and took it back downstairs. He didn't even want the bottle in the room.

While walking back upstairs, still banging his chest, trying to clear up his system, he decided to try to go to sleep. He got back in bed and started thinking about Diamond, wondering how she was. He knew she was lonely, but okay, because she wasn't a homebody type of female. She would find something to keep herself entertained.

Lucky felt bad about the whole situation. She was the one to get a raw deal. He was never going back to her. That's why he gave her so much money and the house. It was a hard decision, but a man couldn't choose another woman over his family. Lucky understood Diamond was deeply in love with him, and he only hoped she didn't take it too hard and tried to hurt herself. He sat back up on his bed, experiencing one of the longest nights of his life.

Right after getting Diamond out of his head, he started thinking about Tamika. He could remember the first day she was born. He'd kissed her on the forehead and promised he would protect her for life. He broke that promise, and now he needed to make it up big-time, because of his drug abuse.

Once he finally saw her in the morning, he knew it was going to be an awkward reunion. A lot of years had passed, but they wouldn't have time to catch up right away because he was going have to tell them about the danger they were in, and about possibly relocating.

When the morning sunlight hit the glass window and the reflection glared off his face, Lucky woke up. He didn't know at what time he'd passed out, but he was happy it was morning. It felt like a Christmas morning.

He washed up, got dressed, and waited for Mrs. Rosie to return. Around ten in the morning, she returned but had a long face.

"Is everything okay?"

"Tasha never showed up. I waited for two hours, and she never showed. That's not like her."

"Maybe she was tired and never got out of bed," Lucky said, hoping that was the case.

"It's still not like her."

Lucky couldn't hold back and play Mr. Nice Guy anymore. "Mrs. Rosie, let me have the address where you were supposed to meet her. If you have her home address, that would be better. Any information would be helpful."

"I'm sorry. I don't know her home address. We were going to meet at Joe's Diner for our usual breakfast meeting. I'm telling you, something is not right. If you want the address to Joe's Diner, here is their card. It has the address on it."

"Thank you."

Lucky entered the address in his GPS system and headed out the door. He wasn't about to sit back, knowing his old partners were out there and Tasha was missing.

While driving, he was so nervous, he couldn't stop shaking, and his heart was pounding in his chest. It was about a fifteen-minute drive, and he drove with caution, looking inside every car he passed. The pounding in his heart felt more like a stampede.

He wanted to stay positive, but it was hard to. He kept saying to himself, "If you touch my little girl, I'm going to kill your whole family."

Lucky noticed the Joe's Diner sign was getting closer. He pulled up to the restaurant, drove around the parking lot first, and didn't see Tasha's car. Mrs. Rosie told him she drove a green truck, but didn't know the make of the car. Lucky thought, *Maybe she got the colors confused,* so he parked down the street and walked to the diner.

He went in, glanced around the dining area, and didn't see anyone who resembled Tasha or Tamika. He asked one of the waitresses if she knew where the post office was located.

The waitress pointed out the window. "It's right across the street, mister."

Lucky thought quickly and asked for a table. "Well, since I'm already here, I might as well eat something."

Lucky was able to get a seat right by the window. He figured he would sit there until Tasha showed up. He ordered three pancakes, scrambled eggs, and a beef sausage. He was starving.

After eating his meal and drinking three cups of coffee, he noticed this one car had been parked in the same spot for the past hour. What was odd was, the driver had been sitting there for almost an hour with his engine running. At first, Lucky thought the driver was waiting for someone, but he thought it was crazy to keep your car running so long.

"Shit, not even getaway cars keep the shit running that long. But who's the suit in that car? I'm going to have to take a closer look. Something is not right," he said to himself.

He signaled for the young, pretty blond waitress to bring his bill.

"Here you go, mister. Thank you for coming to Joe's. Come again."

"I sure will come whenever I'm in town."

"Oh, you from out of town, too. Are you with John?"

"I'm sorry. Who?"

"With John. Him." She pointed outside to the car Lucky was about to check out.

"No, I'm not with him, but between us, he's been there for like thirty minutes," he said, trying to bait her into giving up more info.

"Thirty minutes, yeah, right. More like all morning. When I came in this morning, they were parked there. There were two of them this morning, but now I just see one."

Lucky gave her a fifty-dollar bill and told her dumb ass to keep the change.

Then it hit him. "They must know about the P.O. box address." Lucky walked past the car on the driver's side, close enough to see that the car doors were unlocked. When he walked back, he noticed John was barely keeping his eyes open. They must have been there all night.

Lucky moved in quickly. He went around the passenger side, opened the door, jumped in, and pressed the barrel of his gun against his face.

"What the fuck is going on here? I'm a federal agent. You sure you want to kill me?"

"A federal agent? Get the fuck out of here. Why are you watching the post office? Did Captain Tuna from New York send you here? If he did, then you a dirty agent."

Agent John tried to play it cool. "No, I'm just waiting for my wife to come out the postal office."

"Bullshit! You think I don't know you been here since eight o'clock in the morning? Where is your partner? Who else came out here with you?"

"Again, I don't know what you're talking about. I'm here waiting for my—"

Lucky cocked back his gun. "Go ahead and say you are waiting for your wife again. Go ahead and say it."

John froze like a statue. He knew he was dealing with someone who would pull the trigger. "Okay, yes, you're right, Tuna sent us out here, but I came out here by myself."

Lucky pistol-whipped John and split open his head, and blood splattered all over the steering wheel and dashboard.

"I'm going to ask you one last time. Who else came here with you, and where are they at? Are they inside?"

"Okay, okay, I'm sorry. Don't hit or shoot me."

"I won't if you tell me what I want to know."

"I came out here with Loose Cannon."

"Loose Cannon? Where is he at?" Lucky's heart started pounding again when he heard that name. His aggression level went sky-high.

He grabbed John by his collar and raised his gun to strike him again, but John started talking.

"He's inside the post office, watching the boxes. We know about your P.O. box."

"Put the car in drive and go around the back of this diner," Lucky ordered.

As soon as they pulled around and parked, Lucky began pistol-whipping him until he was unconscious. Blood was pouring out of his skull like a faucet. Lucky left him alive, but with a chance of bleeding to death if help didn't find him quickly. He didn't care if he was a federal agent. Dirty is dirty. He cleaned the blood off his gun, put it back on his hip, and fixed himself up. He looked around the parking lot to make sure no one was watching before exiting the car.

Lucky wasn't going to waste time and wait for Loose Cannon to come out the post office. He was going inside to kill him. He started walking toward the front door, his mind already set on shooting on sight and disappearing.

As Lucky was walking up the steps of the post office, out came Loose Cannon. This was the one confrontation where you couldn't pick a winner, because neither was afraid to die. They both hated each other's guts, so killing the other was not going to be a problem. It was like one of those old cowboy movies. Whoever drew first and shot would survive another day.

As both men approached each other, Loose saw right through the fake disguise and knew it was Lucky.

Lucky saw he was mad, drew his weapon, and pointed at Loose Cannon, who also had his weapon drawn, but was pointing at the head of a hostage.

Downtown Cape Cod went hysterical once someone yelled, "Gun!"

People were running and screaming all over the place.

Lucky thought Loose made a dumb move by grabbing a hostage. "What the fuck are you doing? I don't care about any goddamn hostage."

"Well, you dumb son of a nigger! Take a closer look at who I'm holding!"

Lucky, for a quick second, took his eyes off him and looked at the hostage. It was Tasha. He couldn't believe it at first, until he heard her voice.

"Donald, I'm sorry, baby."

Lucky quickly refocused his attention back on Loose Cannon and tightened his grip on the gun.

As Loose was walking forward, Lucky was backing down the steps, not losing his focus or aim. Loose started to yell different shit at him about dropping his gun, but Lucky couldn't hear him. He was spaced out, thinking about his days at the academy, where he won all those awards for his precise shooting.

He aimed, saw an opening, and fired one shot. As the bullet left the barrel, Lucky heard both of them scream before the bullet knocked them to the ground. He ran toward them, hoping he hit the right target.

Tasha was lying stiff on the ground, and Loose was still moving. Lucky thought the worst, that maybe he shot his baby girl. He walked up to Loose Cannon and shot him twice in the head before even checking to see if Tasha was all right.

He then dropped to his knees and flipped Tasha over. She was bleeding from her head. There was blood everywhere. Lucky was in tears, and he could hear the sirens coming. He sat there rocking Tasha back and forth. He didn't care about the sirens.

"Baby, are you going to rock me to death or help me get up?" Tasha said as she gained consciousness.

"Baby, you're okay. I thought I lost you for a second." He looked down at Tasha, and she looked right back at him.

When he'd first shot Loose Cannon, the impact of the shot slammed both bodies hard to the concrete. Tasha landed headfirst, explaining the blood.

Lucky jumped to his feet and quickly attended to her. "Wow! Baby, you bumped your head pretty hard."

"Yes, I'm still a little dizzy, but I could manage. We need to hurry up and get out of here."

"I'm parked over there," Lucky said, pointing up the streets to his van.

"Let's take my car, Donald. Plus, I know the way around here."

Within thirty seconds, they were in the car and speeding through some back roads.

As Tasha was driving, Lucky was thinking about the shot he just took. He kept visualizing Loose Cannon lying there with his head split.

They finally pulled up to Tasha's house, and he snapped out of his daze.

"Where is Tamika? Is she inside?"

"No, she's at Mom's house."

"Mom's house? Your mother lives out here too? I thought you guys didn't have a good relationship."

"Why you think I begged you to buy a summer house in Cape Cod? Both my parents were living out here. After my father died, our relationship grew to the next level.

"Wait a minute. Mrs. Rosie, that's really your mother, right?"

"Yes, that's her. How you knew?"

Lucky started laughing out loud.

"That's a good one. Wow! Good cover-up. I thought it was kind of funny because I saw a few pictures around the house. But when Mrs. Rosie mentioned she was babysitting, I just thought this lonely old lady treated my daughter as one of hers. It never hit me that that was actually her grandmother. I can't believe I couldn't see right through it."

While they made their way inside the house, Tasha said, "Donald, we need to talk. I know we don't have time, but baby, I need you to sit down and listen."

"Oh-oh."

"Don't be silly," she said, laughing.

"Okay, I know you're trying to be serious, so let me sit down. But if you are about to tell me about other men, please save it. I'm not tripping."

"Boyyee, sit down! I don't want to talk about other men. I want to speak to you about you. Right now, I have to make a decision to hit the road with you and relocate, or tell you, 'Fuck you! Keep it going.'"

"Wow! It's like that?"

"Yes, it's like that. You haven't been around for a long time. For years, I had to lie to our daughter defending you. That way she didn't grow up hating you. I held all that anger and pain inside, and I raised us a great little girl. I figure, why ruin her happiness just because I'm not happy?"

"Baby, I never wanted to hurt you."

"But you did, Donald, you did. Let me finish, please. Just listen. I want you to understand that a lot of things I did for you were because I loved you, not because I wanted to do them. I hope you understand the difference."

"Tasha, listen, I'm willing to do anything to have my girls back in my life, especially Tamika. I just have to take care of some things first before I could give you my full commitment. I'm a new man, but I just have to clean up a little more laundry."

"Are you referring to all the stuff I been reading about you and your former partners on the Internet? I'm assuming the guy you killed today was one of them."

"So you know?"

"Of course, I knew. That's why I went by my mother's house and fixed your room up, I knew you were coming. You took so long, I thought maybe, they . . ."

"What? That they killed me?"

"Something like that. It got to the point I was checking the Internet every day to see what else you did. That way, I knew you were alive. What took you so long to come? And who's this female partner the media keeps saying you have working with you?"

"You can't trust the media. I don't have any partners. I can't trust anyone anymore. I shook the city up, huh?"

"You sure did, but now what?"

"I don't know, but please let's grab what you need. I want to see my daughter. It's been almost seven years now."

"Baby, please don't waste my time. These past seven years were tough, but they were quiet. Do you promise not to fuck that up? Do you swear on your mother's grave you are giving up your old ways for good?"

"I swear on my mother's grave, baby. I'm sorry. I was the one who made the wrong choice. I will work hard to gain the trust and respect back. I haven't used drugs in almost two years, since the night Perry Coleman was killed. I'm focused. I have found peace in my life. I just have to close a few more chapters before I close this old book of mine."

As they were packing, Lucky was smiling because he was able to dodge the bullet about Diamond.

Within twenty minutes, Tasha had all the belongings she needed, and they hit the road. She parked her truck in the garage and drove her '02 Chevy Impala.

Lucky was impressed with the way she carried herself, always keeping a backup plan. He remembered why he fell in love with her.

As they got closer to her mother's house, he began to get nervous. He didn't know how Tamika would react to seeing her father for the first time in seven years.

"Tasha, how you think she will react once she sees me?"

"Oh, don't worry about that. I made sure she always respected you. You will actually make her day with your presence. She is always asking about you."

When they pulled up to Mrs. Rosie's house, Lucky almost caught a nervous breakdown. He knew Tasha just said everything was going to be all right, but he still was a little leery.

As soon as Lucky walked in, Tamika ran toward him. "Daddy, Daddy, you're finally home. I missed you so much, Daddy."

"Hey, baby. I missed you so much. Look at you. You have grown so much."

"Are you here to stay?"

"Yes, baby. Daddy will be around a lot more."

They spent about twenty minutes hugging and talking to each other. Even Tasha and Mrs. Rosie teared up watching them bond.

Tamika went back to the kitchen to finish helping her grandmother fix dinner.

Lucky walked over as well. "Mrs. Rosie?"

"My real name is Angela. You can call me Angie or Angela. Please, no *Mrs.* in front of it."

"Angela, again thank you. I'm sorry we had to meet like this."

"That's okay. My daughter explained everything years ago. I understand. She said one day you will be back, and here you are. But I see you have some drama to take care of."

Before Lucky could answer, Tasha ran back in the kitchen and asked Lucky to come and watch the news.

Chapter Fourteen

Headline:
"Two NY Cops Found Dead in Cape Cod"

"Good evening. My name is Robert McClouss, for BETV Channel 20 News. We are live in downtown Cape Cod in front of the United States Post Office. Today, we are here to report that two New York police officers, one of them a federal agent, were found dead. According to reports, one of the officers is named Steve Stanley, currently on trial for shooting an unarmed African-American in New York City. The other officer's name, at this moment, is still not available, but our sources are confirming he was a federal employee.

"According to witness statements, Officer Steve grabbed an unidentified woman by her arm and forced her outside. The lady kept screaming for him to let her go. When Officer Steve made it outside, he was confronted by another unidentified African-American male. The African American male and the officer both were pointing their guns at each other. We have another witness' statement

that alleged she saw the officer point the gun to the woman's head, and that's when the African-American male shot him and got away with the unidentified female.

"The other officer was found dead in a black Caprice across the street in the parking lot behind Joe's Diner. There are still a lot of questions to be answered here. We are still waiting for an official statement from the police department. This is Robert McClouss, for BETV Channel 20 News, reporting live from downtown Cape Cod."

"Lucky, I thought you said you didn't kill the federal agent?" Tasha asked.

"I thought he was still alive. I guess he didn't make it. I only pistol-whipped him a few times. But fuck him, anyway. They were up here to try to kill or kidnap Tamika. Let's not forget that."

"But wouldn't you get in more trouble if a federal agent pops up dead?"

"Yes, I would, but by the same token, this is a dirty federal agent, and the government doesn't protect or support dirty agents. They will realize he was corrupt because he had no business out here in the first place."

Back in New York, Captain Tuna was going ballistic over the death of one of his best friends. Speedy and Agent Kuntz tried numerous times to calm him down, but they couldn't. Tuna was tearing up everything in sight. He even took a few swings at both of them.

"Get the fuck off me! Don't you two realize what just happened here? Two of our brothers were just murdered. We are in deep shit, and we still don't have a clue where Lucky is located. I'm sure he will disappear along with his whole family."

"Tuna, one of my agents was killed too. I'm going to be in deeper shit myself, but we need to stick together and figure a way out of this mess."

"You know what, Agent Kuntz? Go fuck yourself! And get the hell out of my apartment! This all happened because of you. You were the one who made us aware of the whereabouts of Lucky's daughter. This is why I don't like working with the feds. Our business is over. You go deal with your superiors, and I will handle mine."

"C'mon, Tuna, we need to stick together."

"Work together how? You see how they released Loose Cannon's name in the media, but not your boy John. They startin' to protect him already. My guess is the feds will come up with a story about how John's murder wasn't related to the shooting between Loose and Lucky. Please, get the hell out of here now. I have to call the commissioner."

William Kuntz tried to plead his case, but he realized Tuna was under too much stress, so he left the apartment.

Speedy and Tuna were clueless on their next move. Lucky did enough damage to ruin not only their lives, but also the commissioner and a few high-ranking officials. Tuna kept delaying his call to the commissioner. He needed a break and was praying for a miracle.

Speedy, on the other hand, knew they were doomed. There was no coming back from this mess. And with Loose out of the picture, Tuna would most likely fold under pressure and maybe start cooperating to save his butt. Speedy already knew the commissioner wasn't going down on his own, but with so much evidence out in the public about all the dirt they each did, cooperation wouldn't help too much. Their key to freedom was capturing Lucky, and at this point, that was like hitting the lotto. They had their opportunity in Cape Cod, but once again, Lucky outsmarted them.

Tuna sat back on the couch and broke down in tears. He couldn't hold it back anymore. His best friend was just murdered, and his boss had been exposed because of him. Tuna knew he would end up in jail, or maybe even dead. That was enough to break down any man.

Speedy didn't have time to sit back and mourn. "Captain, do you think the commissioner will turn his back on us to save his ass?"

"Yes, I do. He already told me he will flip the script on me and my crew."

"Captain, I will be back later."

"For a second, I was about to call you a coward for trying to leave, but I'm about to go home myself. First, I have to call Loose's wife and go over funeral arrangements. Damn! I can't fuckin' believe he caught Loose Cannon off guard like that," a tearing Tuna said.

Speedy and Tuna embraced like it was the last time they were going to see each other as free men.

After Speedy left, Tuna started to empty the money out of his stash house. There was a little over two hundred thousand dollars in cash, and about another fifty thousand in drugs in the safe room.

While he was packing up his money and destroying the drugs, his cell phone started ringing. He didn't want to answer the call and hear the commissioner run his mouth about how he fucked up, but the phone continued ringing. He looked at the caller ID, and saw it was a restricted call. He finally answered.

"Hello, this is Tuna. Who is this?"

"I'm sorry about your loss."

"Who in the fuck is this? Is that you, you piece of shit?"

"I'm coming for you next. I know where you're staying. If you a man, you would wait for me. If you a coward, then I guess I will catch you another time."

Tuna didn't know if he was bluffing or not. He knew Loose would never talk, but he wasn't sure about John. "Whatever. You don't know where I am."

"I know you in Spanish Harlem. Let me guess—You're at your old-ass uncle's building. You're forgetting I know everything about you. Once that stupid agent said somewhere on Lexington Avenue in Spanish Harlem, I figured out the rest."

"You want me to wait for you? C'mon, you cocksucker! I'm tired of chasing you."

"I will be there in twenty minutes, bitch." Lucky hung up the phone laughing. He was still at Angela's house in Cape Cod and just wanted to let Tuna know he knew where he was at.

On the other hand, Tuna took the threat seriously. He called Speedy's cell phone, but it went straight to voice mail. He had no choice but to call the commissioner.

"About time you fuckin' call me. What the fuck happened out there?"

"I don't really know. I sent Loose with one of the agents, and somehow Lucky outsmarted them and got to them first."

"Damn, Tuna! Who are we really dealing with here? He's like a RoboCop or something. Why didn't we make him the golden boy of our team?"

"Remember, sir, he's Black."

"I know, but damn, I didn't know he was this good. We should have promoted or killed him back when we first saw his potential. Now look at how he's destroying us one by one. We will never find him."

"He just called right before I called you. He said he knows I'm on 102nd Street and Lexington Avenue, and that he would be here in twenty minutes. I need some help. I'm here by myself. Speedy left and went home."

"I will have people over there in ten to fifteen minutes. You just hold on tight. Do you have weapons there?"

"Yes, I'm well armed. Hurry up and get me out of here."

Tuna hung up the phone then grabbed his money and went up to the fifth floor. He went in the closet and pulled out a loaded AK-47 and two hand grenades. He leaned back against the kitchen wall, from where he could watch both the front door and the windows connected to the fire escape. Those are the only two places where Lucky could enter through.

Tuna was sweating, and his hands were shaking. He kept switching from different aiming position every ten seconds until help arrived. His cell phone started ringing again, and it was the commissioner.

"I hope you have good news. I'm sweating up here like a little bitch."

"Calm down. They're outside. There are three of them, and they're sweeping the area. Hold your position for a few more minutes."

"Okay, hurry up."

"Wait five minutes and come downstairs. Once you see them, you will recognize who they are. Remember, five more minutes."

"I got it. Five minutes."

Tuna started to feel a lot better knowing he wasn't alone. He put the AK and the grenades back in the closet and pulled out his 9mm Glock. He grabbed his bag full of money and drugs, and proceeded to go downstairs. He took his time, stopping and looking around at every step, aiming his gun everywhere. He didn't trust Lucky. He was good at sneaking up on people.

He finally made it downstairs and opened his front door. He walked outside and noticed who the commissioner sent. He'd called the mob and got him some Italian help.

Tuna quickly ran to the car they were standing by, jumped in, and told them to hurry up and drive away. He kept looking back, making sure no one was following them. The Italians drove him to a secret apartment, where he could relax while all the heat on him died down. They drove to the Bronx, Little Italy off Fordham Road.

When Tuna arrived, the commissioner was there waiting for him, looking like a hot mess. The recent allegations against the police force were breaking him down mentally and physically.

"Brandon, are you okay?" Tuna quickly asked. "You don't look good."

"Of course, I don't look good. By tomorrow morning, the headline will be another blow to the police department and City Hall. I'm almost positive they will reopen the Cardinal case. I'm not really worried about myself. I will be okay and beat these charges. But this won't help the case against you and Perry Coleman.

And I'm hearing they're about to release both Rell Davis and Juan 'Pito' Medina."

Tuna shot back, "Are you serious? They can't."

"They will. That means they believe Lucky and the evidence backing up his claims. That also means, at the end of the day, I will lose my job. The media is already talking about who's going to replace me."

"I'm sorry, boss, but we can't quit. We need to find this pig and somehow flip this whole thing around on him. We need to look into his past and find something sentimental besides his daughter. There has to be something we could find. I remember, when we were after M&M, he got close with that gangbanger name Thirty-eight. We all thought Lucky had turned his back on us for him. I know for a fact Thirty-eight will definitely bring Lucky out of hiding."

"So where is Thirty-eight? How can we find him?" Commissioner Fratt asked.

"I don't know, but I know I can find him a lot quicker than Lucky."

"Okay, that's our last resort. I have some people who might be able to help you find him."

"I got this one, trust me. I will find him. People like him don't leave their neighborhoods."

"Just give me till the morning, Tuna. I'll have someone for you. Meanwhile, get comfortable and relax. We have a long night ahead of us."

They decided to talk about different scenarios and strategies.

Meanwhile, Lucky was sitting at Angela's kitchen table, going over a few last-minute details. First, they needed to discuss where they were going to next, because Cape Cod was no longer safe.

"Okay, Tasha, you tell me where you want to go, sweetheart."

"Atlanta. A friend of mine lives there. Actually we used to work together. I visited her last year, and I love it out there."

"Atlanta, that's not a bad choice. Call your people and tell them to get you plugged in with a realtor, because we are on our way."

"Are you for real, baby? We are moving to Atlanta? Thank you so much. I thought you wouldn't go for Atlanta."

"Baby, it's all about you and Tamika. If that's where you want to live, then let's do it."

Tasha, jumping up and down like a little girl, went to tell her mother the great news.

Everyone was excited about moving to Atlanta. Tasha made reservations with a villa company, and they put a four-bedroom villa on hold for sixty days while they get settled in Atlanta.

While the girls were packing, Lucky was outside sitting on the porch thinking about Diamond and how much he was really missing her. He only hoped she was safe and didn't grow to hate him. In his heart, he knew he did the right thing, but he knew he was wrong for the way he played it.

For a quick second, he thought about disappearing and never showing his face ever. He thought he had done enough damage. But there was another side of him that couldn't let him quit until he killed both Speedy and Tuna.

Tasha came outside looking for him. "What's up,

baby? Why are you out here by yourself? What's on your mind?"

"I'm just thinking. I want to stop and just stay in Atlanta and never show my face again, but then I still have business I need to close. I don't know what to do."

"Well, baby, I think you should close those open businesses, and do it now. That way they don't haunt you forever. We will wait for you. We waited seven years. What's another few weeks? It's in God's hand. If destiny wants us together, I will see you again."

They both sat there in silence for about thirty minutes, until Tamika came outside and asked her mother for something to eat. Tasha went in, and Lucky stayed out there until everyone finished eating.

They loaded up Tasha's car and hit the road. Lucky even left his van parked by the diner. There was nothing in that car that would connect anything back to him, except the New York license plate.

Tasha barely spent any of the money Lucky sent her, and so she had over a hundred thousand dollars saved up. It was about a twenty-five-hour drive to Atlanta, so Lucky had plenty of time to think about his next move. He was still undecided.

While Tasha and Lucky drove through the night, Tuna was up himself thinking about his future. He wasn't sure if he would be around any longer. At this point, there were only two choices—getting killed or going to prison. He didn't like either one.

Tuna didn't sleep at all. He couldn't wait for the morning news to come on. He wanted to know what the latest news was. He wasn't the only one. Everyone was waiting for Destine Diaz's report.

When the morning came around, the commissioner

was right about the media. They were hanging the police department and blaming them for everything that had occurred.

"Good morning. It's Destine Diaz, Channel 5 News. I have the latest update on the two New York officers killed in Cape Cod. We know for sure one of the officers was Steve Stanley, better known as Loose Cannon, who was currently on trial for the murder of Perry Coleman. We still haven't received any information as to why he was in Cape Cod. While on bail and on trial, you need permission to leave the state. We are still investigating to see if that permission was filed or even granted.

"The other officer was a federal agent, and his name has still not been released. The federal government doesn't release the identity of their employees, but they are confirming one of their own was found dead. He was found across the street from the post office behind a diner, beaten to death with a blunt object. The feds are denying any involvement or connection to the standoff between Officer Steve Stanley and another unidentified African-American male, in which another woman was taken hostage. Despite their denial, the evidence doesn't look good. There are witnesses putting both Steve and this federal agent inside the same car parked across from the post office for hours. Post office cameras show Steve Stanley inside, watching the area where the P.O. boxes are located. One could only speculate about the woman Stanley was after, and about that unidentified male who confronted Stanley as he stepped outside. We will have more on this story as it unfolds.

"At five o'clock today, we'll also have more updates about those five folders that Officer Donald Gibson sent us. I have updates on the releases of two inmates, and more on the cardinal. I might also have an update on Perry Coleman's case and trial. This is Destine Diaz, Channel 5 News."

Tuna sat there in disarray, on the verge of insanity. For a quick second, he thought about cocking back his gun and blowing off his head. He really gave it a serious thought. Losing Loose, his right-hand man, was a hard pill to swallow.

Commissioner Fratt returned from the store with the newspaper. On the cover of one, there was a picture of a police station and the caption "Corrupt City."

"Tuna, look at this. This is just cruel. After all we've done for this city, this is how they treat me over one lousy mistake or allegation? Listen, I have someone coming down this afternoon to help you find Thirty-eight," he said.

"I don't need help. I know the area. I'll be back before noon. I'll call you if I find him."

"Are you sure?"

"Positive. We don't have time to wait until this afternoon. You sit tight and stay away from these papers. Don't believe what you read."

Tuna snatched away all the newspapers he bought and threw them in a large black garbage bag. He got dressed, took the trash out, and headed for the projects. He jumped on the Bronx River Parkway, merged onto the Bruckner, until he reached Third Avenue, and then he parked.

He decided to walk around and try to get a closer

look. Tuna was unshaved, and his clothes were not ironed, so he figured he would blend in. He looked like just a poor White man living in the projects or a crackhead.

He started walking and realized things had changed since they shutdown M&M. He noticed a lot of freelance dealers. A few years back, only one gang was allowed in the projects, not multiple associations. As Tuna was walking around, this young kid was signaling for him to come his way.

When he got closer, the kid said to him, "What's up, White boy? What you need?"

"What you got? I just came home yesterday. I'm used to buying trays."

He laughed. "Trays? Damn! That's old-school. Get in the building. I got you."

Tuna followed the kid in the lobby of the building, where there were two of his friends. It was ten o'clock in the morning on a school day, and three seventeen-year-old kids were pushing crack and smoking weed.

"Hey, you. White boy here just came home. He's looking for trays," the young hustler said.

His two friends started laughing, and Tuna played along, laughing with them.

"How much time you did, White boy?"

"About ten years. I was drunk and high behind the wheel, and I crashed into a family van. I killed the driver."

"Damn! That's ill. At least you're home now. I guess your skin saved your ass, 'cause if that was me, forget it about. Anyway, enough fuckin' talking. Let's get down to business. I got dimes, big fat rocks for you. Since I like you, three for twenty-five. We family."

"Sounds great. I'll take the three. Man, I remember when M&M used to run this shit here. That's when I used to fuck with that dope."

"Oh, you remember M&M? Well, they all dead now. The last living member, what was his name? It was after a gun. Oh yeah, Thirty-eight. He was killed last year. He was trying to run shit like the olds days, but too many muthafuckas in the hood own guns. You can't boss people around anymore. Anyway, here you go, White boy. Now, get the fuck outta here. You fuckin' up my swagger."

Tuna, disappointed to hear that Thirty-eight was killed last year, walked away upset. He smashed up the crack he'd just bought, jumped back in his car, and headed back to Little Italy. He was going to call the commissioner, but he figured he would rather tell him face to face.

When he arrived back at the house and told Brandon that Thirty-eight was killed last year, Tuna was surprised he wasn't upset.

"Don't worry about Thirty-eight, Tuna. I have better news. You wouldn't believe the phone call I received an hour ago. I need to you to come with me downtown Manhattan. We have a tip about one of Lucky's hideouts."

"About fuckin' time. Give me a few minutes to wash up and change my clothes."

Tuna was excited to hear about the tip. Hopefully they could find and kill Lucky once and for all.

A lot of New Yorkers were calling on the federal government to help restructure the system and clean the dirt. The voices of the people were being heard loud and clear, so the feds were looking into numerous options, which included dispensing the National Guard into the streets of New York to reduce crime.

City Hall had major concerns about rioting. So the federal and the state governments were coming up with a strategy to build a working relationship in order to climb out of the hole Lucky threw them in.

The governor of New York, Andrew Silver, was overseeing the crisis, and he wasn't a happy camper. He hated dirty cops more than criminals. He visited Gracie Mansion for a quick lunch with the mayor.

"Good afternoon, Governor. Welcome. Please have a seat."

"Thank you. I'm sorry I have to visit to discuss bad news, but our jobs are always taking us to unwanted territory. Anyway, how are you holding up?"

"I'm fine. I'm just fine, Andrew. No need to worry. Let's eat. I'm hungry."

"Cut the bullshit, Ralph. What the fuck is going on here? You think I don't know about Donald Gibson? How come you can't kill one little rat?"

"It sounds easy, but this son of a gun is one hell of a rat."

"Was that a joke? Please, tell me that was a joke. Listen, I've been ordered to come down here and clean house. As we stand right now, so far your name is clean. But the commissioner, he's done. I need you to name his replacement in twenty-four hours."

"I can't do that."

"I'm not asking. You either take care of the situation, or your ass is gone, too. Brandon is done. Ask him to resign, and tell him we'll still pay his salary for the remainder of his term. The decision has been made."

"Yes, I got it, but I need more time."

"You have one week. Where do we stand with this Lucky guy you can't catch?"

"We have one more lead to follow. Hopefully, that will help us get closer. But we know that was him in Cape Cod who killed our two men."

"Okay, keep me posted. I want him dead. We don't need him alive."

"We were thinking of capturing him."

"We don't need him at all in order to win this city back. For us to succeed, we have to be honest. We'll admit these crimes, take the hit, and repair from there. The commissioner and those dirty cops will have to take the fall. You have a choice to make—fall with them, or stay afloat and return this city back to its glory."

The mayor had a lot to think about. The governor was telling him to turn his back on one of his good friends. It was a hard decision, but not a tough one. At the end of the day, the mayor understood looking out for self was always the better option.

Governor Silver excused himself because he had a 1:00 p.m. press conference with the media.

"I have to go now. You take care, and for the next few days—no, weeks—you and I are going to be the best of friends. I know we represent different parties, but we have to put our differences aside through this outcry."

After the governor left the mansion, the mayor was dumbfounded. He didn't know what to do. He felt bad about having to fire his friend.

While Brandon and Tuna were driving downtown, Brandon's cell phone started ringing. He didn't recognize the number.

"Who is this? This is a private line."

"It's me, Ralph."

"I'm sorry about that, sir. How are you doing? Right now, we're following up on that lead. We're getting closer. I think we finally got him."

"That's great, but I called you because I need to speak to you about something else. Can you stop by?"

"I don't have the time right now. What is it, Ralph? I've known you a long time, brother. Talk to me. What's wrong?"

"The governor just left my office at the mansion, and a decision has been made to replace you."

"What! Replace me? C'mon, Ralph, this is not my fault. I'm about to deliver Lucky. Give me one more chance," Brandon begged.

"I'm sorry. The decision has been made, and it was made before he came to my house. They're going to say you resigned because you don't want to cause any more distractions. You'll still get your salary for the rest of your term, along with all your perks."

"This is bullshit, Ralph. I don't get perks in jail. What about these charges against me?"

"Listen, Brandon, I have to go. I will talk to you soon. Take care. They're giving you a week. Make something happen." The mayor hung up the phone.

Brandon looked at his cell phone in disbelief.

Tuna was eager to hear what happened. "What happened, Commish? What did he say?"

"Don't call me Commissioner anymore. My name is Brandon. The mayor said a decision was made, and I have to resign."

"Aw fuck! We're doomed. You know what that means, right? They're going to let us take the fall."

"Ralph is a good friend of mine. We started in the academy together. He wouldn't double-cross me."

"I hate to be the one to break it to you, Brandon, but Ralph just fucked us."

It was getting closer to one in the afternoon, and the governor's press conference was about to begin.

"Good afternoon. I'm here today to promise one thing, a new beginning. I promise to rebuild this police department and gain the trust of this city again. I know, the past few weeks, we have dealt with great turmoil. Our police department has come under scrutiny because of allegations of corruption. I'm here to clean it up, but I can't do it alone. I will need a favor from this great city, just one favor. I need a little patience.

"I'm going to make a few announcements. I'm not taking any questions, not today. I just want to let my fellow New Yorkers know that we are not sitting back and accepting any more damaging allegations. We will get rid of the poison and move forward. Those officers and city officials who acted unlawfully will have their date in court. I'm not just moving my lips. I'm a man of my word.

"I have also granted the release of two young men who were wrongly accused and jailed for many, many years. I'm referring to Rell Davis and Juan Medina. All charges against Rell Davis will be dropped, and Juan Medina will receive a new trial. I have a meeting with District Attorney Johnson in regard to the Perry Coleman case. The rumors that the trial was getting moved to another county were just rumors.

"We have some other things to further investigate,

which I will comment on at a later date. I also want to look into this Wiggins family incident and revisit all the evidence against the cardinal. But, most importantly, we need to capture former officer Donald Gibson and bring him to justice as well. I'm officially placing Donald on the top of the list of the most wanted criminals in New York. I do understand the courageous act he is displaying, but let's not forget he also incriminated himself. We also have reason to believe he was behind the shooting in Cape Cod.

"I want to thank everyone who came out. I will hold another press conference soon, when I will answer questions and concerns, but right now I have a ton of work waiting for me."

After the governor's press conference, the City of New York, for the first time in a long time, felt there was hope in the air. They believed their governor was genuine and spoke from the heart, not a scripted message.

When Brandon and Tuna heard the press conference on the car radio, they were devastated, and so was every other cop in the city. They felt betrayed.

"Damn! Did the governor screw us live on TV?" Tuna asked.

"I think he just did. We're on our own. We have two choices, run or face the music."

"How much time are we looking at? It can't be much. I think we should still find Lucky and have him confess. That will help us a lot. I don't like the idea of running. At least in jail I will get a chance to see my family," Tuna said.

"I really don't know. I'm forty-eight years old. I'm too

old to go to jail. If I'm thrown in jail for these charges, once I make bail, I'm hitting splitsville."

They both started laughing, but they both knew they were screwed. Tuna kept thinking about his family. He knew his wife had to be hysterical back at the house if she saw the press conference.

Brandon kept his poker face on as well, but he knew his only option to escape was suicide. That's what he meant by splitsville. His last hope was the tip about Lucky. Once he heard the new intel, he would make his decision then about whether to face the music or the barrel of his gun.

The Colemans were excited when they heard the press conference. They started thinking, maybe they would get justice for their son's murder. To hear the governor say it live on television that the location for the new trial would not change gave them some relief. They were all in tears.

"Thank God," Laura said. "Our prayers have been answered."

While all this drama was taking place in New York, Lucky was still driving down I-95 on his way to Atlanta, Georgia. He had no clue any of this was going on. He told Tasha to pull out his laptop and see if she could get a signal for the Internet.

"Why do you want the Internet? You are driving, babe."

"I know, but I want you to check the news to see what else they're saying about the shooting. I'm sure they're blaming everything on me. I was waiting for Tamika to fall asleep."

"Boy, you never stop working," she said as she was logging on.

To their surprise, they couldn't believe all that had taken place in the past few hours. They first played back Destine Diaz's news report from the morning news, and then they heard the governor's press conference.

"Damn! I don't think I need to go back and show my face. It looks like they believe everything I sent. My plan worked to perfection."

"So does that mean you're not leaving us?"

"Well, I still have to go up to New York, but only to empty out my storage unit."

"Can you just forget about whatever is up there? I have enough money to buy us a house and maybe start our own little business."

"Sweetheart, we're talking close to five millions dollars. I'm not walking away from that. But, don't worry, it will be an in-and-out situation. I'm not grabbing anything else, just the money. I'm even leaving my truck behind."

"Okay, I understand. I wouldn't leave five millions dollars behind either. But, baby, can you just wait a few days? Maybe a week or two? We have enough money to rent the villa until we're ready to buy. You don't need to run up there right now. Let the heat cool down. You heard the governor say they've made you the number one most wanted criminal in New York."

"Baby, I don't want to wait. I want to close this part of my life. This type of situation will haunt us forever. I don't want to settle in Atlanta then have to move again. Once we get to Atlanta, I will chill for a few hours, catch my rest, and then I'm off to New York."

"That's too quick. You're going to need more than a few hours of rest. I understand you need to get up there as soon as possible, but please get some rest."

"My bad. I'm just hyped. This kind of drama excites me. They're falling right into my trap. I'm glad to hear the Perry trial won't be moved. You are right, baby. I will get my rest before I bounce. As a matter of fact, let me start now. I'm pulling over at the next exit, and we'll switch spots. You could drive through Maryland and Virginia."

"I might as well drive the rest of the way. You are so crazy, boy. I don't have any problems with driving, I know you're tired."

Chapter Fifteen

The Final Tip

Tuna and Brandon were just arriving downtown, to Fifty-ninth Street and Third Avenue.

Brandon made a five-second phone call. All he said was, "I'm outside." He turned to Tuna. "I just called my second cousin's son. He was the one who called me about the new tip on Lucky."

"You trust our future on your kid cousin? You can't be serious."

"Let's just hear what he has to say. His job is to answer incoming calls off the crime tip hotline. He gets the information before we do."

"Well, I hope we're not wasting our fuckin' time."

They waited for about five minutes for Brandon's little cousin, Roy Fratt, who appeared to be very nervous when he showed up.

Brandon made the introductions. "This is Tuna. Tuna, this is my little cousin, Roy."

They shook hands.

"Okay, listen, Brandon, let's walk up two blocks to McDonald's."

"Sure. No problem, kid. You look nervous. Are you okay?"

"Yeah, I'm just a little shaken up, that's all. Let's hurry before someone from my job sees me talking to you."

"I understand, but I hope you're not wasting my time."

As they walked two blocks to the McDonald's, Tuna and Roy made small talk about the Yankees and the Mets. Tuna was trying to help Roy relax. When they arrived inside, they all headed straight to the bathroom.

After checking to make sure no one was inside, Tuna placed his left foot by the door to block anyone from entering.

"Okay, Roy, what do you have for me?" Brandon asked.

"Last night I received a call about a storage unit in the Bronx that is used by kingpins to hide drugs and money. At first, I was going to ignore the call, but when they mentioned that Donald Gibson is a silent partner, I sat up on my seat and took down all the information. Here is the recorded conversation on disc, as well as the tipster's name and phone number."

Tuna and Brandon couldn't believe how easily this information just fell on their lap.

"Little cousin, this is fuckin' great. The whole conversation is on this tape?"

"Good job, Roy," Tuna added.

"There's more shit on that tape that you need to hear. Well, fellas, this is the end of the road for me. Bathroom meeting is over," a confident Roy said.

Tuna and Brandon waited a few seconds before walking out after Roy. They almost ran back to the car. They couldn't wait to play the CD and hear the call.

As they were walking, a white van with dark-tinted windows pulled up beside them. The side door opened, and two armed men with M16 rifles jumped out, wearing SWAT team patches on their arms and federal badges hanging from their necks.

Tuna and Brandon didn't have time to react or reach for their weapons, but they were relieved it was FBI and not Lucky. Tuna and Brandon were forced in the van and ordered to sit still. The two armed men sat behind them, aiming their rifles.

The men drove toward First Avenue and jumped on the FDR north toward Spanish Harlem.

While they were driving, Tuna asked, "Where are we going? And are you really the feds?"

One of the armed men tapped Tuna with the barrel of his gun and told him to shut up.

When Tuna turned around to ask why he needed to shut up, the armed officer cocked back his weapon. "I'm not going to repeat myself. Please, shut the fuck up."

"C'mon, Tuna, just turn around and listen to their commands," Brandon told him. "If they wanted us dead, we would be."

After a ten-minute drive, they arrived on 100th Street and First Avenue. The driver parked the van, and the passenger up front, the only one wearing a three-piece suit, turned around and started speaking.

"My name is Special Agent. I don't give a fuck, but everyone calls me Mr. Asshole. Personally, I'd rather play with my dog's shit than to work with dirty cops.

We were ordered to help you eliminate the target. Hand over the CD, and let's see what this tip is all about."

"How the fuck you know about the CD? And why the fuck you couldn't just introduce yourself? What's up with the whole kidnapping scenario?" an angry Tuna asked.

"We've been following you ever since the Cape Cod shooting. When one of our agents gets murdered, we move quickly, unlike the NYPD. The kidnapping thing was just for fun."

"Hey, listen, asshole, enough with the insults and jokes," Tuna shot back.

"Just hand over the CD, sit back and relax, and see why we are the FBI."

Brandon handed the CD to them and asked if he could talk to Tuna outside the van. At first, Mr. Asshole was hesitant, but since he had the CD in his hand, he figured there was no risk, so he agreed.

Brandon just wanted to make sure Tuna understood his options. "Listen, Tuna, I know you're used to running your own team and being in charge, but right now, today, you no longer have that luxury. We're in no position to be turning down help. I hate working with the FBI, but they have the manpower and connections to capture him a lot quicker. Let's get back in this van and remember our number one target is Lucky, not Mr. Asshole."

"Okay, I understand where you coming from."

When they went back in the van, Mr. Asshole said, "Hey, listen, let's start over. My name is Fred McCarthy, not Mr. Asshole, although I could be one at times. I will be honest. I don't want to be here working on this mission, but I am. So let's make the best of it.

Let's get this muthafucka and cut his head off. By the way, where is your other partner?"

"Now we are talking. Hey, no worries. I understand why you don't want to be here. Right now, I'm at your mercy. The commissioner too. All the help will be greatly appreciated. Speedy, he's at home, depressed. I will call him after we listen to the tape and bring him up to speed."

Lucky was getting ready to leave for New York. He didn't listen to his own advice about resting. He kissed his daughter and told her, "I love you, baby girl. Keep taking care of your mommy for me. I will be right back."

"Are you sure, Daddy?" Tamika replied. "Please come back."

Lucky turned to Tasha and kissed and hugged her as well. "I will see you real soon, sweetheart. Trust me, nothing will happen to me. I will be in and out."

"You promise?"

"Yes, baby, I promise. Get with your friend and start looking at houses."

As Lucky was driving up to New York in Tasha's car, he kept thinking about his last conversation with Tasha. It was almost exactly like the one he had with Diamond. He'd lied to Diamond, but he wasn't lying to Tasha.

He started thinking about Diamond and how much he missed her. He was thinking about stopping by to visit her in Maryland on his way up to New York. He wanted to, but he knew that was a bad idea. If he stopped and visited, she would try to keep him there for a few days, which he didn't have to spare. But he missed her so much, the risk was worth taking. He had a lot of hours to debate on whether to stop by the house or not.

Diamond was the type of broad any man would want to marry. It was just so hard to walk away from a lady with a full package.

Lucky rarely second-guessed himself, but the more he thought about Diamond, the harder his dick got. That's when he realized it was all a sex thing. He loved how she fucked and fed him, but he needed more. And that's where Tasha came in the picture.

He refocused himself and started thinking about the mission ahead. He was going to need help.

Once he touched New York, he would stop by and holler at Divine and his two boys. He always liked how they operated. He thought it was finally time to give them another shot.

After a few hours went by, Lucky was hitting North Carolina. Those thoughts about visiting Diamond were coming back to his head. He was able to keep shaking them off, but he decided on his way back to Atlanta he would stop by to see her and also come clean about his decision.

As Lucky was driving up, his old partners were regrouping at a new hideout in the Bronx. Captain Tuna called Speedy and gave him the address. When Speedy arrived, he didn't know what was going on.

"Speedy, I'm glad you made it. My name is Special Agent Fred McCarthy, and we are with the FBI."

"I could see that, but what the fuck is going on here?"

"I will let your captain explain."

"They are here to help us find Lucky."

"But didn't the last two agents we met also imply they were here to help? Now, Loose Cannon is dead."

"Speedy, these guys are not dirty. We have a recording. A call came in where a caller told us about a storage facility in the Bronx where they believe Lucky is storing his money. We finally got him, Speedy. We finally got him. We have the address, but we were waiting for you to arrive. Are you okay? Two days ago you couldn't stomach this shit anymore. I need to know if I can still trust you with my life."

"Hell yeah, I'm okay. I'm back, Captain. Can I hear the tape and make sure it's not another setup? Remember how he fooled us in Central Park?"

"You're right, Speedy. I was so caught up in the moment, I forgot how he fooled us before. C'mon, let's go to the other room and play back the CD."

Speedy was still very skeptical about the whole tip. Knowing Lucky, he was just setting them up once again. He went into the room with his mind already made up. He sat down next to Tuna and listened.

"Thank you for calling crime tips. My name is Roy Fratt. How can I help you?"

"Hello. My name is Diamond. I have some information for those cops that are on trial for shooting the unarmed Black kid."

"Okay, Diamond, I'm familiar with the case. What kind of information do you have?"

"Well, the kind that can help you find Donald 'Lucky' Gibson. He keeps his money in a storage facility in the Bronx, actually off Gun Hill Road, called Put-It-Away. Lucky is a silent partner, and the owner is one of his childhood friends."

"How can we make sure you're not pulling my leg? We get all kinds of calls coming in through here."

"I'm not lying. I'm the girl that everyone thought

was shot and killed in front of that police station in Harlem. That was all a setup. If you want to find Lucky, then watch the storage facility. He will pop up. He has a few million dollars hidden in there. In fact, all types of high-profile drug lords stash their money and drugs at this location."

"Okay. I will pass this information over. In the meantime, do you have a callback number?"

"Yes, it's 347-555-1212. My real name is Tracey Sanders. Please call me back because I'm going to need protection. I'm on my way to New York."

"Can I ask why you are coming forward with all this information?"

"Let me ask you something first, Roy. Do you have a wife or a girlfriend that you love?"

"Yes, I do. I've been married for five years now."

"Well, always treat her right. You don't have to be loyal, just treat her right. Don't ever lie or misguide her because one day she will wake up and smell the bullshit. This muthafucka thinks I'm stupid. He buys me a house in some hick-ass town and gives me all this money. I know why. Because he's not coming back. He abandoned me. Payback is a bitch."

"Point well taken. Well, I'm glad you called. Lucky is number one on the most wanted list. I will have someone call you back to arrange protection."

"Thank you."

Tuna got up and turned the CD player off. He said, "So, Speedy, talk to me. Is it legit?"

"Wow! I don't know, but it sounds real. I guess the only way to really tell if she's telling the truth is to, one, check out the storage place, and two, run her name. She said Tracey Sanders. Also, did anyone try calling the number she left?"

"We tried calling, but she gave us a bogus number," Tuna replied.

"Why a bogus number? That's a red flag. Let's run her name through the system. Check the national database for runaways, and let's see what comes up. We need some background on this girl. It sounds like she's emotionally distressed."

"Damn! I have to hand it to you guys. I'm looking at real police work. I guess all the media drama is overshadowing some good police officers," Special Agent Fred said. "I'm really impressed on the chemistry you guys have."

"Are you shitting me, Fred?" Tuna shot back. "You just gave us a compliment. Well, let's not dance just yet. Let's go watch this storage facility and see what we come up with."

All the men agreed and decided to wait until after hours. They figured, if the place was a drug safe house, most of their activities would be at night.

As they were planning their operation, additional charges surrounding the Rell Davis case were filed against Captain Tuna, Speedy, and Lucky. The DA was able to receive a rapid indictment, and warrants for their arrest were issued.

The mayor called Brandon up. "Hey, my friend, have you heard the latest?" he asked.

"No, I haven't, but by the tone of your voice, I know it's not good."

"New warrants have been issued for Tuna and Speedy. Where are you?"

"I'm following on this hot tip on Lucky. We finally got him. He was the one who killed the girl in front of the precinct. But his luck has finally run out because we know about his stash house."

"Sounds good. Let them handle it. I need to see you. We need to talk more about your resignation."

Brandon got off the phone, upset. He didn't even bother sharing what Ralph had said about the new charges, not wanting to further stress them out right before a stakeout.

"Hey, listen, you guys are going to have to handle the mission without me. I have to meet with the mayor."

Speedy and Tuna understood. They drove around the perimeter a few times and noticed two things that struck them as odd. There were two high-tech cameras covering the front and back, and the storage facility looked old and in need of a few repairs.

Tuna parked two blocks down. "Speedy, why would a shitty place need surveillance? I don't understand."

"I don't either. Now I'm thinking Diamond's story is legit. Let's stay here. I can see the front. I don't want to get any closer, not with those cameras."

They sat there for two hours and didn't see or hear a thing. Tuna was getting a little impatient and wanted to get a closer look.

"Captain, you know a stakeout is unpredictable. We've only been here for two hours. Go ahead and get some shut-eye. I got it from here."

"Speedy, now that we're alone, I want to share a few things. Loose Cannon was like a son to me. I didn't mean to shut you guys out the way I did. I still can't believe he's gone, but it was nothing personal."

"I can't believe he's gone, either. We had our differences, but he was one hell of a cop and partner. There was no one more loyal than him. I miss him a lot. Let's mourn at another time. This is not a great location to start crying."

"You're right. I just needed to say that to you. Also, I'm sorry you didn't know about Tango. We had to kill him. Tango was working with Internal Affairs."

"Captain, please get your shut-eye and let's stay focused."

As Speedy and Tuna continued to watch the storage facility throughout the night, Lucky was entering Washington, D.C. Only about four hours away, he figured he would drive straight to the storage and pick up his truck. Plus, he wanted to holler at Divine about closing this final chapter of his life. He needed ready-to-die soldiers, and Divine and his boys were perfect.

Unaware of the new charges brought against him, Lucky was only thinking about one thing—killing Tuna and Speedy.

As it was getting into the morning hours, the newspaper was starting to circulate, and of course, they were bashing the commissioner and his dirty unit. New Yorkers were shocked to see the number of charges filed. Charges were also brought against the cardinal for child pornography, child prostitution, and child molestation. New Yorkers were also waiting to hear the latest on the Perry Coleman trial. In fact, there were rumors that a plea deal would be offered.

Around five o'clock in the morning, Lucky was pissed the fuck off as he sat in traffic on the New Jersey Turnpike. He didn't understand why.

* * *

Tuna and Speedy were still watching the storage facility when Special Agent Fred showed up.

"What's the status?" Fred asked. "Any movement inside?"

"Nothing. A Cadillac Escalade showed up about an hour ago. That must be Lucky's friend who owns the place. So, right now, we know for sure there are two bodies inside."

"Two bodies?" Fred asked.

"Yes, when we drove through the front, we saw someone sitting by the front desk. Since the Escalade got here, we haven't seen anyone else exit."

"Got it. Well, I'm here. I'm going to make my way toward the roof across the street and see if I can get a visual," Fred announced.

Before Fred could exit the van, they all noticed headlights approaching.

"Okay, here we go. Who is that driving by?" Speedy asked, referring to Lucky, who'd just passed their car.

Lucky instantly knew they were watching the storage place. The windows on the minivan were tinted, so he couldn't see inside. He didn't know if those were cops watching him personally, or maybe one of their customers. Lucky had no choice but to enter the storage unit. He only had a 9mm on him. If he got pulled over, he would be a sitting duck. He couldn't start a war with a handgun. At least inside he had an arsenal of guns.

When Lucky drove by, Speedy said, "Look at the license plates on the car. They're from Massachusetts. That has to be Lucky returning from Cape Cod. If he goes inside, then we know that's him. Call for backup."

"Backup? We're on our own here," Tuna replied.

"Well, then fuck it. Once he goes inside, we make our move," Fred said.

"But, Captain, if that is Lucky, then he knew we were cops when he drove by. I doubt he would stop and go inside," Speedy added.

Lucky made the left turn and drove into the storage facility. He knew something was wrong because Divine came out the office and greeted him as he exited the car.

"Lucky, what are you doing here?" Divine asked nervously.

"Why? What's wrong? Is this about the cops parked down the street? How in the fuck they know about this spot? Who is snitching? is the million-dollar question."

"I don't know who's talking, but Pee-Wee picked the pigs up on the camera. He said they circled the block twice and parked. About an hour ago, another cop got in the minivan."

"So there are three men. That's great news. They can't call for backup because they've been suspended from the force. If I know Tuna like I do, he will make his move in a few minutes. Let's get our guns ready. Lock up all the rooms and doors, and let's head to the roof."

While Lucky and Divine headed upstairs to the roof, Pee-Wee remained downstairs watching the front door, two shiny chrome 40-calibers sitting on his hip, both clips full. Plus, he had a box full of bullets sitting right next to him. His job was to make sure no one came in the door. Pee-Wee sat on a chair about twenty-five feet from the front door, aiming a 12-round street sweeper shotgun. He was going to blow off the first head he saw creeping through the front door.

Pee-Wee wasn't just your average graveyard worker. He was one of Divine's main hitmen, and a ride-or-die soldier. His brother Blood was out of town in South Philly. Pee-Wee wouldn't have any hesitation killing cops, especially the dirty ones who killed Perry Coleman.

Lucky and Divine were on the roof watching the van. Divine was looking through the scope of a high-powered rifle. He couldn't see if anyone was in the van.

Lucky, holding the same rifle as Divine, kept running from one side of the roof to the other, looking for movement, but couldn't see anything.

"Dee, do you see anyone in the van? Because I don't see any movement. These muthafuckas are up to something. Stay on your toes and watch everything," he yelled at Divine.

"I'm watching. I don't see any of these muthafuckas. Radio down to Pee-Wee and ask him."

"Pee-Wee, you see anything?" Lucky asked in a low tone.

"It's all clear down here. I can't see shit," he replied.

Lucky and Divine were a bit confused. How could they exit the van so quickly?

Divine kept a close look at the van, hoping to get a little visual of anything so he could blow it to pieces. It got to the point where he was getting frustrated and losing focus.

As he was about to call Lucky over, he noticed the red dot on the side of Lucky's head. He yelled, "Lucky, duck down!"

Lucky didn't hesitate, and just dropped to the ground.

Two loud shots went off.

As Divine was running toward Lucky, more shots were fired.

Special Agent Fred, who came up as a marksman in the federal government, was across the street on the roof of an apartment building. For him to get back behind a rifle and look through that scope again was natural.

Divine reached Lucky and realized he'd cheated death. Lucky wasn't shot or grazed. He'd either ducked super fast, or Fred was a bit rusty and didn't know how to shoot.

Divine helped Lucky get up off the floor, and they ran for cover.

"There's someone on the roof across the street shooting," Divine said.

"I see him. Let's split. You go that way and cause a distraction, and I will pop up and knock him the fuck off. That muthafucka tried to push my wig back, Dee."

"You sure you know his location? Don't have me run out there and get shot and killed," a nervous Divine said.

"Have I ever let you down before? On the count of three, I need you to run like bullets are chasing. All I need is three to five seconds to take him out. You ready?"

"Yeah, I'm ready, dog. Let's do this," a more confident Divine said.

Before Lucky could count to three, they heard more shots.

"Wait, Dee," Lucky quickly said. "He's shooting at us. Don't run out right now."

"It sounds like the shots are coming from downstairs. We need to get down there and help Pee-Wee out."

Just as Divine said that, they heard more shots, many more than the first round.

Divine added, "Damn! We need to hurry up and help Pee-Wee. It sounds like they're using high-powered rifles."

"I hear you, Dee, but we first have to take out the marksman on the roof."

"With all the commotion going on, I doubt he's not distracted already. We don't have time to wait. I'm making my move now. Get ready and take this pig out."

"Hold on, Dee, we need to make sure he didn't move his location."

"Hold on? C'mon, Lucky, we need to get back inside, dog. Get ready on my three, all right?" Divine said, looking into Lucky's eyes.

"On your three," Lucky said as he gripped his rifle.

After Divine counted to three and made a dash for the roof exit, Lucky jumped up and aimed his rifle, hoping his target didn't move.

When Fred saw Divine make a run for it, he opened fired, not realizing Lucky had spotted him.

Lucky didn't hesitate to pull the trigger, letting off two shots as he watched through the scope. His shots ripped through the body of Special Agent Fred McCarthy, one bullet penetrating the left side of his neck, the other bullet entering through his chin and exiting through his cheekbone. Fred hit the floor and was dead on arrival.

Once Lucky saw his target fall, he then turned and started running toward the staircase, only to trip over Divine's motionless body.

Divine was shot twice in the head and was drowning in his own blood. He'd only taken a few steps before Fred shot him down like a dog.

Lucky was so focused on his target, he didn't realize

his boy since junior high school, his partner, and brother he never had, was shot and killed.

"Oh shit, no! Oh hell no! C'mon, Divine, I need you to get the fuck up!" Lucky kept yelling as he kicked Divine's lifeless body.

Lucky knew Divine, pieces of his brain hanging out his bullet wounds, was dead, and he just didn't want to accept it. He dropped down to his knees and held Divine's hand.

"Wake up, bro. It's not your time. Wake up!"

As bad as Lucky wanted to pay back his old partners, he didn't want to lose those close to him. For a quick minute, he almost lost it while he was on his knees staring at yet another dead body.

Lucky snapped out of his daze when he heard more gunfire coming from the first floor. He quickly turned around and started heading toward the staircase to help out Pee-Wee.

Right before he reached the stairs, another option opened up for him. Instead of running down the staircase and blazing his rifle like a wild cowboy, he could just jump onto the next roof, a getaway. He leaned against the wall and thought for a second. He explored his options—jump to the next roof, or run down and help Pee-Wee on a suicide mission.

Lucky remembered he'd made a promise to Tamika that he would be back. He was still undecided, as he heard gunfire being exchanged in the background.

As soon as he started hearing sirens, he went with option B, jumping to the next roof, and disappeared within seconds. Leaving Pee-Wee behind wasn't as difficult. That wasn't his boy. He only knew him through Divine. Lucky felt bad, but there was no way the two of them were going to win the war. He wasn't a coward or scared to die. He just wasn't prepared to die at that particular moment.

Pee-Wee fought every step of the way. He kept looking at the staircase and was wondering why Lucky or Divine didn't return. He thought maybe they were shot dead on the roof by snipers. He panicked and ran back to the stash room, grabbed two gallons of gasoline, and began emptying them all over the first floor. He figured he could start a fire, burn down the place, and hide in the stash room for a few days.

As Pee-Wee was running around the first floor and pouring gasoline all over, more cops were arriving at the scene. He was outnumbered a hundred to one.

An officer yelled on the bullhorn, "Donald Gibson, you have fifteen seconds to come out with your hands in the air. If you fail to comply, we will be forced to use deadly force!"

Pee-Wee became even more nervous once he heard them call him Lucky. He began to sweat heavily. One of the gallons slipped out of his hand, and when it hit the floor, gasoline splashed on his pants. "Shit! I got gas over my new fuckin' jeans."

He wiped himself off and ran to the office. He looked at the surveillance monitors, and all he saw was cops outside with heavy artillery. He only had about five seconds to start the fire and lock himself in. He disabled the security system, so the sprinklers wouldn't come on, and grabbed a book of matches out the office.

After Pee-Wee had sparked a few matches, the flames grew fast, and the fire began to get closer to him, like it was chasing him. He started running toward the stash room, but the fire caught up to him first. Within seconds, his whole body caught on fire.

Instead of running into the human safe, he ran and

jumped out the first-floor window, banging his head on the concrete and losing consciousness. The force of landing actually helped put out some of the fire.

A few officers ran toward him with blankets and patted his body with them until all the flames were put out. Pee-Wee's body was burned so badly, they all assumed it was Lucky.

Tuna and Speedy were standing over Pee-Wee's body, convinced it was Lucky, but they wanted DNA proof just to make sure.

Everyone present was pronouncing Pee-Wee dead, until one of the medics yelled, "I found a pulse."

They gently rolled his body onto a stretcher and rushed him into the waiting ambulance, where the paramedics began working on his burned up body, hoping to keep him alive until they arrived at Montefiore Hospital.

When the ambulance pulled off, the fire department was asking officers on the scene to move away from the burning building. By now, the entire storage facility was up in flames. Firefighters didn't waste any time in containing the fire, not wanting it to spread to other buildings.

While the fire was being contained, so were Tuna and Speedy. They didn't resist the warrants for their arrest because, with Lucky in custody, they were satisfied.

Chapter Sixteen

Where Is Lucky?

"Good evening. This is Destine Diaz reporting live from downtown, in front of One Police Plaza. We are waiting on a press conference where we believe both Commissioner Fratt and Mayor Gulliano will address the city. According to our sources, early this morning, around two o'clock, gunfire erupted in the Gun Hill area of the Bronx. Our sources tell us that Donald Gibson and a childhood friend owned a storage facility called Put-It-Away. Police officers believed that this was Lucky's hideout. When they tried to serve a warrant, they were fired upon.

"At this moment, it is still unclear who discharged their weapons first. However, according to the police department, Captain William 'Tuna' Youngstown, Jeffrey 'Speedy' Winston, and Donald 'Lucky' Gibson are all in custody. There is also confirmation of two dead bodies found at the scene,

one in the burned-up building, and another across the street, believed to be that of another FBI agent. This is where the story becomes very confusing, so we will wait until we have further information on the identity of these two victims.

"Donald Gibson is in the hospital with third-degree burns all over his body and in a coma clinging to life. Captain William and Detective Jeffrey, both on suspension, shouldn't have been close to any gun battles. What happened next is what Commissioner Fratt is going to explain to us all. Did the city serve an illegal warrant that turned deadly, leaving yet another federal agent dead? Who burned Lucky? Was he found burned before his arrest, or was he burned while handcuffed? Donald drew a hefty list of enemies amongst the force when he testified. This is Destine Diaz, Channel 5 News."

Destine's report sent chills throughout the millions of viewers watching, the most popular reaction being, "Oh shit."

They were all shocked to hear that Lucky was burned and was lying in a coma. Lucky was hated among the police community, but not in the streets. New Yorkers grew to love him for his heroism. They couldn't wait to hear the commissioner's press conference. Many New Yorkers didn't understand the word *patience*; they'd never heard of a "rebuilding process" before. They demanded quick results. They expected the commissioner to come out and hand out promises and guarantees on the changes the city was going to make.

The Colemans were in tears after they heard about

Lucky's situation. If it wasn't for him, they would have never received any kind of justice for their son. They owed a great deal of gratitude and respect for his actions.

"Okay, sweetheart, turn the volume up. The press conference is about to start," Laura said to her husband.

They sat there holding hands, hoping to hear Lucky would survive.

Right before Commissioner Fratt was about to start his press conference, the mayor's spokesperson, Richard Claiborne, came out first.

"I'm here today on behalf of Mayor Ralph Gulliano. I have a few updates, and I will answer a few questions."

"So are you saying neither Commissioner Fratt nor Mayor Gulliano will be speaking tonight?" one reporter asked.

"That is correct. Trust me, they both wanted to be here and speak. They are still currently in the middle of the investigation. Please hold your questions until after my statement. First, let me clarify one thing. We have not confirmed that's Donald Gibson in a coma. I know you guys read the papers this morning, and it quoted that Donald Gibson has been captured. The unidentified male victim was badly burned. The details of his wounds are too graphic to explain. We are still investigating the whole ordeal that took place this morning. We are questioning the officers involved and in contact with the federal government. Tomorrow afternoon, we will hold another press conference when Commissioner Fratt will have full details."

"So now the burn victim in a coma is not Donald Gibson? Did you guys get the DNA results?"

"The blood test was inconclusive," Richard replied.

"What about dental?" the sharp reporter shot right back.

Richard ignored the reporter. *"Next question."*

"Any new charges been filed for the two suspended officers at the scene discharging their weapons?"

"I can't discuss that at this time. Next question."

"What about Perry Coleman's trial?"

"I can't discuss that, either. Listen, guys, the investigation is ongoing. I promise by tomorrow we will have more information. I just wanted to come out here and give a brief update. The answers you are looking for, I don't have at this moment. I want to thank everyone who came out. Have a good night."

Richard left that podium like he was taking part in a hundred-yard dash competition. He did a great job of dodging all the bullets the press fired at him.

The governor paid another visit to the mayor to talk, and hopefully bring closure to the nightmare that was destroying the image of the police force. The mayor wasn't surprised to see him, but he was shocked. He thought maybe he would get a phone call, not a face-to-face talk.

"Ralph, we need to talk and strategize."

"I agree."

"What's the latest on Donald Gibson?"

"We still can't prove that's him in a coma. There's no way we could go out there and say we have Donald Gibson in custody," Mayor Gulliano declared.

"I understand, but we can't say it's not him, either."

Ralph understood what he was trying to say, but then he noticed his private line flashing. He knew it was Richard calling, so he pressed the speaker button, to allow the governor to hear as well.

"This is the mayor."

"Good evening, sir. It's Richard. I just wanted to inform you that the burned victim at the hospital didn't make it. He died about five minutes ago."

"Damn! We don't need another dead body. Are you sure?"

"Correct, but this actually helps us, sir."

"How does it help us, Richard? Please, enlighten me."

"Now we can perform a full autopsy. With the victim still alive and in a coma, we were limited. I'm on my way to the hospital now. I have a forensic team meeting me there. I will call you once we are done."

"Sounds great."

After getting off the phone with Richard, Mayor Gulliano was a bit more relaxed.

Governor Silver popped the question. "What are we going to do with those two dirty cops?"

"What do you mean? They have suffered enough. Captain William and Detective Jeffrey both are facing murder charges already. You want me to file more charges? Let's not forget, two FBI agents popped up dead as well, which means we all have dirty laundry."

"I understand the great deal of respect you have for them, but they still broke laws. I will make sure additional charges are filed against them."

"You see, Andrew, this is where we clash. You think you could bring your ass down from Albany and run my city. Stop disrespecting me in that manner. I will handle the situation."

"Let's stay focused. I'm not here to see whose dick is bigger. We should start thinking of plan B, just in case

Lucky is still out there," Governor Silver shot back, ignoring Ralph's invite to a verbal match.

Governor Silver and Mayor Gulliano hated each other's guts, but they had no choice but to work together. Andrew decided to hang around until Richard called back.

While they spent the next forty-five minutes discussing strategies, Ralph's private line rang again. It was Richard.

"Boss, the dead body is not Donald Gibson."

"Are you positive?"

"Yes, the body was identified as Dwayne "Pee-Wee" Mooks, a career criminal. His rap sheet includes a few gun charges and manslaughter charges. He's a known associate of the other dead body we found, that of Bernard "Divine" Dooley, another career criminal. He's one of Donald's closest friends. His name is on the lease for that property."

"Great job. Anything else?"

"No, sir. I will start on the paperwork and get everything ready for the press conference tomorrow. Should I let the media know that Lucky was never in a coma? If we don't say it, the information will leak."

"You are right, but make sure you make them aware that the two dead bodies were dangerous criminals and associates of Donald. Make sure you smear the storage facility. It was a place where criminals hid drugs, guns, and money. Donald was a partner and provided protection and confidential police information. Tomorrow, when I read the morning paper or see the news, I don't want to hear or see any different," he said as he hung up the phone.

"So we have ourselves a big problem," Governor Silver said.

"Why? Because if he's still alive, we will catch him."

"You sound like a broken record, Ralph. I can't keep trusting you with the integrity of the city."

The governor picked up his cell phone and called Internal Affairs. He walked away from Ralph and spent about two minutes on the phone with IA.

When he returned, Ralph quickly questioned him. "Who was that?"

"Internal Affairs."

"Didn't I just finish telling you, I will handle the situation? Why are you pissing on my backyard? I have it under control. I can understand the concerns, and I welcome your help. But, please understand, I run this city, and you are standing in my house."

Ralph picked up his cell phone and called Richard back.

"Richard, I have another assignment for you. This requires your immediate attention."

"No problem, sir. What is it?"

"I want you to head down to Central Booking and advise both the captain and the detective to keep their mouth shut when IA approaches them. Got that?"

"Internal Affairs? Why? What happened?"

"There is no time to ask questions. Please head down to Central Booking and call me after you speak to them."

The mayor hung up the phone, and turned toward Andrew.

"You see, you're not the only one who could pick up the phone and make things happen."

"There's nothing you could do to stop IA. Those officers will be questioned, and they will be questioned now. Please don't obstruct a pending investigation. This could get you in trouble."

"Was that a threat?"

"I don't make threats, Mr. Mayor, I make promises. Get in the way of this investigation, and I will come after you."

Mayor Gulliano laughed. "Come after me? Well, I would like to see you try it. Since you like giving out promises, let me give you one. I promise IA won't interview the captain or the detective tonight."

"Is that right?"

"Keep ignoring me when I say I run this city. Now, will you excuse me? I have work that needs to be done."

"Are you kicking me out?"

"No, I will never do that. You kicked yourself out."

The mayor didn't walk the governor out, and so he left shocked and upset. Andrew couldn't believe the level of disrespect displayed by the mayor. Andrew thought he was being nice, not taking over the whole investigation when he'd first arrived, but since the mayor wasn't willing to cooperate, he changed his mind. By the morning, he was going to meet with the a select House committee to have the federal government replace certain divisions in their police department, such as homicide and narcotics. The governor was also going to bring in his own special unit to run the streets and hunt down Donald Gibson.

The mayor called the commissioner once Andrew left.

"Brandon, we have major issues. The dead victim at the hospital laying in a coma is not your guy."

"Yes, I know."

"You know, so what's next? The governor just left here highly upset, but not before calling Internal Affairs."

“Internal Affairs? Damn! This is now getting uglier by the day. Can you stop them from interviewing my guys?”

“Maybe for a day or two. That will give you enough time to go in there and see them before IA does. You have about twelve hours. The press conference has been changed to tomorrow around noon. Hopefully, you will have some good news for me, because so far, you keep coming up empty. I will speak to you tomorrow. Oh, let me remind you again. I’m not taking the fall for this mess. You and your wild goons are on your own.” Ralph hung up the phone and didn’t give Brandon the opportunity to respond.

Brandon knew he was in deep hot water, especially now since two dead FBI agents had popped up. The federal government would demand answers. Brandon was clueless on his next move, but he wasn’t about to turn his back on his two officers in custody. His main concern was getting them released and reunited with their families.

He wanted to go home and catch some rest, but with all the drama going on, he couldn’t afford any sleep. He headed down to Central Booking to see Captain Tuna and Detective Speedy. When he arrived there, he noticed Richard Claiborne had also just arrived. He approached his car.

“Richard, what’s up? Are you here to see my boys?”

“Yes. The mayor sent me down here to make sure I see them before IA gets ahold of them.”

“Right. Well, you go interview Speedy, and I will go see the captain. Just tell him to keep his mouth shut no matter what. I will handle everything.”

“Okay,” Richard replied.

Commissioner Fratt went inside to see Captain William.

"Didn't I fuckin' tell you not to add any more heat? What the fuck happened out there?"

"I'm sorry, boss, but shouldn't we be celebrating? We finally caught him."

"Oh, you want to celebrate, Tuna? Well, let me be the first one to stomp on your parade—Lucky is still alive. The only thing you caught was more charges."

"What? Get the fuck out of here! Then who was that?"

"I don't know. I just wanted to come down and let you know that he's still out there roaming the streets. Now Internal Affairs are on the way to see you and Speedy. Why would you work with another FBI agent? One was already murdered. Now we have two dead agents, and their blood is on your hands."

"Man, what do we have to do to catch this son of a bitch? Remember the girl that was shot in front of the police station? Well, that wasn't the girl we were looking for. Lucky set all that up. The real girl, her name is Tracey "Diamond" Sanders. She was the one who told us about the storage facility. She also gave us this address in New Jersey where Lucky owns a condo under a different name."

"Where is this Diamond girl right now?"

"We don't know. After she gave up Lucky, we offered her protection, but she declined."

"Why did she give up Lucky? You think they set this all up?" Commissioner Fratt asked.

"No, she was pretty upset and mentioned something about payback for leaving her."

"Well, give me the address, and I will send a police squad to watch the condo."

"Brandon, you can't send regular cops or detectives to watch the address. Lucky is too smart for that. Look for outside help on this one. This will be the last lead we have on him. After what happened this morning, I'm assuming he will disappear forever."

"I understand. In the meantime, you make sure you keep your mouth shut when IA shows up."

"You don't have to worry about that. The one we have to worry about is Speedy. A few days ago he was talking about how he couldn't take this anymore."

"Do you think he will run his mouth?"

"More like killing himself, but if he doesn't commit suicide, he will most likely open his mouth and try to strike a deal."

"Okay, I will keep my ears open. Trust me, if he starts talking, I will be one of the first ones to know about it. Right now, just worry about yourself. I will work on getting you released."

Commissioner Fratt called Mayor Gulliano.

"It's me, Brandon. I just finished seeing Captain Tuna, and to be honest, I think he finally has lost it, my good friend."

"What do you mean?" the mayor asked curiously.

"He just doesn't look right. I looked into his eyes, and I could see he's tired of all this drama. I'm not second-guessing if we should even help him out. He just doesn't look right, boss."

"Well, we can't leave him in jail. Once we get him out, we'll just provide the proper help he needs to get by. Remember, he also lost one of his best friends. Sitting in a cell gives you a lot of time to think. What about the other detective?"

"I didn't see him. I let Richard interview him. When I finished with Tuna, I left out. I have to follow up on this tip he gave me. I have to find this witness who told them about the storage facility. She has to have more information."

"Okay. Don't forget tomorrow we have a press conference. I will need as much information about the whereabouts of this son of a bitch who is turning our city upside down. Once the city reads the papers, and they know that Lucky was never captured, I'm afraid we may have a riot on our hands."

"According to Tuna, the witness that's cooperating said Lucky owns a condo in New Jersey. We have an address. I'm already sending over two detectives. Hopefully, the tables turn our way, and we run into some luck."

"Keep me updated. Also, a new trial date has been set for the murder of Perry Coleman. The district attorney is willing to work out a deal, but I'm hearing they won't go for manslaughter charges. We're looking at murder one."

"Murder charges? I think I'm going to pay the DA a visit and remind him what side he should be on. I need at least the captain charged with manslaughter."

"I will see what I can do, but he will have to be released through bail. I will call the judge when we get off the phone. But, Brandon, I need some hard-core evidence to damage Lucky's credibility. Find me something."

"Thank you, Ralph. I'll call you when I get to New Jersey. What if we don't find Lucky before the press conference? Can you cancel it?"

"Not again. We're both going to have to face the

music. We could still blame him for everything, even in the murder trial. I will come up with a strategy. Plus, I'll find new lawyers. Anyway, we'll speak about that later. Hurry up and call me as soon as you find anything."

After Brandon hung up with the mayor, he called up two detectives from the 76th Precinct in Brooklyn. The same precinct where an African-American male was raped by police officers in a holding cell. Some of the most corrupt officers worked out of there.

Brandon needed detectives he could trust, and the first two that came to mind were detectives Sean Lee and Mark White. Those two were similar to Captain Tuna and his crew, but they didn't work in multiple divisions. They were only homicide detectives. They would do whatever it took to solve a murder case.

Brandon called Mark's cell phone. After it rang about six times, Mark finally picked up.

"Commissioner, what's up? This better be good. Tell me how much first, or I'm hanging up."

"Twenty thousand," he quickly shouted.

"I'm about to click this red button on my cell," Mark replied, raising his voice in disappointment.

"Maybe forty thousand, if you could agree to my terms."

"Now I'm listening." Mark jumped off the bed and started to get dressed, while holding the phone with one hand.

"It's about Donald 'Lucky' Gibson."

"I was wondering when you was going to call me."

"Well, I'm calling you now. I have an address in New Jersey I need you to check out. It's out of our jurisdiction. Are you available?"

"I'm almost dressed. What are the terms?"

"Well, if you capture him and keep him alive, we will give you forty thousand dollars, if you kill him, then only twenty."

"That sounds fair."

"I need you to call Sean."

"Wait a minute, if Sean has to come, then we need to double the price tag."

"Not a problem. I will double the pay. Just catch the son of a bitch," Brandon said while cutting Mark off.

"I will call Sean now. Give me the address. I will see you in New Jersey."

About an hour later, Brandon and his two new dirty detectives were across the street from Lucky's condo, and there were no signs of him anywhere. They waited until about nine in the morning before they called off the stakeout. They didn't see any reason to waste time in one location.

"Listen, fellas, I will make it an even one hundred thousand dollars, that's fifty apiece, if you could catch this rat by noon today," Brandon said, a desperate look in his eyes.

"Are you serious, Brandon?" Mark said. "Please stop fuckin' with us."

"For a hundred thousand dollars, we will not only find him, but we will hunt down every person related to him."

"We need to speak to the witness who told you about this location. Where is she?

"No problem. I'll write the address down. She gave us a bogus phone number. Hopefully, this address is legit, but it's in Maryland. You won't have time. I have a press conference at noon. I need him located by then."

"So, we are fucked. We need more time. Plus, if you want us to head down to Maryland, we're going to need more money. I think you're leading us to a dead end."

"You might be right. I just need him found and caught. The hundred-thousand-dollar offer stands, if you guys could catch him. That includes going down to Maryland. Anyways, thanks for coming out. I'll send five thousand for the trouble. I'll be in touch."

"Cool. Thanks for the money. We will think about it. Maybe only one of us will go."

Brandon left and headed to Manhattan to his apartment in the city. He wanted to jump in the shower and get ready for the most difficult press conference of his entire police career. He was about to face the press with no answers as to the whereabouts of Lucky and what exactly took place in the Bronx that left three people dead, including an FBI agent.

He didn't even bother calling up the mayor. He headed straight to the apartment, took a shower, and threw on one of his better suits, hoping to at least buy a little sympathy from the public. He headed down to One Police Plaza where the press conference was taking place.

He picked up his phone and finally called up the mayor. "Ralph, it's me."

"I know it's you. Where the hell have you been? What's the latest? You better have some great news. I have the feds crawling up my ass."

"I'm sorry, boss. I still don't have anything."

"What! Are you serious? I sometimes wonder if I

hired the right man for the position. You are really disappointing me. This kind of nonsense should have never escalated. Where are you now?"

"I'm on my way to One Police Plaza after I stop and get something to eat."

"Well, I'll be there at noon. I'll see you then. Make sure you call Richard when you arrive to go over your speech."

"What speech? I thought I was just going to answer a few questions."

"Just call Richard."

Mayor Gulliano hung up in disgust and mumbled to himself, "A few will burn with you. Let's see." He made a few more phone calls before getting dressed to head downtown. It was going on eleven o'clock. He was running late and didn't care, not wanting to be on the podium in the first place.

By eleven thirty, a half hour from the press conference, the streets were crowded with reporters and news vans. Everyone was desperate for answers as to what was going on. When reporters didn't even have a clue, it usually meant corruption was involved. All the files and evidence so far had been labeled top secret. There were reporters from several states and foreign countries present. The press was eager; so were the few hundred protesters who were out there singing that Marley tune once again, "No Justice, No Peace."

Commissioner Brandon and the mayor's spokesperson, Richard Claiborne, were both in a conference room, rehearsing the prepared statement while they waited for the mayor. It was going on twelve fifteen, and no sign of Ralph Gulliano yet.

"Okay, I don't know where Ralph is, but we need to start this press conference before we have a riot," Richard said as he looked out the window. "I see a lot of angry protesters out there."

"Are you sure we should start without the mayor?" a nervous Commissioner Fratt asked.

Before Richard could answer, the mayor walked through the door. "I'm sorry I'm late. Are we ready?" he asked the both of them.

"I'm ready," Brandon quickly responded, happy to see Ralph. He thought maybe the mayor had bailed out on him.

"Well, let's go downstairs, face the city, and let's hope God helps us all."

As all three men walked down the hallway and made their way outside, they noticed everyone they walked past was looking at them like they were criminals. They were all shocked because those were people in uniforms who were turning up their nose. When they reached outside and were up on the podium, the whole crowd went silent. You could hear a mouse pissing on cotton. That's how quiet it was.

Brandon made his way toward the microphone. It was only about twenty feet from him, but it seemed like it took him almost three minutes to reach it. He cleared his throat.

"Good afternoon, New York. Today I come, my friends, with a few updates that may be positive or negative. I'm not going to stand here and fool with the people of this great city. I will never insult your intelligence. I understand in the recent weeks, a lot of allegations, eyebrow-raising accusations, were made public against the great police force that protects our freedom. These allegations couldn't come at a worse time. We are still dealing with the murder trial against the police department where Perry Coleman was killed. I also have an update on that trial as well, but I first want to speak on what I think everyone wants to hear about.

"Yesterday, around one or two in the morning, Captain William Youngstown and Detective Jeffrey Winston were following up on a lead. They were told Donald 'Lucky' Gibson was hiding in a storage facility, which, by the way, according to our sources, was used by kingpins to store large quantities of drugs, guns, and money. These two officers, who are currently on suspension, acted on their own to watch the facility in hopes of catching Donald Gibson. Their plan backfired. They were hoping they could at least catch Donald and retrofire the embarrassment they've been put through.

"When the officers approached the establishment after witnessing Donald Gibson himself walking in, they were met by flying bullets. The officers fired back, and as they retreated, they called it in and waited for backup. In regards to the dead agent we found on the roof, we are still investigating what role he played as we piece this puzzle. We indeed have two other dead civilians, both of whom are career criminals.

"I know the number one question everyone is asking. The answer is no, Donald 'Lucky' Gibson has not been captured. But I do have a message, Lucky. I know you are out there watching. I will guarantee this. Your luck will run out one day. Trust me, old friend."

Bang!

Commissioner Fratt's head jerked back so hard, it almost touched his back. A bullet entered between his eyes, blowing off the back of his head. The force of the bullet knocked him off his feet, and he landed about five feet from the microphone. He was dead before he hit the ground.

All the TV channels went blank, either switching to the weatherman or the sports anchor. But it was already too late. Commissioner Brandon Fratt's assassination was just carried live on national TV.